HEATH

R.M. NEILL

For my husband.
Always and forever, my Croatian Sensation.

CONTENTS

Chapter 1

MARKO

"Is that a guy with a peacock?"

Maybe someone switched my coffee to decaf and my brain isn't fully online yet, but my lone employee, Curtis, confirms.

"Yep, that's Heath."

"The peacock or the guy?"

"The guy. I don't know if you name birds. Do they even come when called?"

Sipping my coffee, I stare as the man enters the Screaming Bean coffee shop across the street with the bird following behind him. He exits shortly with a coffee and a... cup for the bird.

"What does he get the bird from a coffee shop?"

Curtis shrugs and walks back to his station. "I don't know. A double-double? Do birds even like coffee?"

Watching this guy and his fucking peacock, an actual peacock, have coffee together at 9 A.M. on Main Street captivates me more than it should. Why do I even care if the bird has a name?

"Who is this guy, anyway? This Heath dude." I call over my shoulder.

"He works at the Broken Horn Ranch." Curtis's voice carries down the hall from his tattoo station. "It's an animal rescue and they do a lot of community stuff. I think he handles the petting zoo." A cupboard slams and a string of curses follows from Curtis. He probably forgot he left it open and just smashed his head... again. "No, I'm *positive* he does a petting zoo thing. I remember the pig."

My attention remains on the colourful duo outside as the bird ducks its head into the cup, spilling it, and I snort. Water, of course. If the guy actually had coffee with a peacock daily, I'd seriously have to reconsider my move to this dot on the map town. And I'd likely need stronger coffee. There's weird and then there's coffee with a peacock kind of weird.

My first client isn't due for another thirty minutes, so I drain my mug and turn away from the scene outside to review the notes I took from our phone consultation. I never thought my random sketches and doodles would ever turn into a lucrative business, but here we are. And I couldn't be happier about it.

Turns out all that daydreaming and drawing as a kid came in handy. Which is kind of funny when I remember my dad always telling me art wouldn't pay. Well, neither did breaking the rules of the Security Commission, Dad.

"Hello?"

Putting my sketch pad aside, I turn to the front of my shop to greet the voice. A smiling man waves and I offer a hand in greeting.

"You must be Jacob. I'm Marko. Nice to meet you."

His grip is firm for his slight build, and he nods.

"Yes! I'm so happy you opened a shop here. You'll love it. It's a great town. Have you met any members of the business owner's association yet?"

Jacob babbles as I lead him to my station, a sure sign of nerves for a first-timer getting ink done.

"I haven't yet, no. I'm not really a people person."

Mostly because I'm tired of people ghosting me once they find out who my father is. I'll take the solitude of the open road and my bike any day. Less judgment that way.

"Oh, that's a shame. We're a great bunch, and once a month, we meet socially—usually at the brewery. It has the most space, and the food is amazing." He shifts from foot to foot and looks around the small area. Jacob's wide eyes try to take it all in, but his gaze stops on the chair in the center of the room.

"Have a seat, Jacob."

I point to the chair, and Jacob swallows before seating himself and continues the nonstop chatter.

"I don't know if there's anyone local who could source supplies for you. I don't know very much about tattoos."

With my sketchbook on my lap, I roll my stool over to face him.

"What is it you want to know?"

He chews at his lip and looks away, a flop of brown hair falling across his forehead and the lightest pink spreads on his cheeks.

"Um... okay, don't get mad."

My good mood sinks. Not this bullshit again. My instant like of Jacob dissolves. Why do people waste my time on appointments when they have no intention of ever getting a tattoo?

"Listen, Jacob, you seem like a nice guy, but this is a business, and you should do research before taking up my time if you're not serious about it."

His eyes widen as he waves his hands. It's like jazz hands after too many *Red Bull*.

"No, no." He blurts. Colour drains from his face as he rushes on. "It's not like that! I want a tattoo eventually, but I wanted to meet you first and invite you to the business owner's social."

Oh. Well, now I feel like an ass for snapping at him.

"What?"

"Listen, Marko, you haven't been here long and I'll be honest. People talk. They think you're kind of scary and you never get your business involved with the community. They think you're a nefarious businessman doing crimes instead of tattoos." He laughs with a nervous trill and his gaze meets mine. "I was on the committee to approve your business licence. I think you're a good guy, and I want to extend the hospitality that Bloomburg is known for."

Running a hand down my face, I gaze at the ceiling.

Small town is great, they said.

People keep to themselves, they said.

All of it lies.

"You could've just come in and dropped off a pamphlet or something."

He grins as he shakes his head. "I could've. That's true. But it's harder to turn down an in-person invite."

A smile tilts my lips without permission and I laugh softly.

"You're good at this. And you're right. Give me the info and I'll be there." If he went through the trouble of booking an appointment to invite me to a meeting the least I could do is accept.

He pulls a folded-up paper from his pocket and hands it to me.

"It's this Saturday at the Tilt-A-Whirl Brewery. I put my number on there in case you don't want to go alone. I could drive you." He rushes on. "Or not! I just want you to meet the other business owners and know we're a friendly bunch who look out for each other."

Could this guy be any more wholesome? I'd be an asshole to turn down any of it and as much as I keep to myself, maybe this once, I could try to make friends.

"Thank you. I'll be there, but I'll drive myself if that's okay."

He nods, eyes glowing like he just had the best news ever.

"Totally okay." He gestures to the sketch pad. "But I want a tattoo. I just wanted to meet with you and see everything to make sure I can handle it. It's my first time."

His ears turn red as he presses his lips together and I chuckle despite my earlier urge to just get him out the door.

"I love ink virgins, and I'll do my best to set your mind at ease. But first, let me show you what I've sketched based on your description over the phone, and we'll go from there."

Jacob fills the hour with conversation about the tattoo he envisions, and together we work on a sketch he's happy with. A surprise for his husband, he said, and the simple statement makes me all gooey. He speaks of him with such reverence and love it brings back that ache I've buried for years.

"He sounds like a great guy, and he's lucky to have you. How did you two meet?"

I add the changes to the sketch and when he doesn't answer my question, I look up to find him with tomato red cheeks. "If it's an embarrassing story, don't tell me, Jacob. I was just trying to get a feel about how you met."

"Um, it's no longer embarrassing. Much. Not really." He clears his throat as he sets his shoulders. "But, ah...I picked him up at a bar, and it was supposed to be an anonymous thing, but it turns out he found me."

I bark a laugh. "No shit? That's a cool story. How did he find you?"

Jacob chuckles and runs a hand down his face as he relaxes again.

"By accident. He was my brother's teammate. My brother used to play in the NHL. He's retired now, but he was huge then. Matts joined his team, and I had no clue who he was." He laughs softly and spins the wedding ring on his finger with a shy smile. "Sometimes things just happen like they were meant to, you know?"

I don't know, but I pretend I do.

"That's so romantic. I love how he found you like that. I hope your brother didn't give you the gears about it."

Jacob sighs, lost in his memories, but also far more comfortable here now than when he first arrived. We might have got off on the wrong foot, but I think I could get along with a guy like Jacob.

"At first, he did. But it's all good. One big happy family, as they say."

My smile fades as I refocus on the sketch. Happy family isn't something I can relate to. "Cool. Anyway, what do you think about this? It's still rough, but I could add some of what you just told me in there to make it more unique and next time we meet, if you like it, I can start the outline."

Jacob smiles down at the paper. "Wow. I love this so far! Definitely what I've been thinking about." He clears his throat. "Ah, when I actually have it done, can I have a friend here? For moral support? I want to do this, but I'm actually kind of scared."

"Absolutely. People ask for friends to join them all that time."

Jacob nods in relief as he puffs out a small breath. After he rises from the chair, I walk him out. He pauses outside Curtis's area and listens to the buzzing of the tattoo gun. "I can do this," he says softly, and again, his open vulnerability and genuine warmth are so endearing I can't help but to look forward to our next meeting. Sometimes I like people and Jacob seems to be easy to like.

"I'll see you at the meeting then, Jacob."

"Please call me Jake. And I'll see you Saturday!"

With a wave, he exits my shop, and my next client enters, leaving me no time to over think Saturday.

***

The Tilt-A-Whirl isn't that far out of town. Sure, there are farm fields and dirt roads, but it's just inside the town limits and easy to find. And it's a fucking gem of a place.

Easing my Harley Classic along the packed dirt, I manoeuvre the bike into a parking spot near the building's entrance. After removing my helmet, I run a hand through my hair and glance around the property. Rustic signs for walking paths and a community garden bring a smile to my face. I'll need to come back and check that out. I've always wanted a vegetable patch, but living in the city never gave me a yard to do it.

Entering the brewery, the din of boisterous voices greets me along with the mouth-watering aroma of grilled meat. A small merchandise area is directly in front of the entrance, selling their beer in cans and branded items like T-shirts that say, '*I got tipsy at the Tilt-A-Whirl.*'

When I turn towards the dining area, Jacob waves as he walks over.

"Marko! Hi! I'm so happy you came!"

"Well, you said I couldn't turn down an in-person invite, remember?"

"Heh, I did. Come on and meet the few of us that came out tonight."

He points to an empty chair, and I shrug out of my leather jacket while Jake points and introduces everyone. "This is Colby, Dom, Owen, and this beautiful creature is my husband, Matts." He kisses the attractive blonde man on the cheek and takes the seat next to him. "Everyone, this is Marko and he's the owner of the new tattoo studio, Dark Horse."

The man next to me, Owen, gestures at my jacket.

"So, you ride a bike? How do you find it on the country roads?"

Reaching for the beer menu, I shrug. "It's not horrible. I've definitely seen worse out there."

"Bikes are babe magnets," Dom offers as he leans across the table with an outstretched hand. I accept it with a laugh. "My man wants me to get a bike, but I've not been on one since I was a teenager. I don't even know if I could still drive one."

Dom's eyes crinkle at the edges when he smiles and I grin back, pleased to find another bike lover in the small group. Even if he no longer rides, the understanding of what it's like to own the open road is there and nice to share with someone.

"Oh, you should! I bet you could still drive just fine. There's nothing like a growling beast between your thighs as you drive down the highway. It's amazing."

"That's what Matts says whenever we take a road trip," Jake says with a snort.

"Oh, you have a bike too?" I didn't peg Jacob as the type to ride a bike. He comes across as more of a minivan-driving-the-speed-limit kind of guy.

Matts sighs and shakes his head. "No. He's talking about road head, and I can't believe he just said that. Did Zane put something in your *Coke* tonight?"

The friends all laugh and tease the pair, and I allow myself to feel like I'm part of this group. Jacob seems to have more layers than I thought, and I'm grateful for the invitation now that I'm here. Laughing along with the friendly crew, my smile feels real for the first time in forever. For many reasons, I've never had a close friend group, but I came here to start fresh. That should include making new friends.

"So, what's good to drink here? Is the stuff on tap passable or the usual draft I'll be pissing out in an hour?"

"It's all good," Matts offers and the others snicker.

"I feel like I'm missing a joke."

Owen elbows me. "Matts is one of the owners here, FYI."

"Owen!" Jake laughs.

"What? The poor guy doesn't need to be embarrassed. He just got here."

More guffaws and ribbing go around, and Owen leans closer.

"They're a good bunch, but the jokes get old. My favourite is the apple pale ale if you'd like a suggestion."

The server stops by and I order what Owen suggested while Jake speaks briefly about the business association and his role. Of course, I agree to join. It has no downside and while I've only just met these men, I feel a strong sense of loyalty here that any business can benefit from. Friendship might be a side effect. One I'm not opposed to.

Owen is the quietest of the group. With his tight black T-shirt stretched across his chest and muscled arms, he's also a little intimidating. But I'm covered in tattoos and drive a motorcycle. I know it could just be a façade with him, too.

"So, what business is yours in town?" I sip at the beer he recommended. "This is good, by the way. Thanks for telling me."

He nods, a wordless '*you're welcome*,' and I instantly just like the guy.

"I own the Screaming Bean. You've been in a few times, I hear."

"No kidding? I stop by almost every day. I don't know where you get your coffee beans, but your vanilla bean latte and mocha coffee are amazing. And those sugar cookies? I've never tasted a cookie that good."

Owen smiles, genuinely appreciating my words.

"Thank you." He clinks his glass to mine. "The cookies are my husband's. He owns the Crumb and Cake Bakery, but still provides the Bean with desserts."

"Still?"

Owen smirks with a wink. "He used to work for me."

"Small towns." I laugh as I shake my head. "I gotta get used to all this being in people's business. And speaking of... what's with the guy and the peacock every morning?"

If anyone can give me details on the pair, it would be this group.

Owen's laugh booms and the table shifts focus back to us.

"Colby! Switch places with me. He just asked about the guy and the peacock." He says that with air quotes, and Colby, another very attractive blonde man—what is it with this town?—switches seats and Colby plops down beside me.

"Let me tell you about Heath."

Chapter 2

Heath

"**G**oddammit, Jeff! You can't just peck my ass like that!"

I swear he has no clue about the power he has in one peck. Rubbing my ass cheek, I scold the rogue peacock, who somehow became attached to me. In his weird little peacock brain… I'm his mate. And every time mating season comes around, I have to pretend I'm a damn peahen, so he feels fulfilled and stops attacking all the other ranch hands.

If I didn't care about the damn bird so much, I'd hate it. But he's lonely. If I can improve his life by pretending to be a bird, then I'll do it. Because life is too short to be unhappy. Even for peacocks. Although I draw the line at actually dressing up as one.

I wish we could find him a friend, though. I had hoped the chickens would at least keep him company. We don't have any other birds here at the ranch and it made sense to me they could hang out. Feather to feather kind of thing. But Jeff ignores them most days. Or he attacks the wire on the coop and adds to my chore list because he makes bad choices.

Jeff screeches at me, and I turn to glare his way. I may love the dude, but he's trying my patience today.

"Honestly. Sometimes I wonder why I put up with you."

"Some days we say the same about you."

Spinning around, I find Alec leaning on his deck rail, watching me with a small smile.

"That's not nice, Alec."

He laughs and walks down the steps over to where I'm repairing the chicken coop, thanks to Jeff.

"I suppose it isn't. You know I'm kidding. It was a perfect setup, so I couldn't resist."

His blue eyes twinkle and I playfully punch his shoulder.

"I know you're teasing. What are you still doing home? I thought today was the dairy barn rescue?"

"Blaze left without me." He shrugs, but laughs as he drinks from his coffee mug.

"Something tells me you missed him on purpose."

"Maybe." Alec smiles again and looks back at his small ranch house in the corner. "Zane isn't working until noon, so I'm starting late too. I'm sure Blaze will need help when he returns with the cows. I'll be here."

"If you need help, I'm not far."

"Thanks. I'll keep that in mind." He drains his coffee cup and touches a finger to his black *Stetson*. "I'd best get back. Zane should be awake and I like to make his first coffee for him when I can."

Alec turns back to his house and jogs up the front steps before disappearing back inside.

For too long of a beat, I stare after Alec. He's so happy with Zane and I love that for him. For both of them, really.

Jeff squawks again as I gather up my tools around the chicken coop.

"What's the matter with you today? You're extra cranky. If it's because you spilled your ice water again this morning, that's not my fault. I can leave you at home, you know."

I wouldn't though. People think I'm odd for taking a peacock around with me, but I'm just as attached to him as he is to me.

If I could find a person as loyal and faithful as this bird, my life would be complete. Ugh. Is it pathetic that the only fulfilling relationship I've had is with a peacock? But that's life, I suppose, and I make the most of it. Peacock sidekick and all.

Jeff follows me along to the small animal barn where all my other babies wait. I love animals. Since coming to the Broken Horn Ranch and getting the family I never had, I also got all the pets I never had. It's a lot of work to care for all these sweet animals, but it's worth it and I love every minute.

Hank, the mini donkey, is the only animal here who wasn't a rescue. He was for sale because the owner was downsizing their herd. I wanted to buy two, but he was the last one, and thankfully, he gets along well enough with the other animals so far.

I bought Hank with my first paycheck. The better and more responsible thing to do would have been to save for a better vehicle, but I really wanted a donkey. Dan agreed he could stay here, and that was all I needed to justify the purchase. I still don't regret it.

I set to work cleaning stalls and turning out animals for the day, and Jeff takes his perch on a stack of hay bales to supervise. When the barn door creaks open, I raise my head to see who it is and set aside my shovel with a smile.

"Hi, Dan! Everything okay?"

My boss and one of several father figures I have on the ranch smiles his easy smile as he squeezes my shoulder.

"Right as rain, Heath. How are things with you out here? Is everything going well? Do you need any help?"

"It's swell! You know I love this job more than anything."

Dan's smile is soft as he steps forward and ruffles my hair. He's the only one I let do that.

"I know, kiddo." He laughs to himself. "I suppose I shouldn't call you that anymore. You're not a kid. You've been here a long time now."

"I don't mind, Dan. But I suppose it's true. I'm almost thirty."

He winces and passes a hand through his dark hair, now peppered with grey. Time stands still for no one. Although Dan has aged well and the grey suits him.

"You're definitely an adult now. An adult whom I'd like to ask to manage a special invitation for the ranch."

"Yes!"

He shakes his head.

"I haven't even told you what it is yet."

"I know I'll love it, that's why. So, when and where do you need me?"

Dan does that thing where he looks at me with so much affection that it makes me want to wrap him in a giant bear hug. I never knew my father and Dan is as close to one as I'll ever have. Well, him and the other men of this ranch, but Dan was the first to believe in me. The first to make me feel useful and the first one I called whenever I needed something.

"There's a community day event in town. It showcases Main Street businesses and the ones in the surrounding area. Since it's a family-themed event, I thought it would be nice to offer the petting zoo. The ranch can have a presence and provide something fun. Maybe even draw people out for the day."

"Yeah! I can do that. Just let me know the details."

Dan pulls out his phone and taps while he speaks. "I'll send you the info from Jacob. It was his idea, and I know the boys at the brewery mentioned doing something family friendly. I think Zane might cook or what not. So maybe check with him if he wants to partner with you. We work so closely with the brewery growing their barley and hops, so it's only natural for us to present something together."

My phone flashes with the email notification and I confirm to Dan I have it.

"It's only two weeks away."

Dan grimaces. "Yeah. Sorry. Martin and his dad's health distracted me. It slipped my mind completely until today."

Dammit. I forgot Martin's parents had a scare with his dad needing heart surgery on short notice. Dan was a frazzled mess until only recently, when Martin came home from helping his parents. We were all on edge for a while until Martin's dad was discharged from the hospital.

"Sorry, Dan. I didn't mean to upset you."

"You didn't. I'm just sorry for dropping it on you without even asking if you have plans. Maybe there's a date I don't know about?" Dan lifts his brow with a hopeful smile and I shake my head.

"No. No date. Sorry. Jeff having coffee with me in the mornings is as close to a date as I'll get."

"If you ever want to talk, you know I'm always here. So are the other guys. You work a lot, Heath. Don't burn yourself out."

Dan's heart is in the right place. I know he only wants me to settle and be happy. But I'm still happy here on my own. At least, I'm pretty sure I am. I'm surrounded by animals. It's impossible to be unhappy. What else do I need?

"I know. Thanks."

With another squeeze to my shoulder, he says his goodbye and I return to the stalls.

One of these days I'll meet someone. I'd make a kick-ass boyfriend, of that I'm sure. It's just that finding the right one is harder than I thought.

Not that I'm afraid of hard work. It's more like every time I do date someone, it never seems to go anywhere. And the last girl wasn't keen on Jeff. No way am I leaving him because someone else doesn't appreciate his uniqueness. I'm a laid-back guy and I don't get upset often, but if you threaten the peacock always by my side, I get defensive.

Hank kicks up a fuss, braying and running around the pasture, so I leave the shovel to go see what he's so excited about.

"What a dork." I laugh as Hank runs across the pasture with a squeaky chicken in his teeth. He goes through the dang things pretty fast, but it's worth it just to watch him shake it around and spit it out, only to pick it up and run around again. He does this half-honk, half-wheeze noise while he plays with a rubber chicken and it always makes my heart burst.

"C'mere Hank." He comes trotting over and when my hand disappears in my pocket, he spits out the toy like it's poisonous, stopping at the fence in front of me. I offer him the biggest carrot I have as I scratch his ears.

"When I asked if you were getting any ass lately, that's not what I meant, you know."

Dante snickers as he rests his arms on the fence next to me and I roll my eyes.

"Ha, ha. I'm sure that joke hasn't been used before."

He turns to face me and, like always, my gaze drops to the tattoos on his arms. Tattoos he got for Colby when they were apart and he missed him. Dante has fantastic arms. A lot like mine, all toned muscle from manual labour. The natural muscle makes his ink look even better. I have a thing for tattoos, especially arm ones like his. There's just something about them that makes me all fuzzy.

A sigh escapes my lips, and Dante pops a brow in question.

"Those kinds of sighs shouldn't be aimed at me, dude. I'm taken."

"Don't be an asshole." My cheeks burn. I can't believe he heard that. "I just like your ink, you know that. It's romantic that you got them for Colby. They look amazing."

He faces forward again and laces his fingers together as he leans on the fence.

"It wasn't romantic. It was a way for me to survive without him. Obviously, things are different now and it still means a lot to Colby. I don't regret it." He clears his throat before staring at me again. "I don't mean to pry, but you've been different lately. I know I sometimes tease you about sex, and if I offended you, I'm sorry."

"Oh god, no. You didn't do anything wrong, Dante. It's just..."

Tell him you don't think you'll ever meet anyone to date who accepts the peacock.

Dante, thankfully, doesn't push me. He knows me well enough to know I'll just spit it out when I'm ready. Eloquence is only a word I know and never practice.

"It's cool. Just...if you ever need me, you know I'll listen." He taps his fingers on the fence before turning to me. "Actually, Colby is cooking tonight. If you want to come over for dinner, we'd like to have you."

Food will always get my attention. I wonder if that's why I work so well with animals? Food as a motivator works just as well with me.

"Oh my god, yes! I'll take a home cooked meal. You don't have to ask me twice. What time?"

Dante chuckles and checks his phone.

"Whoa. Soon. I told Colbs I'd be home by 5:30 tonight. Can you be there at 6:30?"

"I'll kick things into gear and be there. Thanks, Dante!"

Something cooked by Colby will beat my noodles in a cup any day.

With renewed enthusiasm, I pick up the pace to finish my tasks.

***

Colby and Dante's house is nothing less than adorable. It's a tiny century home that they've been renovating since they bought it three years ago. At first, I thought the horse paintings and decor were over the top, but Colby's horse is a family member to them.

Which makes my chest ache when I think too much about it. I feel the same way about Jeff. All my animals, actually.

If they can balance ranch animals and a relationship, maybe there's hope for me too.

"How was the chicken? Did you like it?"

Tapping my fork on the empty plate, I grin at Colby. "Did you hear me complain? It was delicious. I can't thank you again for having me. You know I don't always cook well and this was gourmet by my standards."

Dante chuckles as he clears the table and glances at Colby. "Want me to pack him leftovers?"

"Of course." Colby laughs. "I'd hate for him to waste away on his cup of noodles."

"I like my noodles." There's just something comforting about instant soup in a cup. It's like a hug and food in one. "I don't always have the patience to cook like you."

We chatter over the table and Dante brews us all herbal tea before we sit in the living room with our mugs. The two of them snuggle together on the loveseat and I take the over-stuffed chair near the window.

"I love what you two have done with this house. It's so cozy here."

"Thanks." Colby grins at Dante and kisses him on the nose. "We're happy with it. Dante is very good with a saw and a paintbrush."

Dante ducks his head with a small smile, and I have to look away. These two always share intimate glances and touches that make me feel... weird. I'm happy my friends are in love, but tonight it makes that ache in my chest throb something fierce. That's been happening a lot more lately and I've yet to figure out exactly what it means.

I thought it was heartburn from tomato sauce at first, but it keeps happening more often. Like now. As much as I intended to talk to them tonight about how hard it's been to find someone to share my life with, right now, it's the last conversation I want to have.

The room feels tight and I just want to leave.

"I don't mean to rush out, but we've got early mornings coming." Draining my still very warm tea, I stand. "I'll let you enjoy your evening."

I'm at the door getting my shoes on before Dante catches me.

"Hey. Are you sure everything is okay? What happened?"

"Yeah, I'll be okay. I'm just..." Huffing a breath, I absently rub at my chest. "I don't want to talk about it right now?"

He nods and steps back. "Yeah, that's cool. Oh, let me grab the leftovers for you at least?"

I nod as he disappears and Colby leans on the doorframe, his brow furrowed as he watches me fiddle with the hem of my shirt.

"Drive safe, okay?"

"I will. Sorry for rushing off."

Colby shakes his head. "You don't need to explain, Heath."

Dante hands me the container, and with another thank you, I rush out to my beat-up old *Honda*.

After making sure the door latches properly—sometimes it takes a few tries and I have to jiggle it—I ease it out of the driveway and head home.

I wish I knew why this keeps happening.

It would be easier to figure out if it was the tomato sauce.

Chapter 3

Marko

"There you go. All done."

The young lady peers at the top of her foot where I finished the colour on her rose. It's quite pretty. Tattooing flowers is a favourite of mine.

"Super! Sviđa mi se! It's gorgeous!"

I stiffen at her use of my first language.

"You speak Croatian?"

"Just a little. I dropped out of Croatian school." She laughs, pure and carefree, while I smile to hide the uneasiness in my chest.

"That's cool. Glad you like the rose." I reach for the home care instructions and go over it with her. When I'm finished, she's staring at me more intently than I'd like.

"You remind me of someone, but I can't place it. Did you ever go to the Croatian school in Rosevale?"

"Nope."

Who needs Croatian school when you live it every day with your *baka* teaching you to remember where you came from?

My client stands with a shrug and carefully slips on her flip-flops.

"I'm sure it will come to me. Have a great day!"

Normally I'd walk my client out, but my nausea rolls. What if it comes to her, and she figures it out? I don't think this town will be as kind as they've been if they learn the truth about me and my family.

"Hey, you okay?" Curtis leans on the doorway at my station as I run a shaky hand down my face.

"Yeah…just…I'll be okay." The itch to run again covers my skin, and I stand, sending my stool flying. Curtis reaches a hand out and I shrug it away.

"Marko, what's wrong?"

"Can you lock up? I just… I need to take a ride."

Curtis studies me before nodding and stepping aside.

"Of course."

Ignoring the deep crease of his brow, I brush past him, grabbing my leather jacket on the way.

"Hey, Marko?" I pause with my hand on the door. "Can you call me tonight? Let me know you're okay?"

I nod once. I owe him that much.

"Yeah."

And without another word, I exit the back door into the small space behind my tattoo shop. After unlocking the small shed there, I open the doors to find my pride and joy. My *Ducati Panigale V4*.

"Hello, gorgeous. It's been a while, but I need to drive fast and clear my head."

After securing my helmet, I back the bike out of the shed and lock up behind me. Once on the street, I start the engine, roaring the bike to life. My adrenaline spikes as I race away from my fear, squealing rubber as I accelerate far too fast down Main Street. It takes all my patience to wait until I'm on the major highway to open her up—and fly. Every shift of the gears takes me farther away from the claw gripping my chest and my breathing steadies.

It's only when I see the sign for the next town that I finally pull over. There's a small hill advertising a scenic lookout, and that's where I find myself, staring out over a river and watching the sun disappear as I curse my father.

Ivica Dasovich.

The thorn of the business world. The thief reported to the Ontario Securities Commission and me, the stupid son who believed his father would never steer him wrong.

Walking over to the picnic table, I remove my helmet and the all-too-familiar anger bubbles to the surface every time I think of him.

"*U pičku materinu!*"

My curse echoes back to me, and I bury my hands in my hair.

He stole my childhood and tainted the memories of a father who I thought loved me more than life itself. With the help of my *baka*, I grew to understand I wasn't responsible for his faults, only my own. But I'm tired of being alone because of them. I want to be proud of who I am and where I come from, but every time someone makes comments like my client did, my gut twists. I changed my last name to my mother's to avoid the instant judgement that followed his name. When people tell me I look familiar or even mention anything about him, the urge to hide always bursts to the surface.

Always. I fucking hate it.

Pulling out my phone, I hit the button for my grandmother and wait as it rings.

"Jura, my boy, nice to hear from you."

The happiness in her voice warms me, even if she still uses my first name. When I came to Canada, I used my middle name,

Marko, instead. It was easier to blend in that way. Not to mention pronounce.

"*Bako*. I've missed you."

"Then come visit. I'll make the apple strudel and we can watch football. Croatia looks good this year."

Baka loves her football, and it makes me smile.

"They do. Hopefully, they don't crumble when needed." There's a pause in our conversation as I work for the words. "*Bako*, someone spoke Croatian in my shop. They said I looked familiar and I panicked. I don't want this life taken too." My free hand curls into a fist. "I hate him so much and I don't want to keep running."

"He may be my son, but I hate what he's done to you." Her voice softens. "I don't know how to make it better, Jura."

She's been down this road with me a few times. Always listening when I have these episodes.

"I know. I just... maybe I should tattoo it on my forehead. Son of Ivica Dasovich and no, I didn't know what he was doing."

"*Dragi*, you can't lie." She scolds me and loses some of the softness in her voice. "You knew, but you turned an eye because he was your father and believed he was a good man. We all did. But honesty is always best."

That's the part that I can never shake. If only I had said something earlier, maybe it would be different. If I had said no to him, maybe I wouldn't be in this never-ending loop of guilt.

"I need to stop running and hiding. Maybe I should just accept that people will judge me because of him. We both made mistakes."

"People will judge because of your tattoos anyway, so why not?"

She laughs a raspy laugh and the tightness in my chest eases.

"I love my tattoos. Leaving finance was the best thing for me. I get to do what I love now, and I love drawing people's visions and having them come to life on their skin. It's where I'm meant to be."

"A silver lining then."

"Yeah."

A buzzer sounds in the background and my grandmother sighs.

"That's my bread dough. We can talk again soon. Remember, you have more good than bad in you, Jura. You have more of your mother than anything, and no one was more angelic than her. Remember that."

I swallow back the lump in my throat. *Baka* has a way of making me feel like there's hope.

"Thanks, *bako*. I love you. I'll call again soon."

After the call ends, the silence of the lookout is profound.

My grandmother's words linger, though.

Honesty is always best.

I know she's right. Honesty is huge, but how do I tell people my father is the biggest financial criminal this county has seen in fifty years and that I let his crimes happen until I was brave enough to blow the whistle? That I negotiated a deal to avoid jail by turning over everything they needed to arrest and convict my father?

How do I just bring that up in a normal conversation?

I'm guilty by association. Which is true. I helped him steal money from innocent people, and ignorance is no excuse. He used my unwavering trust in him to defraud unsuspecting people. It's always been my battle since then to take solace in knowing I did the right thing eventually. Even if I didn't the first few times.

He was my father. It was so hard for me to accept that the same man who taught me how to ride a bike and read me bedtime stories could use me that way.

It still is.

It's why I keep to myself as much as I do. People who I thought were my friends vanished. They didn't want to be tied to me in case it jeopardized their careers. I had no criminal record, but I was required to leave the finance world. Which was the silver lining, as *baka* said. I never wanted to be there. Art held my heart, but back then, I'd do anything for my father's approval.

But my *baka* is right. I need to remember I'm not him. I've let him steal my happiness for too long.

Running and hiding all the time is tiring. I need to take back control of my life.

It's time to start fresh. That's why I moved here after all. A new start.

Placing my helmet on and starting my bike, I head back towards home. The panic that sent me running has lifted and a new purpose has rooted.

There's no better time to start new than now.

It's time for me to take back my life.

*****

The guy with the peacock is across the street for coffee again.

I've moved on from being irritated that someone owns a peacock they take everywhere, to being amused that he appears to have coffee with it every day.

Colby told me about him at the business owner's association meeting. Heath. A veritable Snow White with animals of all kinds, which is how my fascination with him shifted, to where I now want to say hello.

To take that first step towards my happiness, maybe. The fresh start I came here for. I can do this.

"If you're not careful, I might think you have a thing for the guy."

My hand lurches, sloshing coffee over the edge of my mug.

"Jesus, Curtis. Don't sneak up on me like that."

He joins me at the storefront window with his coffee and a knowing smile. A smile I absolutely don't like.

"So, spill it. You watch for him every morning. It's been weeks, Marko. When are you going to say hello?"

Turning to him, I give him my most intimidating glare.

"You're an observant fucker."

He laughs as we both watch as Heath pets the peacock and tosses the water cup. Fuck, he has the prettiest eyes. Long dark lashes I can see from across the street. Damn right I've been watching him.

There's a thud to my shoulder and I glare at Curtis.

"May I remind you I sign your paycheck?"

"It's direct deposit." He snorts.

"Okay, I push the fucking button to pay you, then."

"Marko, dude... the only thing you haven't done is one of those dreamy lovesick sighs. Why don't you just go out there and say hello?"

I've been rolling around that exact question in my mind for the last few weeks. But it's been years since I've considered asking anyone on a date. Years. I break out in a sweat thinking about it. But the fact is, I *have* been thinking about saying hello. I just needed to work myself up to it.

"I'm planning to introduce myself this afternoon at the community days thing. I only have one client this morning."

Heath laughs and waves at someone on the street as he strolls away, the peacock trailing behind him, bopping his head and constantly watching for threats. Are guard peacocks a thing?

Curtis is right, though.

I'm only missing the dreamy sigh, because I'm definitely infatuated with the man.

"That's a fabulous idea! Even if he says no, it's a step in the right direction for you."

"You think he'll say no?"

"I mean, I don't know if he dates men. So, it's possible. But I know you'd have a friend at the very least. I've never met anyone who doesn't like Heath."

Thinking back to when I met Colby, he told me Heath was one of the sweetest guys he knows and that he loves that peacock. He's single. That much I know, but Colby never gave me a clear sign if Heath dated men. That's an important part I should have pressed for.

"Well, I guess I'll find out soon enough."

If the nerves don't get the best of me, that is.

Curtis has a sly grin when he tips his chin towards a gentleman coming towards the shop.

"That's my client. We'll likely be here for a while." He slaps me on the shoulder before retreating to his station. "Tell him I'll be right out."

"Okay..."

Curtis usually stays in the front when he's waiting for a client, so this is interesting. Maybe I can tease him back about something, too.

The door opens and the man steps in. He's tall, very fit, and seems much older than Curtis.

"Good morning. I'm here to see Curtis."

"I'll let him know you're here. Can I get your name?"

He clears his throat. "William."

With a nod, I poke my head into Curtis's station to find him leaning against the wall with his arms crossed.

"William is here." I search the area, and he doesn't seem to have anything set up for a tattoo. Not even a sketch pad. "Curtis, do I need to be concerned?"

He shakes his head. "Not at all. Good luck today."

The door chimes, and this time it's my client. So I take Curtis's word for it and get to work.

"Hey man, you must be Jackson. I'm Marko."

He takes my hand in greeting, and I almost wince at the strength of his grip. The guy has a handshake that might break bones.

"Nice to meet you."

After leading him to my chair, he removes a piece of folded paper from his jeans pocket and hands it to me.

"Do you think you can do something like this?"

Carefully unfolding the paper, I find an image of a steer with the word '*champion*' and what I think is the logo for an event. It's pretty straightforward, and I can probably just take this design and run it through my stencil machine to start his outline today.

"I can do this. Do you want to start today?"

"If you can do it today, I'd be thrilled."

"You're a rodeo guy?"

He grins again. "I'm a champion steer wrestler."

Checking the time and confirming where he wants the tattoo, I hand him the questionnaire while I prepare the transfer.

"I can work on it until 1 P.M. If it's not finished, you'll need to come back. Would that be a problem?"

Jackson pulls out his phone and taps around. "I'm only free until Wednesday. Then I can't be back for another three weeks. Would that work?"

"We'll make it work."

"Excellent!" He passes me his health history and after confirming a few things, I place the transfer to his inner left bicep.

"So...what's it like to be in rodeo?"

Better to talk and pass the time than stare at the clock. And bonus, I'm learning about bull-riding.

If Heath works on a ranch, rodeo might be a thing he likes.

Once Jackson starts talking, it's very clear he is a passionate cowboy.

And I'm all ears.

Chapter 4

Heath

Why isn't Jake here to deal with this clown? The town's bylaw officer, Klaus, is a royal dick.

"You should've checked with me first, Heath. You can't have the tent so close to the fire hydrant. If you take it down now, I won't give the ranch a ticket."

"I can't just take it down now! It's shade and shelter for the animals!"

"Then I have to fine you."

"I followed the map that was approved! Come on Klaus! This is bullshit and I'm not gonna let my animals get heat stroke!"

Klaus calmly pulls out the map and points to our location. "Actually, the map here for your booth says to set up six feet back from the hydrant and to leave enough room between your feed station and tent for a vehicle to pass. It's right there, Heath. You read it wrong."

My cheeks burn and I press my lips together. I know what he's implying with his condescending tone. It's not the first time I've been accused of stupidity. People seem to equate my love of animals with a low IQ. I don't know why being a compassionate human makes me a target, but one thing I won't do is follow his orders and risk the animal's well-being.

"Then write the ticket, Klaus," I seethe. "Now if you excuse me, I have a job to do here."

Spinning on my heel, I head over to the booth with feed where a line of excited kids wait. He can kiss my lily-white ass if he thinks I'm going to disappoint the townspeople and take the animals away so soon after arriving. Fuck that guy.

Hank loves kids and even in the small space, he goofs around with his squeaky chicken and accepts food as a reward. The people love him. What's not to love about a fuzzy, friendly, squeaky ass?

Jeff roams around with Hank and occasionally fluffs his feathers for people, but only if I'm nearby. I also brought the pot belly pig today, Hammy. She's adorable and missing an eye, but she loves people. Rounding out the menage is one of Dante's llamas. The llamas are always a hit and this one loves attention and ear scratches.

It's just a tiny crew, but it's enough to keep me busy and the crowds happy. And to fade the sour memory of Klaus suggesting I remove the tent. I rarely get mad. But when you display such a disregard for an animal's welfare, well, I'm going to show my fangs. They aren't that sharp, but still.

The afternoon is a steady stream of people. At the first lull in the crowds, I fumble around under the counter for my lunch bag and travel mug.

Taking a sip from my mug, I wrinkle my nose. "Damn it. I hate cold coffee."

"I guess I picked a great time to show up then."

A massive pair of tattooed hands set a drink tray in front of me. My eyes scan up the stranger's muscled arms. He has a shitload of ink and it looks quality. Damn.

Finally, I remember my manners.

"Oh, uh, thank you. Which one is for me?" I point to the tray and the stranger swallows. His mouth opens and closes before he finally points to a cup.

"That one. The white one is for your cock. I mean, your peacock." He mutters under his breath and rubs a hand on his neck. He forces a smile and sticks out a hand. "I'm Marko. I own the new tattoo studio, Dark Horse, and I hope that didn't sound too creepy."

Jeff squawks when I shake Marko's hand and we both chuckle.

"It's nice to meet you. I'm Heath. Let me give this to Jeff. Unless you want to?"

His brow crinkles and I realize how confusing that must sound.

"Jeff is my peacock's name."

"Oh!" he huffs a little laugh that makes me smile. "Um, yeah. I could. What do I do?"

"Walk up to the gate and take the lid off. He knows the sound. Set it on the ground after he walks up. I'll come with you."

I don't know what it is about this massive man covered with tattoos, but I already like him for bringing Jeff a cup of ice water. Opening the gate to the pen of animals, we both step inside and Marko removes the lid. Jeff was already strutting over as I knew he would be. He side-eyes Marko but when he notices the white cup, he chirps and dips his head in it after Marko sets it down.

"Can I pet him? I've never been this close to a peacock before."

"Uh...probably not. He's very protective of me, and he takes a while to trust new people. But bringing him a cup of ice water just earned you mega points."

Marko nods and stuffs his hands in his pockets.

"What about a donkey? Ever petted a donkey? Hank loves everyone."

"I don't think I ever have."

Marko moves towards Hank and the donkey happily comes over. He bumps his nose into Marko's pockets and pulls at the hem of his shirt with his lips. Marko hesitates, but then laughs when Hank noses into him harder and places his hand on Hank's neck.

"He's looking for carrots or sugar cubes. When people are in the pen like we are, we have pockets full. Well, I do, and he knows it. Here."

I pull a few remaining baby carrots from my jeans. They're covered in fuzz and probably sugar, but I take Marko's hand and uncurl his fingers.

"Just roll out your fingers and keep your palm flat like this. Okay?"

He nods as his gaze darts to mine. "Yeah. Okay."

Pressing the carrots to his palm, I push Hank back so Marko can hold out his hand. After he does, Hank steps up and takes them as gently as he always does, and I swear he smiles at Marko. Hank honks once and prances away.

Marko stands motionless, and I place a hand on his forearm.

"Are you all right?"

"Yeah, sorry. I'm...that was fucking cool." Marko laughs and smiles so big I swear I see his molars. He's a really attractive guy. Dark beard trimmed short with matching dark hair. His eyes are a deep, warm brown, and when he smiles, they dance with little creases in the corner. Very cute.

"Hank is pretty cool." I notice there are a few kids waiting outside to feed the critters and I motion for Marko to take my chair. "Would you like to wait while I let these kids do their thing? We can talk more after?"

"Yeah. Can I help you at all?"

"Nah. I don't want to put my new friends to work the first time I meet them. Maybe in another hour, though." I wink and laugh, and he returns a crooked smile that makes my belly feel swoopy... and okay, that's odd. I'm probably just hungry.

Marko sits and watches as I take kids with their single cup of feed, two at a time, to the animal pen. Unlike other petting zoos, I'm very careful of what they get fed and how often. Some animals will eat until they make themselves sick and while mine don't do that, I keep a very close eye on them. Except for Hank, the other animals love the attention more than the food. Hank is all about the goofing around, and the kids love it.

So do I. I love seeing their happy little faces when the pig grunts and smears them with drool or they feel how soft the llama's fur is. Usually, Jeff is fine while I do this, but sometimes he's a dickhead and squawks to scare them. But I carry a giant dog crate with me just in case. If he's too disruptive, I have no choice but to corral him at these kinds of things. But he never wants to be left behind and it's the compromise to deal with his mood swings.

More time than I expected passes and I fully expect to see an empty chair, but Marko still waits. A small smile dances on his lips and his giant hands rest on his thighs.

"I'm so sorry about that. Sometimes I get carried away." I reach for the coffee cup, and, of course, it's cold—though I drink it, anyway.

"Perhaps we should meet properly over a hot coffee. I'm sure this one is just as cold as the one in your travel mug by now."

Laughing, I place the cup back on the tray. "I'm sorry you wasted your money on this one. But I'd love to meet you for coffee."

He nods and when he smiles, there's a small part of a dimple visible on one cheek. It just peeks past his beard, and why do I think that's as adorable as a newborn barn kitten?

"Do you... ah, is there a day that works for you? For coffee I mean."

"I can make Wednesday work if you'd like. I'll leave Jeff at home and maybe we can do lunch instead? More time to get to know each other."

"Yeah." His voice is breathy, and he hands me a business card. "If your plans change, that's my personal number. Call anytime. Well, I mean, call if you want to. But if something comes up and you can't make it, let me know. I'll be done by noon."

"Great!" I pocket the card and we stare at each other until he nods and waves as he walks away.

Huh. That was nice of him to bring me coffee and Jeff water.

I wonder if he does his own ink? He sure has a lot. Nice ones too.

Pulling out his card, I examine the logo with the horse on it for Dark Horse Tattoo. It's very elegant, and the horse's mane flows like it's running fast, nostrils flared, and its eyes glow. It's beautiful. I wonder if he designed it too?

If he chose a gorgeous horse for his logo and wanted to pet a donkey, he obviously likes animals. And that's an instant friend in my books.

I can't wait to learn about him when we go for lunch.

And maybe see more of his ink.

***

"That asshole gave you a fine on a community event day?"

Dan reads over the ticket before raising an eyebrow.

"Yep. He said I set it up wrong, and he's right. I didn't read the whole thing. I just wanted to get the animals on the grass and not the pavement. It's my fault for not understanding."

Dan shakes his head and removes his reader glasses.

"It's not your fault, Heath. Nobody blames you. And Klaus has always been a dick. He should've ignored it. It was an event to build community spirit and awareness for local businesses. The businesses who help pay his salary." Dan scowls at the ticket before motioning for me to join him at the table. After pulling out a chair, he settles into one next to me. "I heard you had a visitor Saturday who you brought into the animal pen with you. An adult visitor."

"Sure did!" He was the highlight of my day. "Marko is his name. He owns Dark Horse tattoo. Really nice guy."

He also has gigantic hands and fantastic ink up his arms. But I keep that part to myself.

Dan nods. "And he brought water for Jeff, I hear. How do you think he knew about that?"

Until now, it wasn't something that crossed my mind. Except that it was an incredibly thoughtful gesture.

"I...don't know. I never asked. But I will when I meet him for lunch today."

"Oh. You're meeting him again?"

Dan's eyebrows raise so high they might push his hat off. What's that about?

"Yeah, he asked if I'd like to go for coffee sometime. He waited for me to be done with all the kids. The coffee he brought me got cold, so I said let's do lunch. He even petted Hank, so why not? Is that not good?"

Oh shit. Did I break a rule? Dan's face is all scrunched up like he wants to spit out a cherry pit or something. Maybe I'm not allowed to meet up with people after they've come to a Ranch-sanctioned setup.

Dan rubs at his jaw before clearing his throat.

"No, it's fine. It's just... he asked you out, Heath. You know that, right?"

"Yeah, as a friend."

Dan cocks his head and crosses his arms. "When's the last time you've been on a date? A real one."

I take a hot minute to comb my brain for the answer, and I almost need to take out my phone and scroll back through my calendar. Almost.

"Two years in June. Stacy Laforge. We went to a concert in Rosevale."

"And what happened after that?"

I shrug as I recall with some sadness that she ignored my messages after that night. After many unreturned calls, I just gave up. "She never called me again."

Dan sighs. It sounds painful. "Heath, I won't pry into your private life but... Marko probably asked you on a date. A romantic one. Didn't you think it was different for him to bring you and Jeff something when he came to say hello? He could've just stood in line like anyone else, but he specifically went out of his way to talk to you and make an impression. If you're not into men, tell him that right away. I feel like he was asking for more than a friendly meeting."

"What? No. He's a friend. He'd never petted a donkey before or a peacock. He was making friends, and I was being nice to the new guy. That's all."

Dan stares at me long and hard. He opens his mouth, but then closes it and stands up. "Just...be careful, okay? If you ever want to talk, you know I'm here."

"Thanks, Dan. But he's a new friend. There's nothing to talk about. And I'm sorry about the fine."

"Don't worry about it. It was worth it. Mrs. Laliberte from the feed store said she took her granddaughter Maddie and might come by to look at one of the mares we need to re-home. Maddie wants to get into horseback riding, and I think we have two that would be a good fit. So a fine is worth finding a forever home for a rescue."

Dan squeezes my shoulder and wishes me a good day. If we find a home for a rescue, I feel better about the fine. Klaus is still a dick, though.

Jogging down Dan's porch steps, I head over to my loft above the equipment barn. Wednesday afternoons are my free days. Volunteers come to do my chores as part of their volunteer hours for school and Alec always supervises. I don't mind one bit either. Usually on Wednesday afternoons, I end up taking a trail ride or something else that keeps me on the ranch. Today is the first time in, well, since I was dating Stacey, that I'll be leaving the property on my free afternoon.

Charging up the staircase, I fling open the door to my tiny sanctuary and head straight to the shower. I don't need to smell all barn-y when I meet Marko. As the water warms and the mirror fogs up, I step in with Dan's words rattling in my head.

Did Marko really ask me out? People ask to go for coffee as friends when they meet, don't they? And how have two years passed since I had a date?

Rubbing the shave gel on my face, I grab my razor and tilt the shower mirror back. I wonder how Marko keeps his beard trimmed so short? Do they make trimmers for that? I liked how his beard followed his jawline and was just as black as his hair.

Speaking of hair, mine has grown a little shaggy. I wonder if I have time for a haircut before I meet him? Probably not. I'll have to go after.

Towelling off, I stare at myself in the foggy mirror and wonder why Stacey never called me back. Wrapping a towel around myself, I leave the bathroom and find my phone where I left it on the kitchen counter. After I find her number in my contacts, I hit call without a second thought.

"Hello?"

"Stacey?"

"Yes. Heath? Is that you?"

"It is! So, listen, I have a weird question."

"Um...okay?"

"Why didn't you ever call me back?"

No sense wasting time with small talk. I'd just like an answer now that the question is in my brain.

"Honestly? You seemed way more interested in talking to the guy who spilled his beer on you more than anything else. Either I was really boring or you were into the guy."

"You weren't boring! He was just apologizing, and he said he had a farm, too. We just had a lot in common."

Which is true. He used to do rodeo and told me all kinds of stories that reminded me of Alec. He even gave me the info for the ranch he owns and I should call if I ever pass through. Then he offered to buy me a beer and not spill it. I thought he was quite nice. The concert was more Stacey's idea, not my kind of music. But I'll always talk to people about farms and animals. It's just being polite.

"More in common with him than with me, anyway. So I just left it alone. I think...listen, you're a nice guy. It wasn't you exactly. I liked you, but I think maybe you weren't on a date with the right person."

Oh.

"I'm sorry if I made you feel shitty. I liked you."

"Thanks, Heath. You didn't. Just...maybe give yourself time to meet people and explore yourself." There's some conversation in the background and before I can ask what she means, she wishes me well and ends the call.

Glancing at the clock, I notice I only have an hour to finish getting ready and get to the Burgatory on time.

I shoot Marko a text to say I'm looking forward to it and head to my closet.

I hope he wears short sleeves. Those tattoos went on forever and I want to see them again.

CHAPTER 5

MARKO

My phone vibrates on the counter, and I pause from my clean-up to read the text.

Heath assures me he's on time and will be there. Well, that's one source of nerves I can let go of. He's not standing me up, at least.

Another one comes through as I'm holding my phone.

Heath: No peacocks!

"There's only one reason for you to smile that big." Curtis seems to always sneak up on me and if he wasn't the only friend I had in this small town, I'd tell him to fuck off. I'm not a fan of being teased.

"You're giving your notice, then?" I say dryly.

He flashes his middle finger with a laugh and flops into my client chair.

"You're funny. So...you talked to the peacock guy over the weekend, right?"

Locking my phone, I place it face down on the counter and continue with the restocking and clean-up of my space.

"I did. His name is Heath, remember? The peacock is Jeff."

"And? What happened?"

Turning around, I lean my ass against the counter to survey Curtis. He waits with an expectant smile, and since I'm dying to talk about it, I pull up my stool.

"There're no clients here, right? And you promise not to tease or bug me if I ask your opinion?"

Curtis's smile fades a little. "We're empty and I know I tease you, but Marko, I'd never be a dick. If you need to talk about something, I'm always here. It's the least I could do."

Nodding, I agree. He likes to yank my chain, but I can trust him.

"He's adorable." I sigh. "Like, you have no idea how much. He loves animals, and he's so gentle with them. I got to pet the donkey. The peacock seems overly protective, but he's a neat thing. And up close...lord, Curtis...he's..." I trail off, not sure what word best describes Heath. He's so kind and full of life. Like a giant ball of happiness and sun that warms me from all angles. And those eyes. I'd be lying if I said they weren't something I constantly think about.

"Sounds like you hit it off, then."

"I think so? I brought him coffee, and he got busy so he couldn't drink it. Then I offered to have a proper coffee with him away from work and he accepted. Then he offered to make it lunch."

"So, it's an actual date, then. That's why you've been so quiet and jumpy today."

I'm always quiet, but I'll admit the jumpiness is all because of Heath.

"I'm nervous. I really like him. He has the longest eyelashes and prettiest eyes."

I sigh again, and Curtis laughs, so I smack him.

"You said you wouldn't be a dick."

"Sorry. It's just…you sighed twice, and I've never seen you like this. In fact, I wasn't sure you had a heart." I scowl and he holds his hands up. "I'm kidding. But for real, Marko, I don't know what to say because this is a new side of you."

He's right. After deciding to try for a new start, it included me reaching for love again. Not that I'm in love with Heath, but he's the first man in a long time I feel even a little comfortable with about letting in. Something about him makes me want to let my guard down and take a chance.

"I don't like to let many people into my life. You're an exception. Probably because you're as clingy as a bad smell in a running shoe and I have no choice."

He grins at me. "It's my most endearing quality." We both laugh and I smile fondly. He *is* a good friend. There are some people you just click with, and Curtis was one of them. He's been instrumental in helping get this place set up and, at the time, he'd only lived here a few months. Our meeting was one of those right time and place things. He may be my employee and fellow tattoo artist, but he's also a friend and someone I trust with my business.

"Have you ever just been totally mushy about someone and all you can think about is how their laugh sounds or how it felt when they touched your arm? Shit, like the stuff you see on the *Hallmark* channel?"

"You watch Hallmark?" He smacks his thigh. "Did you see the one with the best friend who didn't know his best friend was into him and the family knew? They all meddled and sent them on tasks together for them to figure it out. It was funny and so cute."

"Literally any Hallmark movie ever. But good to know you're just as sappy as me sometimes."

He shrugs. "A sensitive side isn't a bad thing. But to answer your question, yes, I have felt that way before and I'm happy for you." He slides out of the chair and squeezes my shoulder. "Just be you and see what happens. You're a good guy. You deserve the moon, my friend."

Curtis leaves, and I glance at my phone.

Thirty minutes until the first date I've had in years. Here's hoping I don't screw it up.

***

The Burgatory is an interesting place.

Photos of farm animals, cowboys, and burgers cover the walls. Half the floor is wooden planks, and the other half is black-and-white tiles. According to the history of this place printed on the menu, the tile side is a bar after 8 P.M. and they pull a sliding wall out to separate the sides.

Like I said, *interesting*.

Just as I arrived, Heath messaged his car was giving him trouble, and he'd be a bit late. Unsure if I should offer to pick him up or not, I settled into the booth and read the menu. Then I slid around the sugar packages on the table to make a design.

"I'm so, so sorry."

Heath's voice has me snapping my head up and I jostle the table while standing to greet him. "Car problems happen all the time. I'm glad you're here safe." Offering my hand, he scrunches his eyebrows and slides his palm against mine.

"We've already met?" He huffs a laugh as I step into him.

"Not appropriately. Where I come from, we greet people like this."

"Kako si?" I press a kiss to one cheek and then the other, being careful not to linger too long in his clean, soapy scent. His cheek is smooth under my lips, like he just shaved. Blond curls poke out from under his ball cap and he's just about the cutest thing I've ever seen. "That means how are you?"

Heath stares at me and touches his fingertips to his cheek. A flush colours the tips of his ears and I wish I could kiss his lips instead.

"Oh...I'm great. Thank you. That's really cool."

Reluctantly, I release his hand, and he slides into the booth across from me.

"So, what happened with your car?"

Heath rubs a hand across his jaw and leans back into the cushioned booth.

"What hasn't happened is probably a better question." He snorts and removes his ball cap to run a hand through his hair. "It's a twenty-year-old Honda Civic. The odometer stopped working years ago, and it's held together with bailing twine and a prayer."

Heath chuckles, but I'm mortified.

"That sounds like a death trap. I can have a look at it for you, if you want?"

He blinks those enormous lashes at me and I panic that I'm being too forward already.

"Thanks, but Dan, he's the owner of the ranch and kind of like one of my dads, has been on me for a long time about it. He makes sure the car isn't gonna blow up, but he also disapproves."

"I apologize for being so forward. I just don't want you to get hurt."

"It's okay. I know all its quirks and I never drive it where I might get stranded." He swivels his head and looks around the restaurant. "So, what do you think of the Burgatory?"

His expectant grin makes me smile and the concern over his car fades. "It's different. But interesting. What's good to eat here?"

"Literally everything." He slaps open the menu and I tear my gaze away from him as he runs his finger down the laminated plastic. "What are you in the mood for? Any allergies?"

I'm in the mood for you. I bet you taste as sweet as the smile you always wear.

Okay. Clearly, he's under my skin more than I thought. But I'll put a lid on those thoughts until we have a few dates first.

"What's your favourite here?"

"Everything! I love food. I'll try anything once, and here, the food never disappoints. Today I'm in the mood for beef. The mushroom burger is amazing. Messy but incredible."

I don't think I've ever met anyone so passionate about food. He's so animated, too. It's not just words he uses to describe this burger. Heath gestures as he speaks and his face glows with the same excitement he uses to talk about animals.

"And what if I don't like mushrooms?"

"Really? Are you just saying that or have you ever really tried them? It makes a difference between canned and fresh, too."

He's so freaking adorable and he's talking about mushrooms. Fuck me, I've got it so bad.

"I've tried mushrooms and I don't like them. But maybe next time you can try to convert me. I'll have the chicken linguine then. Is that good?"

"*So* good."

He beams another smile that makes my heart melt as the server approaches. I have a suspicion he doesn't even know how attractive he is. It's just the way Heath is. Carefree and happy, with a smile that stops the world and eyelashes that could make men kneel for him. Well, this man would at least.

Heath orders for both of us and insists I try the apple cider. I agree because I like cider, not because his face lights up when I go with his suggestion.

After the server delivers our drinks and we sip our cider, Heath asks me about the cheek kisses.

"So, the kiss thing when I got here, do you always do that?"

He's genuinely curious, so I explain how I was raised.

"I lived in Croatia until I was sixteen. My family immigrated to Canada to give me a better opportunity for education. It's a custom I never really dropped. My *baka*, that's my grandmother, still does it to every single person she meets. I usually do it if I'm comfortable around the person. Like, I wouldn't greet my tattoo clients like that."

"So that's why you have a bit of an accent. I couldn't place it. Not that I know many accents, but I like it. You've got this bit of hardness around some of your words. It's hard to describe, but I think it's cool." He takes another sip and I watch his tongue dart out to lick his lips. "Do you miss it there?"

He likes my accent?

"I miss parts of it. Like the sea and the lavender fields on Hvar. We used to vacation there, and it was stunning." I laugh. "And the way we can turn swearing into an art form. I miss that."

Heath laughs, and his eyes sparkle with amusement. Lord, his eyes are my undoing. His lashes brush his cheeks with every blink, and his warm brown eyes make my insides melt.

"If you miss lavender, I can take you to a lavender garden at the brewery. It's grown over the years and there are a few of them now, but it's open for the public."

"Really? I'd love that."

The server places our meals down and we continue effortless conversation. He's so awkwardly charming and funny. I haven't laughed this much in forever. Heath is like a giant teddy bear, and the urge to squish him against my chest is alarming.

"Here." He picks a mushroom off his plate that fell out of the burger and brings it to my lips. "It has the best barbeque sauce on it. Seriously. If you don't like this mushroom, then I'll leave it be."

He's feeding me.

With his fingers. In a public place.

With a lopsided grin, he waits for me, and like an idiot, I part my lips and lean forward while he slides the mushroom between them. Sauce drips and my tongue flicks out to catch it on instinct. My tongue gets a bit of his thumb.

His eyes widen as he sits back and I forget to chew.

I just fucking licked his thumb. Oh god.

"So? Do you like it?"

No waver in his voice. Okay. Good. It didn't freak him out. Hopefully. Now if I can just do the same.

"It's actually pretty good." Swallowing, I attempt a smile and Heath asks if he can try a piece of chicken from my pasta.

"Oh, sure."

Stabbing a piece on my fork, I hold it out to him. He stretches forward with his mouth open and takes it off my fork with an obscene moan.

"I love their sauce and whatever they do to that chicken. It's just so, so good."

I've never been someone to get my date in bed after the first date, but Heath is definitely pushing me to change my mind.

Somehow, we finish our meals without me lunging over the table and mauling him like a wild animal. It takes all my willpower, but I manage.

"So, do you want to see the lavender field next?"

"I would. Do Wednesdays work best for you?"

"They do. Right now works too."

Frowning, I silently curse myself for not clearing my entire afternoon.

"I have a client in an hour. I only thought we were having lunch today or I would have cleared my entire afternoon. He's from out of town…" Fuck. I'm babbling. He doesn't need to know the details. Just set another date. "Next week? Or…"

He pulls out his phone and taps away before looking back at me.

"Do you work on Sunday? I just checked the weather, and it's supposed to be beautiful. We could go in the morning and they do a bag lunch at the brewery for people in the gardens. It's really pretty there."

Shit. Could he be anymore romantic? I don't even think he's trying. He's just being nice to show me lavender, so I feel less homesick, which isn't sweet all on its own. Nope.

"I can do Sunday. It's my day for housework, but your suggestion is much more appealing."

"Anything outside is more appealing than housework, Marko."

Ugh. He needs to stop smiling like that.

The server brings our bill and after much arguing, we split it 50/50. He seemed very passionate about not letting me pay. Ever the peacekeeper, I relented to his request for an equal split.

When we walk outside, Heath runs a hand through his shaggy blonde curls and replaces his ball cap backwards. It's a miracle my knees don't give out as he offers me his hand to shake. With a questioning smile, I take it and he steps up to me, pushing up on his toes slightly to press a kiss to my cheeks, just like I did to him.

"I have no fancy words, but it seemed like the right way to thank you for your company. So, thanks, Marko. I'll see you again on Sunday."

A laugh escapes me as he walks backward with the most glowing smile and I wave like an awkward idiot.

"I look forward to it!"

Heath disappears with a last wave, entering the barbershop at the end of the street. I hope he doesn't cut all his curls off. I really like how they poke out from under his ball cap.

In a daze, I cross the street back to Dark Horse, buoyed by the feeling of having an amazing date and another one still to come.

Chapter 6

Heath

"Are you planning on helping me today or what?" Dante barks at me as he loads more boxes on the handcart, and I shove my phone in my pocket.

"Sorry, sorry. I just got carried away. Lost track of time."

Rushing out behind him, I help load the boxes of llama product into the delivery van. His llama-based business has grown so much he hires people to deliver the product now instead of doing it himself like he used to.

"How much would a tattoo cost?"

Dante wipes his forehead with his arm, and I follow the flex of one of his tattoos. I've always liked his art. It's so damn sexy.

"Well...kind of depends on how big, if it's colour or black. Is it intricate or not? Lots of factors." He walks back to the storeroom and I follow along at his heels.

"I might get one."

He snorts a laugh and raises an eyebrow. "You? Golden boy with a tattoo?"

"What? I can get a tattoo. Why do you say that?"

He hefts a few boxes onto the cart and I'm no stranger to hard work here on the ranch, but Dante is all sinewy, compact muscle. I'm fit, but not as chiselled as he is. When he works, everything is on display and it's hard not to notice. Especially when he takes his shirt off and you see the whole chest piece he has.

With his olive skin tone and physique, he really is a walking canvas for skin art.

Dante leans on the cart handle and furrows his brows.

"What's going on with you?"

"Nothing! I swear! Why are you asking?"

He glances at his phone and tilts his head to follow him. Leaving my work gloves behind, I follow him outside, where he leans against the pasture fence.

"Listen, Heath. I'm just gonna come right out and say it. It's probably rude, but I love you like a brother and you've been acting weird. So here goes." He mumbles under his breath before exhaling a heavy sigh. "Are you attracted to me?"

My mouth hangs open as Dante waits for a reply.

"No?"

I mean, I find him attractive. I admire him physically, but I'm not attracted to him. Not like what I think he's implying. Pretty sure.

"That's not very convincing."

"I mean, you *are* attractive but like...I just admire you physically and I've really noticed your ink. It's hot."

Dante closes his eyes and huffs a breath. "Heath..." He turns to me with a shake of his head. "You can't just say stuff like that."

"How come I can't say your tattoos are hot?"

"You can. It's just...you've been a little off ever since we had you over for dinner. You took off when you saw me and Colby kissing. You work with a bunch of gay or bi men, so I didn't think that bothered you. Now you're kind of always checking me out, and

I'm not sure if you know you're doing it. But if something has changed—"

"Nothing changed! I just like tattoos. I think." Pulling out my phone, I bring up the website I was on that had me distracted earlier and show him. "I've been thinking of getting a tattoo and this site is full of tattoo models. Did you know that was a thing? Anyway, I like these two guys the most." I turn the phone to Dante. "See that guy? His arm is all flexed, and the dragon goes up the side. It's damn fine and his abs are...chef's kiss."

Dante stares blankly at me before taking the phone. "I can see why you think that," he says slowly as he flips through the ones I marked as favourites. "This guy is rocking the full sleeve well. Epic muscles too. I bet he works out."

"Right!? I really like him."

He hands me back my phone and runs a hand through his hair. "You really like him, or do you really like his ink?"

My brow scrunches as I stare at the images on my phone.

"Um, his ink?"

Pretty sure. I mean, yeah, he's ripped and has amazing arms, but... I don't obsess over the guy. Okay, maybe a little since I bookmarked his page, but it's nothing weird.

"Are you sure there's nothing you need to talk about?"

Why does everyone keep asking me that?

"Well, I have a new friend? We had lunch this week. My car is still running and Jeff still hates it when he's not within six feet of me. And he broke the chicken coop again. Other than that...nothing new."

Dante finally smiles and playfully punches my shoulder. "Just know I'm here. And that peacock is...damn lucky he found you. I'm sure nobody else would be as patient with him."

"He's a good bird. He's just misunderstood and lonely."

But Dante is already out of hearing range and I shove my phone in my pocket.

It's easy to be lonely when there's no one else quite like you around. I provide Jeff comfort and sure, he's a peacock, but every creature needs a little understanding.

Speaking of the peacock, Jeff strolls around the corner of the barn with purpose and stops when he notices me.

"Hey, buddy. You gonna be a good bird and stay in your pen tomorrow? I'll be out for most of the day."

He bops his head and comes closer.

Stroking a finger down his head, I smile when he chirps and fans his tail feathers for me. "I know, buddy. I like you too. But I'm not going anywhere. It's you and me, okay?" His feathers ruffle and he struts around for a few steps before dropping his feathers back to trail behind him. At first, I didn't know what to do with this bird when he came here. He was always escaping pens and a general pain in the ass, causing trouble wherever he went. But he seemed to like me, so I tolerated a lot of his shenanigans.

Even birds need friends.

He follows me into the barn this time, and I continue to help Dante loading the van. When we're done, he heads home to Colby and with Jeff trailing behind me, I follow the smell of grilled meat over to Alec and Zane's house.

"Hey guys! Mind if I join you?"

Zane swivels his head away from the BBQ and smiles.

"Hey, Heath. Nah. Come on over. I can throw an extra steak on. Or would you prefer chicken?"

"Oh, whatever is easier for you. Thanks!"

Zane disappears back into the house, and I take the steps up the porch and settle into a deck chair. Jeff wanders off into the meadow behind the house, exploring. The back door slides open and closed and when I turn my head, Alec carries three drinks and joins me at the patio table.

"Hi, Heath. How have things been? Where's the bird?"

Zane appears again, chuckling by the BBQ as he tosses more food on. If it was anyone else's place, I'd feel bad about just showing up, but Zane loves to cook and entertain and Alec has not once turned me away when I needed help with anything. Alec is very dad-like, much like Dan, while Zane is more of a big brother. I love them both like family and I don't doubt for a minute that they don't love me either.

"Jeff is out back." I tilt my chin to the meadow and crack the beer Alec hands me. "I smelled the grill and wandered over instead of hanging by myself and a cup of soup."

Alec smiles warmly, the crinkles around his eyes only making him more welcoming.

"We never mind you here. As long as you knock on the main door before coming in."

We both laugh because I learned that rule the hard way when I interrupted their morning routine. I'm not keen on seeing two of my closest friends in *that* position again anytime soon.

Zane pulls out a chair between Alec and me. Alec hands him a beer with a murmur and presses a kiss to his temple. Zane turns to kiss him softly and just like with Colby and Dante, I look away.

Not uncomfortable with their affection at all. Quite the opposite. I'm in awe of their love, but that weird ache comes back whenever I see my friends in these tender moments.

My hand rubs at my chest, and I watch Jeff duck around some dandelions.

"What have you been up to, Heath? I heard you had some issues with the bylaw guy last week."

With a snort, I roll my eyes. "He's such a jackass. There was no way I was going to take down the tent. Clearly, he doesn't have animals."

"Dan said you met the new tattoo shop owner. How'd that go?" Alec settles back in his chair and my stomach flutters when I think about Marko.

Okay, that's different.

"Good. He's really nice. He's from Croatia and we had lunch this week. I'm taking him out to the brewery's gardens tomorrow."

Zane raises an eyebrow. "Is he into gardens?"

"Sort of? He said he misses the lavender fields back home, and I told him about Jake's garden and then I guess I just invited him."

"That's nice of you to do." Alec sips his drink as Zane moves to check on the food. "You must have really clicked to invite him to a garden."

We did. He makes me laugh and I love his smile. That's not a lie.

"I never thought of it like that. He just mentioned missing the lavender, and it was out of my mouth before I could think anything else of it. But he really is a nice guy. He brought Jeff a cup of water when he introduced himself."

Alec smiles again, but he cocks his head and those blue eyes see right into my thoughts.

"Sounds like he already knows the way to your good side. Did you appreciate him thinking of Jeff like that?"

"Of course I did. It was very…" I think back to last week when Marko had that crooked smile and offered the water to Jeff. "He's very kind."

Alec lets his gaze roam to Jeff in the field and we watch him in companionable silence. It's the thing I like best about Alec. His presence is comforting without words. The clatter of plates behind us sounds and Alec excuses himself to help Zane, encouraging me to stay put.

With the comforting sound of them plating our dinner behind us, I stare out into the meadow behind Alec's house. Jeff still roams through the tall grass and occasionally snaps at a bug as the sun dips behind the trees.

I've loved the peace of the ranch since I arrived here almost ten years ago. There's so much this place gives me. A found family. The responsibility of caring for animals that I love and, most importantly, a purpose. Without a father and my mother losing herself to drugs when I was young, I was on a path to self-destruction with the wrong people. But the universe must have had plans for me because they put me in front of a judge who was lenient. I served my time in juvenile detention and then I found Dan.

From Dan, I learned how to save money, care for animals and be a part of something. I was now one of the faces of the ranch with all the other guys. I loved them. Even Martin, who still sometimes gives me a stink eye when I park my rusty car in front of the main ranch house.

But there's one thing I still don't have.

Zane and Alec return, placing mountains of grilled food on the patio table and moving together with a practiced ease. With the same love and care I see in every single one of the partnerships here. And the ache blooms more when it finally hits me.

I want to be in love.

I want dinner with someone who kisses my temple at dinner and cuddles on the couch with me to watch movies. Someone to watch Jeff play in the long grass with me. A person who accepts my quirks and odd pets without judgement.

"Hey. You okay?"

Zane's hand on my arm draws me from my thoughts. "Yeah. I was just thinking about stuff." Picking up my utensils, I smile at Zane. "Mostly about eating," I lie. "This smells great. Thanks for feeding me again."

"Anytime. You know that."

By the time I finish dinner and corral Jeff, I'm tired. But it's a good tired. It's barely 10 P.M. and I'm not quite ready to sleep. There's an odd restlessness in my entire body. Picking up my phone, intending to play a game until I fall asleep, I open my messages instead.

I wonder if Marko is awake?

CHAPTER 7

MARKO

My phone chimes and I consider ignoring it, but I set the paintbrush down and reach for it. It's rather late and it could be *baka*. Better to just check instead of worry.

> **Heath:** Hey. I'm wide awake and need something to watch. What do you suggest?

My lips twitch and I wonder if this is his way of flirting. His text messages always seem to be so random, and this is yet another one. It's so Heath.

> **Marko:** If you need to fall asleep, you can watch paint dry.

I snap a photo of the watercolour I'm working on and send it. Normally, I don't share my paintings, but this time, I didn't give it a second thought.

> **Heath:** Wait…is this what you're doing right now? You paint?

> **Marko:** I do. I sketch, paint, and tattoo people. A true artist, lol. This is watercolour, so it's mostly dry already, but I thought you'd like it.

Heath doesn't respond for a while and the little bubbles keep popping up and disappearing. I chew at my thumb while I wait, hoping it's a message of approval, because his approval means more than it should right now.

> **Heath:** Sorry. I didn't know what watercolour was and had to google it. I'm extra impressed. You're really good at this stuff. Did you design your tattoos like this?

My lips curve in the biggest grin with his words, and I lean back to type my reply.

> **Marko:** Most of my tattoos are my designs, yes. I usually sketch them on a pad first. Sometimes I colour them in. Sometimes I just trace them to my skin to see if I like it before making it permanent.

> **Heath:** What's your favourite tattoo?

I smile at the question, because it's an easy one, and pull up my sleeve to snap a pic of one on the inside of my biceps. It's a dragon on a motorcycle. The dragon's tail wraps around my arm and twines with a few of the surrounding tattoos, but it's the dragon and the bike that are close to my heart. Once I press send, it takes a while for it to register as sent and I clean up my paint while I wait for his reply.

Finally, the bubbles dance and I hold my breath while I wait for his opinion.

Heath: Holy shit! I can see why it's your favourite. That's amazing. I love all your tattoos. Seriously.

I huff a small laugh when he sends a string of hearts and fire emojis. My chest warms knowing that he appreciates something my father hates. And I stare at the emojis for a long time before replying.

Marko: Thank you. That means a lot. Do you have any ink?

Heath: Not yet. I've been thinking about it a lot. More since I met you.

Marko: Oh?

My heart races. Is he thinking of *me* more, too?

Heath: Is that weird?

Is it? I have tattoos everywhere he can see... and some in places he can't. I'm a tattoo artist and it always comes up in conversation. People usually start asking about them once they're comfortable. It doesn't seem weird to me, but maybe it's something he's never thought of.

Marko: No. I don't think so. Especially when you admire the art.

Heath: Yeah. I just like it. It's like…idk. I want something special when I get one and I'm nervous, you know? I want to look as good as you.

My hand shakes as I reread his message. I've never been good at reading people. And texting makes it worse. Is he complimenting the ink, or does he really think I look good? No wonder I'm single. It has nothing to do with hiding and more to do with the fact that I can't decipher flirty messages.

> **Marko:** Lots of people are nervous their first time. If you trust me, I'll walk you through it.

The message sits as sent for a long time and I keep tidying up my paints while thinking about tomorrow. I've never toured a garden and had a picnic with a date before. It's not something I'd ever even consider, but now that he's talked about art and I've shown him my painting, I'm looking even more forward to it. It may spur some ideas for new designs.

Or I might get homesick.

Either way, it's time spent with Heath and I'm excited about it.

> **Heath:** I trust you. I'll pick you up at 9 A.M. That way we can grab coffee first.

I laugh at his message because he thinks I live at the studio. While I spend a lot of time there, I rent the apartment above the shop out.

> **Marko:** Would you like my address? The shop is where I work. I have a tenant upstairs. Unless you'd rather meet there.

> **Heath:** Ugh, I'm an idiot. But I want to pick you up so, yes, address, please.

He wants to pick me up!

I rattle off my address with a yawn and head to brush my teeth, even more excited about this thing Heath planned.

Maybe I'm allowing myself to be hopeful, but I really like Heath, and I think we connect. He's such a sweetheart and Curtis was right about me being into him. I'm just not sure where Heath stands. He likes me. I know that, but whether it goes beyond a friendly like is where I'm uncertain.

Whatever happens tomorrow will be great. I'm going to spend the day with a gorgeous man surrounded by gardens that remind me of a happier time in my life.

Things are changing.

And I like it.

***

Tires crunching on gravel and the rattle of a broken muffler enter my yard at exactly 8:57 A.M.

I've been awake for hours, eager to get the day started, but I'm not prepared for the deathtrap he calls a car. Standing in the doorway, I watch as he chugs to a park in the driveway. The tired Honda shudders and backfires and I wince. He shouldn't be driving this.

Heath opens the door with a wave and a cloud of butterflies takes flight in my gut as he steps out. No, they don't just take flight. They're performing aerial maneuvers that should be their own air show. Wearing a white T-shirt and faded jeans with a pair of scuffed-up cowboy boots, he's not exactly dressed for a walk through a garden, but I'm not complaining.

And that dang ball cap with his curls sticking out sits on his head. Literally one of my teenage wet dreams just came to life.

"Hi!"

He trots up to me with a beaming smile and holds out his hand in greeting. Smiling because he remembered how I first greeted him, I take it and step up. "*Bok*." Pressing a kiss to each cheek, I succeed in not burying my face in the crook of his neck and breathing all his *Heathness* in.

"That's a new word. Oh! I almost forgot!"

He returns to his rust bucket car and I enjoy the view of denim stretched over his ass as he reaches inside the car for something. He emerges with two takeout cups and sets them on the ground before using both hands to gently lift and close the car door at the same time.

"I stopped at the Screaming Bean." He passes me a cup and the aroma of vanilla hits me.

"How did you know I like the vanilla bean latte?"

"I asked what the tattoo guy always gets." He flashes a bright smile and fuck me if I don't feel my neck turn hot.

"Thank you. It's one of my favourites." I take a small sip before stepping aside to allow him in. "Come on in. We can drink before we go."

Heath steps inside my small house with a whistle. "Marko...this place is amazing. Do you own it?"

"It has a mortgage, but yeah, it's mine."

Now standing in his sock feet, he's peering up at the cathedral ceiling of my living room with his mouth agape.

"Would you like a tour?"

"Well, if you don't mind. It's gorgeous. I've never been down this road before. How did you find this place?"

Talking while I lead him to the back of the house, I explain. "As an artist, I knew I wanted some property. Being outside inspires me. It didn't need to be huge since it's just me. The only thing it lacks is a garage. I might build one in a few years, but for now, I store my other bike in the shed at the shop."

My small house is one of my favourite things, and when we pause in the sunroom off the back, Heath simply stares. Most of my art supplies are here, and the easel with the painting from last night is still on display. The room looks out into the backyard, which is fenced and has a man-made pond in the center. The previous owners had plans to landscape, but abandoned them when they fell ill and needed to sell.

"This is amazing. A pond! Wow. You should get ducks."

I laugh as he says it so casually, as though I could just walk into a store for them. Can you? I've never thought about buying ducks before, so I don't know how one would even acquire a duck.

"I don't know how to care for ducks, but thanks for the suggestion."

"I'd teach you. I love ducks and their little smacking feet. So cute."

Heath makes a sound that I assume is duck feet and his lopsided grin forces me to look away.

"Come on." I shake my head with a small laugh. Honestly, I just can't get over his cuteness. "I'll show you the rest. It's not big."

There's a hallway on either side of the sunroom. One leads to the spare bedroom, which is mainly full of stuff I haven't unpacked, and the other leads to my bedroom and the bathroom.

Heath pauses at the door to my bedroom before taking a single step inside and stepping back. He whistles again in the bathroom when he notices the large soaker tub.

"I didn't take you for a bubble bath kind of guy."

Throwing my head back, I laugh as he grins and sips his coffee. "I haven't used the thing since I moved here. Maybe I should."

"I can see you in there, suds up to your chest while you lounge like a prince."

Is he flirting? Does he actually think of me naked in a tub? Should I ignore that? Ugh, *why* is it so hard to figure this guy out!?

"I'm no prince." My voice is hoarse and Heath freezes for a moment. Licking his lips, his gaze darts to the door and I clear my throat. "Let's go back to the main room."

Because I don't want to stand here and imagine you naked in my bathtub with me. Nope. That's not happening.

"So that's it. Nothing fancy, but I love it."

We sit on my worn sofa and finish our coffees while Heath describes his plans for us. His voice takes on this excited lilt when he tells me about the garden grounds, then it switches to an almost reverent tone as he speaks of his friends who own it. Heath talks with his hands, almost spilling his coffee several times. Finally, he shoots up off the couch and claps his hands.

"So, ready to get going?"

I could listen to him talk all day and be happy, but he's vibrating to go. He hops from foot to foot and while I share in his eagerness, there's a question I need to ask.

"Um...yes, but...do you mind if I drive?"

Heath smiles again and tosses me his keys. "Not at all. Don't enjoy being a passenger?"

Grabbing the keys out of the air, I inwardly smile at this key chain. It's one of those tiny clear squares you can personalize with a photo and it's a selfie of him and Jeff.

"Not really, but I meant if you would mind if we took my bike."

His eyes widen. "Like a motorcycle?" His voice is breathless, and I puff a little that he seems so enamored with the idea of my bike.

"Yeah. Have you been on one?"

"No. Is it...like what do I do?"

"You hang on and enjoy the ride."

He scrunches his brows. "I won't fall off?"

"I'd never let you fall. I promise."

Heath puffs out a breath before nodding. "Okay. Let's do it."

Oof. His agreement to ride with me shouldn't set my pulse racing like it is.

"You'll love it. I promise."

Leading him outside, I hand him my spare helmet. It's red and glittery and totally badass, but he raises an eyebrow. "A glittery helmet for the tattoo guy? I was expecting skulls or something." He takes off his ball cap and looks at me. "What about my hat?"

I take it and place it in the saddlebag where I've already stored my sketch pad and pencils. After giving him a rundown of how to hang on and what to do and not to do, he confirms he understands. Throwing my leg over the bike, I bring it to life and the rumble beneath me settles my nerves. I'm always at ease when I ride. Even with a man I'm crushing on as my passenger.

Heath's hand on my shoulder as he mounts the bike has me inhaling a sharp breath that—thankfully—he can't hear over the motor.

"Ready?" I shout as I turn my head.

He gives me a thumbs up and I slide my visor down before accelerating out of the driveway. Heath immediately wraps his arms around my waist to hang on.

It's a rush like I've never experienced before. Probably because I've never been attracted to my passenger as much as I am to Heath. My pulse races and heat floods my body. He feels like he's supposed to be there.

When we finally reach the highway and I gear up to go faster, Heath's arms tighten around me and I already know I don't want the ride to end.

Chapter 8

Heath

The ride to the brewery isn't long, but it's enough time for me to wonder if I can ask Marko to take me for another ride. There's nothing about this I don't like.

The thrill of open air rushing by was scary at first. Logically, I knew the wind wouldn't pull me off, but the adrenaline rush that it could, lingered. The rumble of a powerful engine beneath me, controlled by the man I'm clinging to, also makes my heart kick up a notch. At first, I wasn't sure if I should hold on to Marko, but he told me it was fine and he wanted me to feel safe and not scared. Which definitely made me feel better about being on the bike. I had these little handle things I could also hold to stay on, but that didn't feel right to me.

I can't explain it, but as soon as I wrapped my arms around him, I felt... aware. Aware of him in a way that was new. And when he shifted gears... whoa. It was heady to sort of feel him channel the confidence of riding this machine through me. Like I said, I was very aware of Marko.

And I don't know what to make of that. I was just a passenger on his bike, but it felt like I was part of a secret. I don't know what the secret is, but the entire experience made me feel like I was special.

When we parked at the brewery, he told me to wait until he gave his signal before I got off the bike. He killed the engine and steadied the kickstand before tapping my leg and I slid off from behind him, much like I would if I got off a horse. My hands shook as I fumbled with the helmet's buckle because I was still so amped up from the ride. Marko noticed and brought his hands up to help.

Once unbuckled, I pulled off my helmet to find him waiting with my ball cap and an expectant smile.

"Well, country boy? Did you enjoy your first ride on a motorcycle?"

Marko's accent sounds thicker and rumbly. He rubs a hand through his short dark hair, and I'm distracted again by the ink on his arms. Jesus. He's incredible.

"It was amazing, and I'm probably going to ask you to take me again."

His answering smile makes me feel all floaty. Kinda like that time I took one too many painkillers after I had my wisdom teeth pulled. Nothing hurt, but man, did I ever feel like I was walking on air.

"Anytime. Just ask. I love riding."

Marko secures the helmets to the bike, retrieves a small backpack from the saddlebag and throws in on his back.

"What did you bring?"

Holding the door open to the brewery, we step inside to pick up our lunch for the afternoon. I wave at Zane, who signals for me to wait, and I turn to Marko.

I'm not sure why, but his olive skin looks pinkish. Marko rubs at his neck. My gaze follows his tattooed arm up to his fingers that now disappear into the hair at the base of his neck. He must work out. That arm is fine. I should ask.

"Um...it's just a sketch pad and pencils. You said it was pretty here, so I came prepared." His lips tilt in a shy smile. "Artist, remember?"

"Hi, guys!" Zane appears with a cooler backpack and passes it to me. "Everything is in the bag for your lunch, and there's a blanket strapped to the bottom. Just bring back the garbage and toss it out inside when you return."

Taking the bag from Zane, I motion to Marko.

"Thanks. Zane, this is Marko. He's the owner of Dark Horse Tattoos. Marko, this is one of my ranch friends. He and his husband often feed me supper." I laugh and Zane sticks out his hand to Marko. "He's also one of the owners here."

Marko takes Zane's hand and greets him with kisses to the cheek like he did me. Zane, ever gracious, takes it in stride and just asks him where he's from.

"Oh, Croatia. I've been in Canada since I was a teenager, but sometimes the instinct takes over and I greet people like I was taught growing up."

"I've always wanted to go there. Heath says you miss the lavender, and he offered to show you ours. I hope you love it." Zane turns to me with a grin. "Matts and Jake are away this weekend. You'll be safe out there." He chuckles as he turns back to the bar. "Have fun, and it was nice to meet you, Marko."

Shouldering our picnic pack, Marko follows me out and we start the walk to the trailhead.

"Why should we worry about Matts and Jake?"

Laughing, I explain how Matts planted the garden as a gift to Jake because he has a weird hang-up with lavender and it makes him horny.

"Sometimes the guys find them getting freaky and it's always a joke to friends. They don't actually *do* anything in public. Since the brewery opened these gardens to the public, if they want to do it amongst the lavender, they actually give warning and close the paths."

Marko huffs a laugh. "I would never have pegged Jacob for someone like that. And they *like* to have sex outside here?"

The word sex coming from Marko sounds like sin with his hard accent, and I shiver. Must be the sun going behind the clouds. Or maybe I should have peed before we left.

"I was told it only happened once."

Marko's deep laugh pulls my lips into a smile.

"I doubt that very much, Heath. When the mood strikes, you just do it."

Swallowing hard, I push those images from my mind. Is that what Marko does? Just does it? Oh my god, why am I thinking about him having sex?!

Clearing my throat, I point to the other path before we ascend the hill.

"The community garden plots are down that way. If you ever feel the need to plant your own produce, you can rent a square or you volunteer your time to the garden upkeep in exchange."

"That's a cool idea. One day I'll try a garden. I'm not much of a gardener, but I'd like to landscape my backyard one day. That seems like it might be easier than growing food."

"You totally should. That pond has potential. I can help you if you do it."

Marko cuts a glance my way and nods with a murmured thank you.

The summit to the start of the trail is only a few hundred meters, and when we reach the top, our first stop is the largest of the lavender gardens on the trails. Turning to Marko, I point.

"Here's the first—and biggest—one. There are, I think, three kinds of lavender in this garden. There should be markers in there to tell you."

Marko steps up to read the dedication sign that's for Jacob before stepping into the garden and following the paver stones. If you follow the path, all the lavender plants surround you as you go farther in. Marko pauses in the centre and roots around in his bag, pulling out a sketch pad and a pencil.

I stand behind and watch as his mammoth tattooed hand grips the pencil and flies over the paper. A small breeze flutters his ebony hair and he swipes it out of his face. The noon sun isn't here yet, but it's growing warm and there's a sheen of sweat on his forehead.

And again, I'm watching him with something new. There's this different feeling tickling along my spine. Marko loses himself to his sketching and I'm lost to watching him while he creates another work of art. It's kind of cool that I get to see him in action like this. I've never known an artist before.

At least not this kind. Art before Marko was me and Zane making happy faces in the snow with our feet. Or me peeing my name in a snowbank. Which is harder than you'd think, and my cursive is stellar.

His brown eyes raise to find mine and his gaze softens, but he continues to sketch for a moment before finally closing the pad.

"*Oprosti.*" He shakes his head with a huff. "Sorry, I mean. Sometimes I get carried away. This place is gorgeous. Thank you for bringing me."

"Of course. Anytime. There're a few smaller gardens along the way still."

My tongue doesn't want to move as Marko falls into step beside me again—which is odd because I talk a lot—and we continue along the path. I usually talk too much. But right now, there's a vibe going on, and it demands silence. Silence is hard for me, but it feels kinda good as we walk the path together.

The next garden is one full of orange and yellow daylilies, tiger lilies, and hostas. Easy maintenance growers for out here and plants that the animals leave alone.

Marko takes photos and shoots me an apologetic smile as he once again pulls out his sketchbook and pencils. I wish there was something that ignited this type of passion in me, like his sketching does for him. I'm passionate about the animals we rescue and care for, but I don't stop dead in my tracks over them. Not like how Marko focuses on his sketch and sometimes pokes his tongue to the side of his lips.

I have got to stop staring at the guy.

Finding a rock nearby, I sit and watch the butterflies. I love how butterflies just fly around looking pretty. Sure, they have a job to do out here, but they look so pretty doing it. But they also have really brief lives and that makes me sad.

When I look up next, Marko has his hands in his pockets and has moved closer to me. I didn't even notice.

"This place is so peaceful, Heath. I love it here. I can't wait to see where you plan to have lunch."

Pushing off the rock, I grin. "You're gonna love it."

With the summer breeze rustling the tree leaves, we continue on the path. Our feet crunch the gravel, and the songbirds provide a soothing melody around us. It's been a while since I've been out here, and I've forgotten how much I enjoy it.

"So, what brought you to live here in Bloomburg?" Marko's voice breaks through my daydream. "Did you grow up here?"

It's been a long time since someone asked me that question. It's the only question I ever hesitate to answer. I can talk about the ranch and animals all day long, but to talk about myself? Nope.

"Sort of." Risking a glance his way, I find Marko watching me. "Do you want the long or short story?"

"I think there's time for the long version, don't you?"

There is. Normally I answer with the most vague and boring answer I can. I don't like the questions or pity that sometimes come with my honest answer. But with Marko, I feel like he wouldn't judge me. He makes me feel safe and like I'm someone who belongs. Someone worthy.

"Well, it's not a pretty story. I grew up here, but it wasn't great." Puffing out a breath, I swallow. "My mom was into drugs and I never knew my dad. I took care of myself as much as I could. Mom was...well, an addict and not much of a mom, you know? She tried. I don't hate her or anything. But I couldn't help her beat it." Tears prick in my eyes. I'll never shake the guilt. If only I could have done more, maybe things would be different, and she might still be here. "Anyway, she died when I was sixteen and I fell into a rough crowd after that."

Glancing at Marko, I notice him listening, soft eyes fixed on me, and I decide to continue.

"I was arrested for joyriding. That's a funny story on its own." I snort. If you can't laugh at yourself in your darkest hour, you might just stay in the dark forever. Thankfully, I'm an eternal optimist. Getting caught was the best thing to happen to me. "The judge sent me to juvenile detention and when I got out, Dan found me."

"Who's Dan?"

There's no simple way to explain who Dan is to someone new here.

"Dan owns the Broken Horn Ranch. He's been like a father to me. He gave me a job and once my time at the halfway house was up, he offered me a place to stay." My nose burns a little because sometimes it's hard to talk about all this, but with Marko, I feel a little lighter after telling him. Like he understands it more than someone else would. Which is an odd feeling to have with someone I've just met.

"Ah, the same one who looks after your car. You mentioned him before. He sounds like a great guy."

Marko's tone is warm, and I sneak a glance to find him smiling at me.

"They all are. The guys at the ranch are the best people you'll ever meet, and I consider them family. And Jeff, of course."

We both chuckle, but it's true. That bird is part of me.

We crest a small hill and I sweep a hand in front of us as the open meadow comes into view.

"This is it. Our lunch spot."

I watch Marko's face as it lights up. The crinkles deepen at the corners of his eyes, and the bit of dimple he has peeks over the edge of his beard. Funny how I've never noticed dimples before, and his are barely there.

"Heath, this is... so beautiful."

Marko's voice is laced with the same appreciation I feel for any of nature's wonders. My chest puffs, knowing I made a great choice by bringing him here.

Finding a patch of grass in the shade, I crouch to spread out the blanket before laying on it and stretching out. As I figured he would, Marko heads off to the lavender garden. This one is smaller, but it's plunked right in the middle of a field of wildflowers. Buttercups, daisies, wild roses, and flowers I don't even know the names of surround a raised lavender garden.

Matts said it's a place to meditate and find peace, and I agree. It also smells great.

Unpacking the lunches, I place them on the blanket and wait to eat until Marko comes back. Zane left a sticky note with our names on each box, and I leave the drinks inside the bag to stay chilled longer.

Marko doesn't sketch this time and returns quickly, plopping himself onto the blanket and rubbing his stomach with a grin.

"I'm too hungry to get lost in a sketch. What are we having?"

My cheeks heat and I sort of wish I didn't go through this trouble, but Zane assured me it was a kind gesture.

"I, uh…" Clearing my throat, I point to his small brown box. "I looked up some food from the island you talked about. Hvar, you called it."

Marko's lips part and before he can say anything, I just want to spit it all out first.

"When you talked about it, you just looked really happy and I enjoy making people happy. So I tracked down these sugared almonds that might be close to what you'd find at the open markets there. And Zane made the cookies filled with the walnut paste. I wanted to get you a lamb sandwich but couldn't get that on short notice."

Marko opens the lunch box to find the Croatian treats he mentioned enjoying while his family vacationed, and he's quiet as he pokes around. The longer he remains silent, the bigger the knot in my guts grows.

"Do you like it?" I finally whisper because I just wanted to make him happy, not silent and gloomy. He does the broody look well, but it's more of his smiles I want to see.

"Yes, Heath. Very much." His voice has a huskiness that wasn't there before, but he smiles at me as he tastes an almond. "These are great. Not quite exact but close enough. You did good. Thank you."

"Yeah?" My grin grows with his praise and my gut settles.

He grins back. "Yeah. Real good, Heath."

Fuck if my insides don't combust with his words and seal of approval. I'm always trying to please people, but this time it feels a little more special. Something that sits a little warmer in my chest.

"Here, try one."

Marko leans over and rather than take the almond like a normal person with my hand, I part my lips. His brows scrunch, but he places the almond at my lips and I close them together, pulling it into my mouth.

I crunch and lick my lips. "Those are great! I can see why you like them so much."

Marko stares at me with an expression I can't quite read.

"Yeah, they're common, but what makes them so good is that even though they're at every market and you might see them every day…you appreciate them." He clears his throat and turns his attention back to the garden.

I stare at my lunch, unsure of what I'm feeling.

"Do you mind if I sketch a bit more before we head back?"

"Gosh, no! Sketch all you want."

Marko strolls through the gardens, stopping here and there, and all I can think about is how easy it is to be with him. It's a different kind of easy. Not like with the guys at the ranch. With Marko, I feel a happiness I don't get from goofing off in the barns with Dante.

It's like a fuzzy happiness. Like a baby duck, maybe? Nah, that's not right either.

Whatever it is, he sure makes me smile and I already smile a lot, so that's saying something.

***

"Thanks for taking the long way home." I shake my hair out before placing my ball cap back on. Marko settles my helmet on the bike alongside his.

"You seemed like you wanted a longer ride, but I know you still have to get home to Jeff."

Marko stuffs his hands in his pockets, and I do the same. He's right. I need to see Jeff. Hopefully, he hasn't torn apart his coop in anger. He's done it before.

"Um, yeah. It's not fair to him. But thank you for coming today. I had a great time. It's neat to watch an artist do their thing live."

Marko laughs and dips his head.

"Thank you for the invite. It was an amazing afternoon. Beautiful scenery." He pauses and his gaze finds mine. "And amazing company."

I pull my keys out of my pocket, smiling at his compliment. "Be grateful I didn't babble like I always do. I enjoyed watching you draw, and that seemed like something I should be quiet for."

"I don't need quiet to draw. I like your voice."

"Thank you. I don't think anyone has ever said that to me."

Silence hangs, and this weird energy sensation coats my skin. Like invisible goosebumps.

Marko clears his throat.

"I was wondering if maybe next Wednesday you'd like to take a longer ride with me? I usually ride alone, but today it felt nice to have a rider. If you can leave Jeff again, that is."

"Oh. Yeah. I mean...I'd love to ride again. And Jeff isn't always an asshole."

Marko's eyes crinkle at the edges as he laughs. The smile grows on Marko's face, and that tingly, fuzzy feeling is all over my skin again.

"Really? I mean, great! How about I pick you up at the ranch next time?"

"That would be great! Next Wednesday then."

"Yes. Noon?"

My phone goes off in my pants and I slap a hand to my chest. Marko laughs at my reaction as I silence the phone and check the screen.

"Shit. It's Dante. Jeff did some damage. I guess he chose asshole bird today."

As I slide my phone back into my pocket, Marko nods. "I'll see you next week."

I wave as I jog the few steps over to my car. Once I'm behind the wheel, I look up to find Marko still watching me. I wave again as I pull away and rub at the weird ache in my chest.

Chapter 9

Marko

Heath sent me the directions to the ranch last night. He also casually mentioned I'd probably meet a few of the guys while I'm there.

And I'm low-key hyperventilating. I already met Zane, and he seems nice, so the rest of them are probably just as nice, right?

After our time in the gardens, I knew watching Heath through my shop's windows as he got coffee with Jeff would never be enough. I just hope he feels the same way.

When my bike passes under the archway to the ranch, I spot Heath's car and head towards it just like he instructed. Once I kill the engine and remove my helmet, I glance around the ranch yard and don't see a single soul. Which seems odd. It's a busy place, and he knows I'm coming.

Taking out my phone, I find a message waiting for me from Heath.

Heath: When you get here, go to the tiny house in the corner and follow the noise around the back.

Okay. At least that's answered.

The dust swirls around as I walk towards the cute farmhouse in the corner. With its wrap-around porch and painted shutters, the old-time farm feel is so quaint it brings a flutter to my chest. The domestic simplicity of it just punches me in the heart.

Laughter flits through the air as I draw closer, and when I round the corner, all I see is a crowd of cowboy hats and Wrangler-covered asses. A roar comes up, and the crowd parts just as two men run at each other with... lassos? No. That can't be right.

"You made it!"

Heath bursts out of the crowd and another roar of laughter goes up. His flushed cheeks make him appear a lot younger than twenty-nine and his hair is a little damp, clinging to his forehead under his ball cap.

"Hey. What's going on?"

Laughing, he loops his arm through mine and pulls me closer to the crowd.

"Cowboy jousting."

"What the fuck is that?"

He snickers as we stop at the edge of the crowd. "It's easier if you just watch. I figure we have two more rounds before Alec comes out and tells us to get back to work."

Heath still holds my arm and shouts out encouragement to the two... competitors? Both men have lassos—yes, my eyes saw that correctly—and run at each other before releasing the rope towards the other's feet. I flinch when one steps into the perfectly placed lasso and falls to the ground hard as the other man jerks the rope to close around his ankle. The man still standing cackles and offers a hand to pull him up.

"This is what you guys do for fun?"

Heath shrugs. "A few of the volunteers do rodeo and one thing led to another. You've got to be a little bit crazy to be involved in rodeo, in my opinion."

"Heath." A large hand lands on Heath's shoulder and he jumps. Turning, I find a man with eyes bluer than the clear skies and a black Stetson firmly on his head. "Care to tell me why the volunteers on a break are out here doing something stupid?"

Heath clears his throat and drops my arm. "It wasn't my idea."

"Doesn't matter. You should have said something."

He pushes past us and hollers for everyone to get back to their jobs. He's not threatening, just... very in control. And clearly respected as not a single person in the group disobeys. They gather their ropes and hustle back to the ranch yard with murmured apologies as they pass by. The watchers also hang their heads and apologize.

When the group clears out, Heath clears his throat again as the older man approaches.

"I'm sorry, Alec. I just thought they were having fun."

Heath hangs his head, and I ache to console him.

"I know. It's not your fault. But you should know you're a leader here too." He claps a hand on Heath's shoulder again. "Don't be afraid to speak up. It's mostly harmless, but they could have hurt themselves by doing something unsanctioned. Our insurance doesn't cover those kinds of things." His blue eyes shift to me and back to Heath. "What are your plans today?"

Like a switch went off, Heath no longer has the sheepdog look, and he smiles as his hand settles on my back.

"Alec, this is Marko. He's taking me for a ride today. On a motorcycle."

Offering my hand, his roughened palm encases mine. Alec shakes my hand with a firm grip and a tip of his head. His eyes flick up and down my body so fast I almost miss it.

"Marko. Nice to meet you."

"Like wise."

Heath tugs on my arm. "We should get going. Sorry again, Alec."

Alec shakes his head. "Make good choices, Heath. See you later."

As Alec strides away, Heath puffs a breath. "He's not usually that intense. I think I made a mistake letting the guys fool around like that."

We walk up the path back into the ranch yard. Heath seems deep in his own thoughts as we travel the dusty path back to the main ranch yard. The same group of people are now back at work. People collect eggs in the chicken coop or wheel loads of manure out of barns. Someone has a horse out to bathe. It's all very quaint and pokes at the deep want I keep buried.

"He seems to understand you, though. I don't think he's mad."

"No, he's not mad. He's not like that. But I'll talk to him tonight." Heath suddenly spins in front of me, arms thrown wide. "Well, what do you think? Welcome to the Broken Horn."

He smiles and laughs as he spins around again, and I laugh softly. This is clearly his element. Faded jeans and scuffed up cowboy boots with a heart of gold to match his personality. Heath belongs here nurturing the animals.

"It's a great place. Maybe you could—"

A loud screech cuts me off as Jeff appears. The bird runs towards Heath, and I simply stand there, watching. Heath coos to the bird and strokes its head as I take a tentative step closer. Jeff shakes his feathers but doesn't move away from Heath.

Pulling my hand from my pocket, I open the little baggie and toss a few dried cranberries at him.

"I read online peacocks like fruit and nuts. It was all I had in the house, so figured I'd give it a shot." Jeff pecks and swallows one down, then another, and cocks his head at me. I never thought I'd need to win the favour of a bird, or that it would be this intense. I wipe a bead of sweat from my forehead.

Jeff continues to eat the cranberries, and I look up to find Heath's thoughtful gaze on me.

"What?"

"You googled what peacocks eat?"

My neck burns under Heath's stare, and I nod. "Yeah. You said he hates it when you're gone all day. I thought... I thought it would be nice to give him a treat for that."

Heath shifts his gaze back to the peacock for a beat before returning to me.

"That's very nice of you. Thank you."

Heath's voice is soft and my heart thumps out of beat. Jeff finishes the cranberries and steps towards me, so I dump the rest of the baggie on the ground. The bird happily gobbles them up and searches for more.

"I'm sorry. That's all I have."

Jeff bops his head like it's all cool, then shoots forward and pecks my thigh.

"Jeff!" Heath yells as I step back from Jeff and grab at my thigh.

"Oww!"

Heath lunges for the bird, and I rub at the pecked spot. Holy shit, that hurts.

"I'm so sorry. Are you okay?"

"Probably. It's just a bird...peck." Is it a peck or a bite?

Heath's eyes well with wetness as he herds the peacock towards the barn. I trail behind him and listen to him mumble to the bird about how you don't bite guests and it was very rude of him.

I want to smile because it's kind of cute, but when he finally closes the barn door, his sunshine smile is gone.

"I'm so, so sorry he did that. He's just a jealous bird and a bit unpredictable, but he's a good bird usually. I'm just... I understand if you don't want to come around anymore. Or want to hang out."

"What? No. It's not...I mean...yeah it hurts, but he's an animal. I don't blame him or you. I still want to take you for a ride."

He sniffs and raises those soulful brown eyes up to meet mine. Lord have mercy, I can't stand him sad.

"I have an antibacterial cream in my loft. You should check the spot and put some on." He tilts his head towards the barn where his car is parked. I follow him up the short flight of stairs and through a door to stand in the cutest barn loft.

"Nice place, Heath."

He disappears behind the only door in this open space that must be his bathroom. It's all open concept. A low counter separates the kitchen from the living area, and a long couch creates separation from his sleeping area. An enormous king bed flanked by two nightstands sits behind the couch. It's inviting and warm, a lot like Heath.

He reappears with a tube in his hand and, thankfully, his smile again.

"Thanks. It's not much, but I love it here." He motions to me. "Let me see what he did to you."

"It's uh...I'd have to drop my pants. It's on my thigh."

Heath shrugs like yeah, go for it and I unbuckle my belt as he babbles on about the amazingness of this cream. With a breath, I shove my pants down to locate the bird peck. You can't miss it. Right there in the middle of my olive grove tattoo is a red, swollen welt and a bit of dried blood.

"Dang, he got me worse than I thought."

My gaze finds Heath fixated on my thigh with no words coming out of his moving mouth.

"Heath?"

"Oh, yeah. He got you and it's uh, that's going to bruise. Let me ah, I'll be right back." He disappears into the bathroom again and comes out with a different tube. "Arnica." He waves it in the air and drops to his knees in front of me. Just like that.

I clench my molars together and screw my eyes shut while singing the *Baby Shark* song in my head. Seeing Heath on his knees in front of me might have been okay, but then I had to allow him to touch me.

"So, this stuff is incredible for not letting bruises get too bad. I used a lot when I first figured out birds can peck so hard." His fingers gently massage the gel around the peck mark, and I risk opening my eyes to look.

Bad idea.

Backwards ball cap, curls poking out, and Heath at eye level with my junk while he lingers to ogle my tattoo is not a scene I can wipe from my brain. "This is a cool tattoo. What is it?"

His fingers trace a pattern on the branches, and I step back while pulling up my jeans. What the fuck was I thinking?

"It's an olive bush. My, ah, my *baka* loved to walk in the olive groves with me when I was a kid."

"Oh." His voice is soft, and I turn to look at him now that I'm no longer exposed and back under control. "That sounds like a nice memory." He caps the gel and tosses it on the counter. "Do you still want to take me for a ride?"

"Of course. A peacock bite won't keep me off the roads. Besides, you told me there was a great place with homemade ice cream. I want to go."

Heath's beaming smile returns as he reaches for a jacket.

"Yes! I'm telling you, it's the best and if you don't like brownie chunks in your ice cream, we might not stay friends."

Laughing together, he leads me out and after we're settled on the bike; he shifts forward and wraps his arms around me before we're even out of the ranch yard.

And I might have hit a few bumps on purpose just to feel him hold me tighter.

***

"Ugh." I rub my stomach and lean back, sticking my feet out in front of me. "I can't believe you made me eat that entire dish of deliciousness."

Heath bumps me with an elbow as he scrapes at the bottom of his ice cream dish and laughs.

"I wasn't twisting your arm to eat it all."

"No, but you convinced me I could."

We both laugh as Heath mimics me, stretching out his legs.

"Worth it though, right? It's the best ice cream I've ever had. And the brownie?" He kisses his fingers. "Perfection."

At that moment, the sun shines upon us and lights Heath up. Like a gift from above, his curls glow, and I want to reach out and pull his lips to mine. Tell him *he's* perfection, not the brownie.

But I don't.

Instead, I stand and walk over to the little fence and watch some kids playing baseball in the park nearby. Heath joins me, leaning on his arms with a sigh.

"I always wished I had been the kid who had a dad to take him to baseball. I used to watch all the kids play like this on nights my mom was out of it."

It's the first time Heath has ever been anything less than sunny. His sadness bleeds through every word.

"What's your family like? You mentioned *baka*, but nobody else."

My heart rate kicks up. This is the time to tell him. He asked.

"My mother also died when I was young. A car accident when I was six." Heath touches my arm.

"I'm sorry, Marko. What reminds you of her most? For me, it's black licorice. Mom would bring me this black licorice pipe sometimes when she was in a good mood. She thought it was a riot. I'd eat it even though I didn't like it. Her heart was in the right place, you know?"

His question startles me, and I turn to him. He shifts and now we face each other as I war with myself about how much more to tell him.

"My *baka* says Mom was an angel on earth and I'm more like her than I give myself credit for."

Heath smiles. "*Baka* sounds like a smart lady."

"I'm no angel, Heath."

The silence sits between us and his gaze shifts to the ball field again. "Angels don't have to be perfect, Marko. Sometimes it's just how you make people feel."

Heath dips his head and examines his shoes. Since he offered me something, I need to give him something back.

"My mom was an artist, so I guess my painting reminds me of her the most. She always used to have pots of paints all over, and she'd let me mess up canvasses all the time." Smiling at the few memories I have, I turn back to the kids on the ball field. I don't want to tell him about my father. The day has been too perfect, minus the peacock incident.

"That sounds like fun. Better than a stale licorice pipe." Heath tries to smile, but it's not true and I reach out to grasp his hand.

"It may have been a piece of candy you didn't like, but she thought of you, and I know she loved you. It's hard not to." His eyes widen and I stumble over my words. "You were a good son, is what I mean. It's hard not to love a child."

Heath drops his gaze again. A ball pinging off the aluminum bat sounds, and we both swivel to watch the ball fly over the fence for a home run.

We clap and cheer for the ballplayer, even though we're too far away for the kid to hear us.

"Do you think we could go home now?" Heath whispers.

"Of course. If you're ready, we can."

We get our helmets on, but before I start the bike, his hand is on my arm.

"Can you take the long way along the river?"

"Whatever you want."

He nods and climbs on, and before we even reach the highway, he's not just holding me, he's hugging me.

And I'm positive he's turned his helmeted head to rest a cheek on my back.

CHAPTER 10

HEATH

"Okay, Jeff, act cool."

He doesn't.

He spills his drink on the sidewalk, then makes a show with his feathers.

"I was counting on you, buddy." I heave a long-suffering sigh as Jeff poops and screeches. Great, now I need to ask for more water to wash off the sidewalk. "You've failed the assignment, Jeff. Huge, epic fail. Public sidewalk pooping is not cool."

It's a miracle someone like Marko even wants to hang out with me.

Pulling out my phone, I send Marko a text and hope he's free to come outside. Since meeting him, we've met on the street for coffee at least once a week. I want to take more rides on his bike. It's so addicting and I love holding on to him as he takes corners. It feels like my heart might fly out of my mouth when we dip to the side, but life happened, and we just haven't been able to arrange another ride since we went for ice cream.

A moment later, Marko exits his tattoo shop with a giant smile as he holds up his coffee cup.

"Good morning, Heath." He looks over at Jeff and nods. "Jeff. Not liking the water today, big guy?"

Jeff stares at Marko and fans his feathers.

"He's in a mood. Barely drank any of it before making a mess and attacking the cup." I motion to the mess in front of the coffee shop. "Then he decided he needed a good shit. So...yeah. Great day."

Marko tries not to laugh and just watching him struggle with it makes me smile. Makes me... fuzzy. "He's allowed to have bad days. We all do. Maybe not so...graphic but it happens."

Marko watches Jeff bop around on the sidewalk before turning back to me. My palms are all slippery, almost like I've been playing with the slime in the kid zone at the library again. Which I only did once, and you'd think it was the end of the world when I told the librarian what happened to all the dish soap. Some people are so judgy.

"I was wondering if you're free again this Wednesday. For the afternoon."

Marko smiles and sips from his coffee cup. The ink on his hand catches my attention, a stark contrast against the white of his porcelain cup. Very masculine. Very... attractive in an *'I appreciate fine art'* kind of way.

"For you, I can be."

"Um...have you ever ridden a horse?"

Marko licks his lip before his gaze drops to his feet. "No. Can't say that I have."

"I'd like to take you for a trail ride if you're up for it. At the ranch."

Marko bites at his lip. The longer he takes to respond, the lower my hope drops. I hadn't counted on him saying no. And I've missed being with him.

"Yes. I'd love to learn how to ride a horse. What time should I be there?"

My entire body sags while my skin fizzes and pops like a mouthful of *Pop Rocks* candy.

"Really? I mean, great! Um, 1 P.M. would be perfect."

"I'll be there. Thanks, Heath."

We both stand there and, oddly, I don't want to walk away. I enjoy being with Marko. More than anyone I've ever met. On our last bike ride, he felt so easy to talk to. Even more than Dan. It felt like Marko might be the person I've always hoped for in a best friend. Jeff scratches at the concrete and peers up at Marko before preening his feathers and shaking them.

"He doesn't like me much, does he?"

Marko steps away from Jeff with a sad frown.

"Give him time. He's just protective. He probably thinks you're trying to steal me or something." I laugh, but Marko doesn't. Maybe he really is sad that Jeff doesn't like him.

Marko smiles again, but those cute crinkles around his eyes don't pop out like normal. He tilts his head back to his shop. "I should get back. I'll see you Wednesday. It was nice to see you again."

"Yeah. You, too. See you Wednesday."

Marko jogs across the street, and I stare after him. Before he enters his shop, he glances back to find me watching, and he sends the cutest little wave before finally ducking inside.

"Come on, Jeff. I've got a lot to do today." He follows me with no hesitation, and I tuck him into the back of my car, making sure all his feathers are in. He likes to poke his head out the passenger side, so I quickly roll the window down for him. "Stay put for a few minutes while I go wash your shit up." Jeff ignores me and sticks his head out the window, ready to go home.

I throw another glance at Dark Horse Tattoo and wish it was already Wednesday afternoon.

*****

"Mornin' Heath. How have things been? It feels like forever since I've seen you."

Blaze sits on the porch swing at Dan's and I bound up the stairs to greet him.

"Hey! It's been a while, for sure. I'm great!"

Jeff squawks and runs across the ranch yard towards the chicken coop.

"Still have the bird I see."

Laughing, I sit next to Blaze. "Yep. I'm the only one he seems to listen to."

"Did you ever try to find him a mate? Seems like he might be lonely, don't you think?"

Blaze sips from his pink glitter travel mug as he watches Jeff just be Jeff and run amok around the ranch.

"I haven't found any females close by. I've been preoccupied, and it just hasn't crossed my mind to look again. Other than the destruction of his pen or the chicken coop sporadically, he seems fine."

Blaze grins as he focuses on me. "You've been busy, I hear, with a new friend. When do we get to meet them? Me and Dan feel a little left out."

He bumps me with his shoulder and I feel like a kid keeping a secret.

"He'll be here tomorrow. I'm taking him on his very first horse ride."

Blaze's eyebrows raise, but he says nothing.

"What?"

"Nothin'"

Shaking my head, I meet Blaze's smirk. "No. You don't get to do that. Spit it out. What do you know?"

Blaze throws his head back with a laugh. "Simmer down. I've heard through the grapevine you've been datin' a fellow and I was just…" His eyes roam my face. "I want to meet him."

Goosebumps run up my skin and I shiver. "He's a friend. And if you're here tomorrow, you can."

Blaze nods and drinks from his mug.

"Okay. I'll be here."

"Good."

"It is."

Feeling very out of sorts suddenly, I stand and nod to Blaze.

"Say hi to River for me."

Blaze acknowledges he will and I march back towards the barns to continue my chores, but Blaze's words keep ringing in my ears.

'Datin' a fellow.'

I'm not. Not unless dates are sharing ice cream, walking in gardens and going on motorcycle rides. Or talking about families, pets, and careers and texting all the time. And complimenting his tattoos while thinking about where else he has them.

The way his thigh quivered when I smoothed ointment around his bird peck injury.

The way my belly swooped when he was standing there in his underwear and pants down so I could—

My thoughts are all tangled up like a kitten in a yarn basket as I lean against the barn wall with a gasp.

Shit. I *am* dating him, aren't I?

Does he think that too?

My belly gets all swoopy again like butterflies tickle everywhere and I shiver despite the warmth of the barn.

Well.

This is... not an entirely unwelcome revelation.

Now what do I do about it?

Chapter 11

Heath

"Thank you for letting me take Babe out today. Since Marko is new to this, I want him on a steady horse. I don't want him getting hurt, you know."

Colby leans against the stall, watching me.

"Of course. She loves to take anyone on a ride, and I agree, she's a safe bet for a newbie. Who are you riding?"

Looping the reins over the saddle horn, I motion towards the stall for Alec's horse, Domino. "When I told Alec what I was doing, he insisted I take Domino. Probably because the dang horse will guide us home while I'm not paying attention."

Colby laughs at me. "Good idea. Sometimes your directional skills aren't the best. Domino has a built-in compass."

You get turned around in a field once and send out an SOS and they never let you hear the end of it. Great friends I have.

Colby chats about his store and house renovations while he helps me saddle Domino. I don't need his help. I'm perfectly capable, but I don't mind spending time with him, either. While we talk, I'm trying really hard to notice what's different between talking to him and talking to Marko. So far, it feels much the same.

"So, is everyone going to meet Marko today?"

My body gets all tingly and that fuzzy duck sensation comes back after just hearing Colby say Marko's name.

I guess that's one difference.

Pausing, I peer over the horse's back at Colby, who calmly waits for my reply.

"Is that why you're still here? You want to meet him?"

"Oh no. I met him already. I'm just wondering when you'll introduce him to all the dads here."

His eyes twinkle, and his grin is big enough to split his face in half.

"He'll meet whoever is here while he's here." I shrug. "But Blaze said he'd be here and if he is, then Dan is." Colby snort laughs and rubs his hands together. "Besides, it's not like he's a date. They just want to meet him."

"He's not a date?"

Blaze's words from yesterday still roll about in my head. *Datin' a fellow*. And I'm not ready to say it out loud. Not that I don't trust Colby at all, but... what if I *am* right and we're just two friends?

Colby says nothing and I guide Domino outside in silence. Babe waits patiently and the low rumble of a motorcycle engine spikes my heart rate. Dust kicks up behind Marko as he draws closer on his Harley and Daisy, Dan's dog, tumbles down the porch steps and into the yard to greet the new vehicle.

Pointing to a space next to my car in front of the loft, the same place he parked last time, Marko acknowledges and pulls up. Daisy jumps and wags, waiting for the new friend to acknowledge her. Marko removes his helmet and reaches down to scratch her ears. Murmurs of *'good dog'* reach me and I wipe my hands on my pants before walking over. Hopefully, I can still talk, but my mouth is as dry as the farm field after a week of no rain.

"That's the greeting committee, Daisy. Everyone is a friend she hasn't met yet."

Marko smiles as he dismounts and leaves his helmet on the bike. He bends lower to pet her belly and his joyful laugh spreads to me.

"She's so happy and waggy. What a cute dog!" He looks over at me, and that swoopy feeling comes again when he stands and runs his hand through his jet-black hair. Yeah, okay. I don't get that feeling when I talk to Colby.

"Come and meet your horse. She's just as cute."

He joins me as we walk over to the horses, and he waves when Colby walks up to Babe.

"Hi, Colby. Nice to see you again."

"Hey, Marko. You, too. So, Heath says he's taking you on a ride today and it's your first time. Are you excited?"

"I am...and nervous. I've never had to control an animal before."

Colby smooths a hand down Babe's side with a smile. "This is my horse, Babe. She's as gentle as can be and won't do you wrong. Nothing to be afraid of. Here, come and pet her."

Marko approaches Babe with a giant smile, and something about him loving first on Daisy and now Babe has me all tied up in the weirdest way. He pets her neck, then goes around to the front and gives her an ear scratch and Colby hands him a sugar cube to feed her. She's so gentle and scoops it from his hand, then nuzzles his pockets for more.

"Hah! That's so cool. Her nose is so soft." He strokes her nose with one finger and Colby beams.

"She's an amazing horse. Just listen to Heath and you'll be fine." Colby snuggles the horse once more before saying goodbye and going off to find Dante, leaving us alone. So far, no sign of Dan and Blaze, and I'm oddly relieved.

"This is so cool, Heath. I'm excited."

His eyes crinkle as he smiles and I swallow, my mouth still dry and my heart galloping like a horse on the way back to the barn.

What the fuck are all the weird feelings about?

"Yeah, it's fun. Let me show you how to get on and give you a quick how-to. We're just trail riding, so all you need to do is sit and let the horse guide you. Babe knows what she's doing."

After I explain how to mount the horse, Marko nods. Jaw set, he shoves a foot into the stirrup and pulls himself up on the first try. After swinging his leg over, he sits proudly on Babe.

Taking her halter, I turn her around to stand beside Domino. I swing up on the horse with ease and take the reins. Turning to Marko, I find him watching me with a look that makes me blush. A blush! I don't blush. But I sure do like how he's looking at me.

"You ready?"

"Yes!"

His exuberance makes me laugh, and with a click of my tongue, we set off at a slow walk towards the trails. I've taken many people on these trail rides and never been nervous until now. I'm not even sure why.

"So, how did you learn to ride a horse? Was it by coming here?"

Grateful for the conversation, I nod. "Alec taught me. This is his horse, actually. He said I needed to learn to ride if I was going to work on a ranch. He used to do rodeos too. Have you ever been to one?"

"A rodeo? Never. But I'd love to one day." The saddles creak as the horses' hooves plod along the packed dirt path, and I sneak a glance at Marko.

"You'd look good in a cowboy hat."

Marko's eyes widen, and I look away. Pretty sure I made my entire body blush with that comment, if the heat under my shirt is an indicator. When I'm nervous, I talk more than usual. This is one of those times where words just keep coming out of my mouth like clowns piling out of those tiny cars at the circus. They never stop, just like my mouth.

"I mean, you look good on a bike and a horse. It's natural to wear the hat for the full effect. Especially at a rodeo. Chicks dig cowboys."

Oh my god. I need to stop talking.

"I've heard that, but what about the men? Do they dig cowboys, too? Because that's my preference, Heath."

Marko's voice is low and gravelly and... *fuck me*, it's sexy. And he's into men. How have I been his friend all this time and not even asked him if he was dating anyone? Do I want to be dating him?

Oh, lord, what the hell am I thinking!?

"Um, if you ask Zane, he'll say absolutely. He has a thing for Stetsons."

"I'm asking you."

Sneaking another glance, I find Marko watching me, swaying in the saddle like a pro and looking oddly delicious. His question doesn't feel like a blanket statement. He's not asking me what I like. He's telling me he prefers men and if I didn't already have questions about us, I'd think he's into me.

Is he into me?

Rubbing at my chest, I breathe deeply. God… I don't think. I know. Oblivious Heath has left the building, and he's very, *very* aware of the man next to him and the hints swirling around like dandelion fluff in the wind.

This man likes me, and my head feels like it's in the clouds.

And now all I can think about is Marko in a Stetson and nothing else.

"Um, I think…I mean…"

I've never been at a loss for words in my entire life. Thankfully, Marko lets it drop, and we continue the ride in comfortable silence. Well, mostly comfortable. I think something big just happened. At least it did for me.

"It's beautiful out here. I can see the appeal of riding a horse and not a bike sometimes. You can take in the scenery and the noise is gone. I love the growl of my bike and the wind in my face, but this is…completely different."

Marko's soft smile as he takes in the trees and fields around him warms my insides and settles the prickles of nerves.

"I know. There's something that hits different, right? It's freedom on four legs instead of two wheels."

When we reach the clearing where I planned to let the horses drink and rest, Marko fidgets in his saddle. After I've hopped off Domino and looped her reins around the post Colby installed up here, I approach him and Babe.

"Is everything okay, Marko?"

"Um, yes, but…" he huffs a small laugh as he looks down. "It seems like a long way down from here. A lot different from parking a bike. There's no kickstand."

His fingers clench the saddle horn as he exhales a shaky breath.

"I'm here," I whisper as I rest a hand on his leg. "Babe won't move. Just do it backwards. Swing that leg over and drop yourself down. Slide off slow."

He hesitates, but does as I instruct. When he drops to the ground, it's a little too soon for him to let go. He loses his balance, stumbling back against my chest.

"Oof." My arms instinctively wrap around him and pull him up and away from Babe, just as I would with any other rider. Except he's not any other rider. I'm keenly aware of Marko's scent. His spicy cologne and the citrus laundry detergent from his shirt. And the feel of his body under my hands. Solid and unmoving. When his hand brushes mine and squeezes instead of pushing me away, my belly warms, and I press my forehead to his back.

"I won't let you fall."

This time, Marko clears his throat, and both of us step away with awkward laughs.

"Thank you. I guess it was higher than I thought it would be." He steps forward and leads Babe to the creek, and I bring Domino along after untying her from the hitching post. "This is almost prettier than the lavender gardens, Heath. There's so much diversity in nature it always astounds me. There's so much inspiration out there."

"Did you bring your sketchbook?"

He smiles and taps his pocket. "Just a small one. I didn't know what I could take on a horse."

Laughing, I motion for him to lead the horses back to the hitch post. "Lots. They have saddlebags, too. In fact..." Unbuckling mine, I reach in and pull out a bottle of water for him and pass him a small package.

"What's this?" He flips open the box top and gasps. "Are these *kiflice od badema*? Almond crescents?"

Smiling at his joy, I nod. "Yeah. I helped Zane make them last night. Are they good?"

Marko bites into one and closes his eyes. "Heath..." He hums his pleasure as he chews. "My *baka* would be impressed. These are amazing."

"They were kind of fun to make and not too hard. I'm glad you like them. I have more at my place if you'd like."

"I would."

His voice drops and my pulse beats a rhythm unfamiliar to me. I'm... squirmy and it feels like I ate too many pixie sticks. When I glance at Marko, he licks the icing sugar from his fingers and shocking, dirty thoughts burst into my brain so fast I place a hand on Domino and pretend I'm adjusting her saddle.

I'm having a fucking sexual... epiphany? Crisis? What the fuck do you call it when you realize you're not straight and it sort of slaps you across the face?

"Okay, cool. I'll get you more when we're back." Chugging my bottle of water, I hope it dulls the heat building in my groin. I risk a glance to find Marko taking in the meadow. "If you want to sketch something, go ahead. I don't mind. We can go back when you're ready."

He wipes the crumbs off his hands and passes me the cookie box. "Okay. I'll be quick though. I could eat so many more of those."

I pack the box away and exhale a deep breath as Marko wanders off. The scent of Marko is still strong in my memory and I bite my lip, remembering how he felt under my hands. So many hard edges, but I bet his skin is soft. I still can't place the scent in his cologne, or maybe it was his shampoo, but I liked it. And the way he squeezed my hand instead of pulling it away. I liked that, too.

Oh boy.

I'm crushing on Marko.

Now what do I do?

And how come everyone figures this stuff out about me before I do?

***

No amount of coffee will help me today.

I wanted to take Jeff on a morning coffee break into town, but that would mean seeing Marko and after yesterday, I need to unscramble a few things in my brain first.

Not that I don't want to see him, because I really fucking want to, but after a very sleepless night playing back everything since meeting Marko and even events before I met him, I need some time to wrap my head around this.

Dante waves when I find him mucking out the llama stalls and I slump onto the hay bales. After leaning his shovel against the wall, he walks over to join me.

"You look like you've had a bender and need caffeine mainlined. Late night?"

"I think you were right."

He snorts. "I'm right about a lot of things. Care to narrow it down?"

"How does Colby put up with you?"

Dante snickers as I shake my head. "With a smile, my friend. With a satisfied smile." He laughs again before schooling his features. "Seriously, Heath, what's going on?"

Last night, I replayed my entire twenty-nine years in my head. All the signs I missed. All the things I ignored because... well, because I thought nothing of them. I dated women and liked them. I was straight. Or so I thought. The end. Do not pass go.

Seems I've had it all wrong.

"I'm pretty sure I'm bisexual. You were right."

Dante blinks and clears his throat. "Are you, I mean...sometimes it takes a while to discover things about ourselves." He places a gentle hand on my arm. "Thank you for confiding in me. Do you want to talk about it?"

Nodding, I pat the space next to me and he sits.

"Well, I discovered I like Marko. Not only that, but there have been a few other guys over the years who, now that I think about it more...yeah, I was attracted to them, and I guess I never gave it serious thought." Puffing out a breath, I run a hand through my hair and stare at the rafters. "The last date I was on, we went to a concert. A man next to me spilled his beer on me, and we talked all night. And...my date was right. He was flirting with me and I just..." I shrug. "I just didn't pick up on it. But I remember he had nice eyes, they were pretty, and I complimented him on his shirt."

I couldn't tell you what my date wore that night, but I can tell you the man had a warm smile and his eyes were brown with a pretty yellow tint when the lights pulsed just right. His shirt was red and a soft cotton that stretched and hugged him tight. I remember telling him the colour looked good on him. Because it did. He was attractive.

"So how do you feel now knowing this?"

Good question. No different really, except the man who I thought was just a fun friend is really the man I'd like more with... and if I'm right, I think he'd like that too.

"Well, I definitely have a type." Laughing, I run a hand down my face. "Taller, tattoos, and wide shoulders. I've been attracted to guys with those traits before, and Marko isn't the first one. Before, I brushed it away as just admiration. Nothing sexual because, you know, I had a girlfriend or liked women. Even those magazines I'd look at. I just..."

"Sometimes it doesn't make sense, Heath. Lots of people discover things about themselves later in life. We're conditioned to think '*straight.*'" He uses air quotes and wears a sad smile when he says that. "If we were all born with a manual and a sexuality sticker, it might help, but even then, we'd often ignore it. There's no box that you need to put yourself into."

"I should tell him, right? We've been dating this whole time, haven't we?"

Dante grimaces. "From where I stand, it sounds like you've been dating, yes. But I'd go ask him and make sure you both understand what's going on. Don't ever let things go unsaid. Communicate and, worst case, he only sees you as a friend and you carry on."

Before, being friends was all I wanted. If I read it all wrong and that's all he wants, I just might be heartbroken.

And that kinda sucks.

"That's a good idea. I should go talk to him."

The rumbling of the tractor sounds and we both groan.
After the hay is done, of course.
My sexual epiphany will have to wait.

CHAPTER 12

MARKO

My tattoo gun buzzes as I work on my client and I'm unusually detached from the process. I'm confident they could tell me there's an alien in the office, and I wouldn't even hear them. I've never been this unabsorbed from my work, ever.

My mind is with the man with a sunshine smile and a tendency to ramble during conversations. The man who has a pet peacock and baked me almond crescents before taking me on my first horseback ride.

I thought something changed between us that day. Like we were finally going to take this to the next level. But when we returned from our ride, instead of inviting me up to his place, he ran in and returned with another bag of cookies for me. After an extremely awkward goodbye, I went home alone.

But at least I had amazing cookies to take the disappointment away.

Heath hasn't brought Jeff to the coffee shop all week either. I've not seen him for four days and his last text was very short. No random questions like have I ever peed on an electric fence or if an orange wasn't called an orange, do I still think we'd have the colour orange? No late-night texts asking if I'm painting. Not a single word.

And I'm crushed.

Swivelling on my stool, I grab more gauze from the counter. I'm almost done with the shading on this tattoo and all I need to do is finish some colour on the duck feathers. Who tattoos a duck on their body, anyway?

Heath would, I bet. Ducks aren't far from peacocks.

"Do I have time to take a piss? That large *Slurpee* is on its way out."

People who love Slurpees. That would be the answer to who gets duck tattoos, then.

"Yeah, man. Just don't touch the tat."

He bolts off my chair and down the hall to the bathroom while I snap off my gloves to reach for my phone. This is so stupid. I like Heath and I should just tell him that. I'm positive there was a shift after that horseback ride. He baked me another Croatian treat—and I can't forget all the other thoughtful things he's done for me. There's no way I'm imagining it all, and he can't possibly be blind to his actions.

Can he?

"Hi."

The soft voice I'd know anywhere has me fumble my phone, and it clunks on the counter as I spin around.

"Hi. I was..." I clear my throat as Heath steps into my room. "I was just thinking about you." My voice fades away as Heath steps closer.

"Do you have a client? I was hoping we could talk."

His long lashes frame his eyes, and his smile is just a twitch of his lips. *Fuck.* Why does he have to be so damn cute all the time?

"I'm just—"

"Sorry, I went fast, but do you mind if we finish this another day? Is it a good place to stop?" My duck tattoo guy nods to Heath. "Hey, man. You here for a tat? Marko is amazing."

Heath's eyes never leave mine. "He's pretty amazing, all right."

My throat goes dry, and I motion for the guy to get into the chair. "Of course, we can stop for the day. I'll extend the next appointment by thirty minutes, and you should be good to go."

The man is thrilled, and I clean up the area on his skin before applying a bandage with the usual instructions. He says goodbye and bolts out the door.

Silence settles as I remove my gloves and wash my hands before giving Heath all my attention.

"I'm..." He screws up his face before he blurts, "*Oprosti.* Did I say that right?"

"You're sorry?"

His hands fiddle with the hem of his shirt as he bites at his lip. "I didn't come for coffee because we were in the middle of hauling hay. It's, well, you know how they say make hay while the sun shines? It's true. We were doing it all day, every day until it was finished. And then I..." He pauses and huffs a breath. "I didn't call or text you because I—"

His mouth moves and there's no sound, but his eyes are a little misty and my gut clenches, expecting him to have something bad to say.

"Don't explain. Life happens."

He shakes his head with renewed purpose and the curls poking from under his hat bounce.

"Yes, life happens. It happened, I mean, and okay, here's the thing." He inhales a huge breath. "Have we been dating?"

My knees wobble, and I reach for the counter.

"You don't think we've been?"

This is worse than I thought if he hasn't even clued in that we've been on dates. New friends don't do the things we've done. At least not mine. I don't go on intimate picnic dates with friends or let them hug me on my motorcycle. Not that I have many friends, but I sure as shit wouldn't be doing those things.

Heath rubs his face and mutters something I can't hear. Then he meets my gaze.

"I'm screwing this all up. Marko...here's the short version... I'm bisexual. I just figured this out." He sucks in another breath. "I have a lot I want to talk to you about, if you're even interested. And if you're not and I've misread this whole thing, then I hope we can still be friends." He's rambling, and it's adorable. "Because I think even if you don't like me like that, we're cool. I mean, you do tattoos and sketch and you teach me about your country and—"

"Heath."

He blinks like he didn't realize he'd been rambling and even if he was here to tell me he didn't want to see me anymore, there's no way I could just walk away from him. The fact he didn't realize we were dating is just the tip of the iceberg here. There's so much we need to discuss.

And a discussion in my tattoo studio is not the right place for this.

"Do you have Jeff with you?"

"No."

"Okay, first, thank you for coming by and I'd like to talk, but not here. Can we take a walk in about fifteen minutes?"

His shoulders finally drop as he nods. "I'd like that. I'll wait in reception for you."

The moment he leaves the room, I'm working as fast as I can to clean and sterilize my workstation. I take a little longer than fifteen minutes, but he's still waiting when I walk to the front and find him staring out the shop window at the coffee shop across the street.

After flipping the closed sign around on the door and texting Curtis that I'm out for the day, I set the shop alarm and turn to Heath.

"Are you under any time constraints?"

"No. I had Dante cover my evening chores, and I secured Jeff for the night."

"The night, huh?"

His lips tilt in a small smile. "If I wasn't talking to you, I figured I'd spend the night at some karaoke bar singing sad country songs."

I bark a laugh as the tension finally eases, and we walk towards the town's waterfront. "That's awfully specific, Heath."

Our footsteps fall into sync as we walk down Main Street towards the trail that leads us to the waterfront of Dogwood Pond. It's more than a pond from what I've read about it, but it's a cute name and suits this town well.

Heath remains quiet, which is unusual, and rather than wait until we're in some perfect place, I decide to rip the *Band-Aid* off and start talking.

"I want you to know that whatever the outcome of this conversation, I've enjoyed every minute I've spent with you."

Heath peeks up from under his lashes and smiles. "Me too. I've never met anyone like you before, Marko."

The french fry truck at the trailhead smells heavenly, and Heath nudges my shoulder. "It's no sugared almonds, but fresh-cut fries from a truck are like a delicacy around here. Want to split one?"

"Not with the gravy and cheese stuff, though." Heath stops walking, mouth hanging open. "What?"

"You don't like poutine? How?"

"I don't mind it. It's just...not my favourite."

"Okay. I can work with that at least. Just fries. Please tell me you like them with vinegar and not smothered in ketchup, or I might have to reconsider this friendship."

Heath smiles as he steps up to order, and I plunge my hands into my pockets.

"Vinegar is fine with me."

With a bag of hot fries, forks, and enough vinegar to drown in, we walk the path until we find an open bench looking over the water.

Heath quietly tears the bag open and doctors the fries with salt and vinegar. Only after he eats a few does he begin to talk.

"I'm sorry if I've hurt you. It was unintentional if I did. Believe me when I say I'm not one to pick up on obvious stuff."

Shoving a fry in my mouth, I shake my head. "Not hurt, not really. But I was confused when I didn't hear from you after we'd yet to go a day without contact. It felt like...I guess it felt like I was maybe imagining it all and you didn't feel the same way. I thought I screwed something up."

Heath drops his gaze to the ground at his feet and leans forward.

"It wasn't imagined." His arms hang between his legs as he twists his fingers together. "But it took me one sleepless night to put all the pieces together and realize I like you as more than a friend."

My heart leaps at his words. I want to shout and punch the air in victory.

"What changed?"

Heath turns his face to me, and I'll never tire of his gorgeous eyes with those lashes always kissing his cheeks. The way his hair always pokes out under his ball cap.

"Probably nothing, because I've always been drawn to you. When I think about being with someone, it's always you. When I think of growing old, you're there. If I think about a vacation, it's with you. That's probably far too much to say right now, but like I said, I've thought a lot since that horse ride." He swallows and licks his lips. "I can't *stop* thinking about you."

His gaze never wavers, and I have to swallow back the wave of emotion.

"What if we're not compatible with...you know, sex? We've never even kissed yet, and you just learned you're... not straight. While I'm relieved you want to be with me, Heath, there's still a lot about me you don't know. Not to mention this is a huge thing to learn about yourself. There's so much for you to learn and explore and...I'm not a guy who likes to fuck around."

Heath's cheeks flame the cutest pink as he ducks his head.

"Even if it's with me?"

He chews his lip and his knee bounces so fast I wonder if he'll fly off the bench.

"Especially with you."

"Oh. It's okay. I hope we can still be friends." He forces a smile on his normally sunny face, and I replay what I just said.

"Shit." I huff a small laugh. "Seems like we're both horrible at this." Grabbing the pile of fries, I set them on my other side and slide closer to him. His brown eyes track my movements as I slide a palm over his cheek. "When I say fuck around, I mean, not be serious. Casual. I don't do that. If we do this, if you want this, I'm kind of all in from the first kiss. I don't know how to do it any other way." My thumb caresses his cheek and his eyelids flutter. So fucking pretty. "My artist's heart never let me be casual. It was never my scene. Like two paintings at once, I can't do it."

His eyes widen as he finally understands.

"You actually want to be with me?"

"More than you probably know."

"I've never been with a man," he whispers as he licks his lips and inches closer. "I...I've never done casual either. I just know you make me feel like I'm covered in tiny bubbles whenever you smile at me like that."

I smile with a soft laugh. It's so Heath to describe something so meaningful by referring to how it actually feels. This man is always making me smile. But right now, he makes me yearn for so much more.

He makes me fucking hope I can have it all.

"Can I kiss you?" Heath's thigh now presses against mine and he bites at his lower lip.

"I wish you would."

Heath leans forward, and his ball cap bumps me on the forehead. He snorts and turns it around. "I swear I'm not always this clumsy."

Our noses brush and his rapid breath fans across my lips.

"Just kiss me, Heath," I breathe.

His lips press to mine, soft and chaste at first, and then it's on. In a blink, he's gone from shy and tentative, to almost climbing into my lap as he bites at my lower lip. One hand grips my neck and the other one digs into my thigh. He presses himself so close it's like he wants to mould into my body, and I have to tap on his thigh to back up so I can breathe.

"Sorry, I got a little carried away there."

"Don't be sorry." God, I sound so wrecked and it was only a kiss.

"Okay, I'm not. But I want to do it again. Do it more." He closes his eyes and drops his forehead to my shoulder. "I've never wanted anything more than the way I want you right now. Well, the time I bought the donkey comes close, but you still win. Even those french fries aren't holding my attention."

My body shakes with a laugh and my arms automatically circle around him.

"Come home with me," I whisper in a shaky breath next to his ear.

Heath lifts his head and his throat bobs with a swallow. "Yes. Right now? Because we can go right now."

"Yep. Right now."

He bolts off the bench and grabs my hand, then drops it. He scoops the barely eaten bag of fries off the bench and sprints over to a garbage can before jogging back.

Swollen lips, pink cheeks, and slightly out of breath... Heath is stunning. He's something I should sketch. There's no hidden meaning here. No miscommunication. He's one hundred percent into this, and I almost feel like I'm caught in a dream.

But I ask just to be sure he understands what I'm proposing. He didn't think we'd been on dates after all.

"Um, just to confirm we're on the same page here, I want you to come over to get you naked and keep doing what we started."

His laughter scares the seagull that was creeping towards the garbage can. The gull squawks and flaps its wings before lunging at the fry on the ground and running off.

"Thank fuck, because that's exactly what I was hoping."

Before taking off down the path back to the shop, I pull him flush to me and he snaps against my chest with a gasp.

"You're sure? I don't want us to be a regret for you, Heath. I like you too much for this to be something you wish never happened."

He searches my face and takes my cheeks in both hands before pushing on his toes to kiss me. This time slower, but I feel his unspoken words.

"The only thing I wish never happened is my cluelessness to not see my attraction for what it is. Because I wasted time kissing you by being such a fool."

With a shy smile, he slips his hand into mine and we walk back to the shop as fast as we can without tripping over our feet.

Chapter 13

HEATH

Marko still has an issue with riding in my car and insisted we take his bike to his place.

I wasn't about to complain about being smooshed up against his back, nuts to butt and hanging on to the man. If I'm being honest—and I am—hugging him while he drives a bike that actually vibrates under you is a major fucking turn-on. I'd grope him if I wasn't afraid of distracting him and causing an accident.

But as soon as he tells me I can get off, I can't keep that promise. No, I won't keep that promise because since I kissed him, it's like I've walked into a dark room and found the light switch after my flashlight died. Marko did that.

Everything is so clear now.

And I don't want to go back to the feeling of fumbling in the dark. My entire life has been bumbling from one thing to the next and trying to find a place to fit. I thought it was limited to choosing my career path and purpose in life, but it's extended to my love life too.

The bike gears down and he slows as we travel the brief part of his road that's unpaved. Then he's turning into his driveway and stopping under the carport. My skin is bubbly and if I were a shaken bottle of pop, this is what it would feel like right before you pop the lid off.

Marko taps my leg, and I dismount from the bike without causing bodily damage, but my fingers shake and fumble as I try to remove my helmet. His steady hands push mine aside as he unbuckles and slides the helmet off me.

His scruffy grin and messed up hair paired with those damn tattoos are like a direct line to my libido. Marko stands a full head taller than me, and I sort of like that I have to look up at him and pull him down to kiss me.

Pushing up on my toes, I grab his neck, pulling his lips down to mine.

His hands grip my waist as we stumble backward.

"*Oomph.*" My back hits the side of his house, and Marko pins me in place with a thigh between my legs. In one swift move, my hands are over my head, and he peers down at me.

"Sorry." Marko smirks.

"No, you're not." My voice is so low and breathless that I barely recognize it.

He laughs softly as he brings his lips to my neck.

Holy shit, I like that.

"You're right. I'm not sorry. I like you like this." His teeth graze my collarbone, and I stretch to get his lips on mine, but I'm distracted when he presses his thigh harder against my dick.

"Oh, shit..." Rocking my hips, I struggle to touch him and forget he has me pinned. *Everywhere.*

"Marko...let me touch you or something."

The rumble from his chest as he chuckles vibrates through me. "Not yet." Marko pulls away slightly and rests his forehead against mine. "If I let you loose, you'll be like a monkey after a banana. I can see it in those damn eyes of yours." He kisses my neck again. "Slow down."

I bark a laugh, and he grins at me. Marko's dimple shows again, right above his scruff. Good lord, he's hot. Who knew a single dimple would turn me on so much?

"Are you saying there's a banana in your pants? Because that's not attractive and might not turn out the best for you. They make mini bananas, you know."

Marko's eyes widen. "You're..." He snorts and shakes his head. "You're ridiculous." He chuckles and presses his thigh against me again. God damn, this man knows what he's doing. "No banana. You've just got that look in your eyes that means I need you to slow down or I'm going to come far too fast. I don't want that."

His eyes soften as he whispers near my ear. His warm breath across my heated skin somehow causes a shiver to race through me. How does he do that? I'm a quivering pile of goo and nothing has happened!

"You can come twice, then. You're not that old."

Marko's lips smile against my skin before he finally pulls back to let me see him again.

"No, I'm not, and I can, but..." Marko brings his free hand up to cradle my cheek. "I want nothing cheap or rushed with you, Heath. I want to take my time and discover what you like. You deserve that."

He takes my lips in a deep kiss that makes my toes curl, and okay, I can get on board with slow if that's what he wants. I think.

"I'll behave," I mumble and he releases my wrists.

"Good boy."

Okay. Um, that's new. Kinda like it when he says that. I shift my hips again to press on his thigh and he raises an eyebrow.

"Heath." His voice is low but commanding, and I stop.

"You're gonna kill me here."

"But what a way to go, right?"

I snap my teeth and nip at his jaw as he laughs and removes his thigh.

"It would be tragic to leave you, but I'd no doubt leave this world the happiest I've ever been." He takes me by the hand and tugs me to the front door. "Right now, though, I want you inside and naked."

As soon as he turns the deadbolt on his door, it's on.

I tear my shirt off and bounce out of my shoes. The button on my jeans nearly pops off as I rip them open and I've shimmied out of my pants all before Marko has even crossed the room.

He stands in front of me, completely clothed, which is against the rules here, while I still have one sock and my boxers on.

"Do you always rush, *dragi*?"

Marko leans against the kitchen island, calm and casual, like he has all the time in the world.

"You know what? No. But I'm...you..." I puff out a breath and close my eyes. "I just really want to do this with you. And I don't know what you just called me, but I love it when you speak Croatian."

Marko steps towards me and smooths his palm down my neck. My eyes drop closed as I bask in his touch. "It means 'my dear.'"

Everywhere he touches me, it's like he raises the temperature a million degrees. I open my eyes to his warm, hungry gaze.

But there's something else. A fleeting glimpse of something I understand well.

Longing. Aching. Hope.

"The feeling is mutual, Heath, but I'm not quite as...unrestrained as you. I like it though. To know you're that eager to be with me. It makes me feel like a king."

Taking a step towards him, I loop my arms around his neck and stretch up. "I can slow down. I just, I...fuck, I want you to touch me, Marko."

Am I begging? Maybe. I don't care though.

Marko's lips crash into mine and I'm lost for breath as he does exactly what I asked for. His hands are everywhere on my body, leaving trails of heat in their wake. When he squeezes my ass, I damn near explode. The tattooed hands I've admired for weeks are no longer holding coffee cups but cupping my ass, and that's enough to tilt my world. It's not even sex, and it's already the best sexual encounter I've ever had. Nothing has ever felt this consuming or passionate. This *right*.

He releases me to rip off his shirt and toss it behind him, and I slide my hand across the smattering of dark chest hair. Another tattoo near his heart, the Croatian flag, and I trace the edges of it. There's more ink down his left side, and I allow my hand to drift along the edges. His olive-toned skin goes well with the mostly black pieces. My fingers stop at the button of his pants.

Marko grabs my wrist gently and brings it to his mouth, pressing a kiss to my palm.

"Take them off me."

"You don't need to tell me twice."

That's like asking a kid if they want to open a Christmas gift early. They're never going to turn it down, and I've never ached to be close to someone skin-on-skin like I do right now. My hands shake as I peel his jeans down. A wet patch blooms on his boxers, and I gaze up to Marko. He nods and I continue dipping my fingers under the elastic and sliding them over his ass before pulling them down.

Marko is naked. Holy shit. We're naked together and I'm harder than an exposed nipple in January.

Marko's laugh rumbles and I snap my eyes to his amused grin.

"I said that out loud, didn't I?"

"You did." His hands grip my hips, and he presses against me. "*Jebote*, Heath. I want to make you mine."

I'm not a small guy. I may be shorter than some, but I'm compact with muscle from all the farm labour. Marko lifts me like I'm a feather, and I damn near swoon as he walks over to the couch and, somehow, we sit with me straddled on his lap.

Sliding my hands through his hair, I rock my hips and feel our hard cocks touch.

"God...Marko..." I gulp in air, feeling like a fish out of water. My entire body burns as hot as a forest fire and every kiss he plants on my flesh fans the flames.

Lips feather across my collarbone and up my neck. Marko's hands are firm on my ass as he urges me forward in my awkward bucking and grinding. He murmurs more Croatian words near my ear and I lose my mind.

"Fuck, fuck...Marko..."

My groan reminds me of the sound the donkey makes when he has to get up off the ground. It's not sexy *at all*. But my fingers pull on Marko's hair, tilting his head back to me and I smash my lips to his so hard our teeth crack. I should really come with a warning sign. *Caution: Injury may occur, ride at your own risk.*

My balls draw up so tight I fear they might shoot off sideways and I come all over Marko. Panting and shaking, my gaze meets Marko's and I find him watching me with a smug grin.

"Holy shit. Holy. Shit. I just covered you with my cum."

Marko chuckles and removes one of my hands from his hair. He kisses my knuckles, then my wrist.

"You did. I want you to add to it." He leads my hand between our bodies and slides it through the mess I made before placing my hand on his dick. "Stroke it, Heath."

"Fuck, that's so hot."

Marko's answering gasp as I jerk him off with my release is fucking addictive. His cock is so much thicker than mine. It's heavy in my hand and I wonder what it might be like to have it in my mouth. Glancing up at his face, Marko's molten gaze is locked on me, not my hand. Swallowing hard, I don't break the eye contact. I can't. Marko is, well, just as turned on as I am, and it sort of overloads my brain.

"Heath...*tako...*"

I don't know what that means, but it must be good. You don't sound like that and mean something bad. He strings a few more words together that I don't understand, but holy shit, do I love how they sound. His accent is a dick hardener.

Marko tenses and I speed up my strokes, pleased when the cutest whine escapes his plush lips. He comes with a shudder, and he still quakes as I slow my speed, but I can't stop touching him. Even as his dick softens in my hand, I don't want to let go, which is odd. It's not like I can keep my hand in his pants 24/7.

"Heath? Are you okay?"

Marko reaches for my hand and joins our sticky fingers.

"I'm great. Peachy, even."

"Peachy?"

Swallowing, I nod as I explain. "Yeah. I'm all fuzzy like a peach."

His brow furrows. "Is that what it means?"

I shrug. "I don't know, but that's what I think it means. And it's good. I feel fuzzy inside and," I raise our joined hands, "sticky on the outside. Which is the opposite of a peach, I realize, but it still fits. So, yeah, I'm peachy."

Marko's eyes crinkle at the sides when he laughs, and my heart gallops.

"Okay. Peachy is good. No regrets?"

"Only that I wish I figured this out sooner."

He leans up and kisses me, soft and languid this time, and I melt against him. His touch is so...tender? Gentle? I don't know how to describe it, but right now I trust him with all my soul and it all just feels too good to stop.

"Is it too much to offer to share the shower with me?"

"No," I breathe, suddenly overcome with more than just a wanton sexual need for him.

His hand gently taps my thigh, just like when I'm on his bike, and I stand.

"I'd offer you a hand but..." I hold them both up, now coated in drying cum, and I snort. "I guess it doesn't matter, does it?"

Marko pushes off the sofa and stares down at the mess on his stomach.

"Nah. I think we're beyond that now." He grabs one of my messy hands with his own and tugs me after him down the hall to his bathroom.

As he turns the water on and grabs fresh towels for us, I'm not ashamed to catalogue every tattoo, every muscle twitch, and every soft curve and hard line on Marko's body.

I've never felt more alive or comfortable than I do right now. With him.

Marko turns to invite me inside first and once we're under the spray, a whole new wash of desire spreads over me. He's magnificent as he tilts his head back, his black hair now wet and dripping. Water runs a path down his tattooed chest, and he rubs at the mess of cum on his stomach.

"What is it, Heath? You're very quiet."

"Sorry...I was, um, just admiring you. You're like one of the tattoo models I like to look at online. But you're here, and I'm in a shower with you, and I..." I'm babbling again. Probably easier to just show him.

Stepping into him, I reach up and drag his mouth to mine and kiss him until my lungs hurt and I have to step back. Fuck, even my hands are shaking.

"That's what I was thinking. Think you have one more in you tonight?"

Marko's grin slowly spreads, and he presses me back against the tile.

"For you? I have whatever you want."

"Does that include breakfast?"

He pauses and brushes his fingers across my collarbone. "If that's what you want, I'll give it to you."

"I like food."

He chuckles before shutting the water off. "I know you do, *dragi.* I'll take care of you."

Isn't that what we all want? Someone to take care of us?

"I trust you."

My voice is a scratchy whisper, and my heart bangs all over my chest. Because I do trust him and not just with food.

CHAPTER 14

MARKO

Incredibly, after showering, we made it to my bed. Heath voiced he wanted more, but instead of indulging his desire right away, he wanted to...cuddle.

While he was definitely turned on, once we made it to the bedroom, he switched to clinging to me like I might disappear. There was no way I wanted to move him off me. This was nice, lying here holding him. I've missed having someone hold me just because they want to.

"I don't know if I can stay until the morning. The idea of staying for breakfast is so tempting, but I work super early and I don't want Jeff to be alone for so long."

He shifts his head from my chest where he rests, tracing random tattoos on my body with his fingertips. Heath's warm brown eyes carry an uncertainty he didn't have before the clothes came off and I smooth the hair from his forehead.

"I understand. Work is important and I wouldn't want you to neglect Jeff."

His bright smile returns, and he leans up to kiss me. No hesitation. He just does it like it's the most natural thing in the world and it catches me by surprise.

"What's wrong?"

His smile fades and I rush to reassure him.

"Nothing. It's just…you seem so comfortable with me. I was expecting a freak out at some point. You've just discovered something pretty huge about yourself. We changed our dynamic, and I wasn't sure how you'd be."

Heath remains quiet, but I know he's thinking. He always scrunches his eyebrows just a little when he's thinking, and bites at his lower lip. Reaching up with my thumb, I tug the lip out of his teeth. Again, he smiles that damn sunshine my way and shifts to blanket his body over mine.

"I discovered something huge about you, too." He wiggles his eyebrows, and I huff a small laugh.

"I'm serious Heath. I really like you and I want to know where your head is at here." My hands smooth up his muscled back. Lord, I love a farm boy's body.

"No, I'm not freaked out. Don't forget I work with a group of gay or bi men. It's not a new concept and…I've missed a lot of signs over the years. Like, an impossible amount of signs that I like men too. It's hard to explain, but I'm not about to run screaming from your house because I touched your dick." Again, he kisses me. First on the forehead with a tenderness that makes my heart soar, and then again on the lips that turns into something far more than just a simple kiss. "I want to do more than that, Marko. I like you. Very much."

It's like the weight of the world lifts from my body and I wrap a hand around his neck to pull him back down for a deep kiss. Heath answers and grinds his hard cock against mine with a groan. I haven't been this easily turned on *ever*. Heath just has to breathe on me and my dick swells. I'm not that much older than him—I'm only thirty-five—but compared to his enthusiasm, I feel like a damn dinosaur. Only teenagers should think about sex more than once in two hours.

Flipping us over, Heath gasps as I grin down at him. A gorgeous strawberry flush spreads from his chest up his neck as he stares up at me.

"Jesus fuck, you're hot when you do that. Hell, you're hot just sitting here."

Laughing, I slide down his body, trailing kisses along his skin and delighting in his squirms and moans.

Hovering over his hard cock, I wait until he opens his eyes to meet mine.

"I want to suck you off. You okay with that?"

"Am I okay with that?" His voice squeaks as he nods quickly. "I don't think okay is an adequate word here."

"No?" I chuckle and tease a line along his shaft with my tongue.

"Marko...damn. I might come in two seconds. Don't judge me, please." He fists his hands into the sheets and stares down his body at me between his legs. "You're the fucking sexiest man I've ever met. Sinfully sexy and you're about to put my dick in your mouth."

Laughing, I drop my head as I kiss his hip. "That's my plan. You good?"

"So fucking good. I might die because I can't breathe, though."

Heath spreads his legs further, eyes begging me to take him apart and if I still doubted his lack of freak out, I don't anymore. I intended to take it slow and learn his likes and his hot spots and just revel in being with this man I've wanted for what feels like forever, but my cock aches fiercely and my patience is shot now that my face is buried in his groin.

After suckling at his balls for far less time than I should, I lick up his length and take him half into my mouth.

"Fuck, fuck, fuck...Marko!" Heath wants to lift off the bed but my hands pin his hips in place as I take him further down my throat. God, he's perfect for me. Large enough to satisfy my craving, yet not enough to trigger my gag reflex. And, not surprising at all, he tastes sweet. Like he dipped his dick in honey just for me. Which is ridiculous. But then again...it is Heath. Nothing is off the table.

Lifting my gaze as I suck him down, my eyes lock on Heath's molten expression long enough for a shudder to wrack my body and a moan to escape around my mouthful.

"I wanna come on your face," he huffs, and I pop off as his hand flies in to stroke himself to finish. Holding my tongue out, I hover as he explodes. It's on my tongue and I swallow it greedily, my tongue searching for more within reach. I'm pretty sure there's cum in my hair, on my face and probably the sheets behind me. But I'm not complaining.

Heath's chest heaves as he reaches out to wipe a blob from my cheek. He offers it to me on his fingers and I take it, only to have Heath surge forward and smash his lips to mine to chase after it. After some pushing, he's manhandled me onto my back and staring at my hard-on like he's starving.

"I wanna do that to you, too."

"Only if you want to. Don't feel you need to repay—" My eyes roll back as Heath decides today is the day he wants to test my self control and I turn the air blue with a string of Croatian curses.

With zero warning, he grips my dick and wraps his lips around it like a goddamn pro and moans. The vibrations send me into orbit and I thread my fingers in his hair.

"Fuck...Heath..." He sucks, moaning again, and I clench my teeth together. His gaze meets mine while his lips are still around me and it's a vision to store forever. "You look amazing with your lips around my cock. Shit, it's the hottest thing I've ever seen."

That just makes him take me deeper and my eyes roll back again.

"Heath..."

I tug on his hair to warn him, but he stays until I'm shooting into his mouth. He pops off while I'm still coming, licking his lips and with cum on his chin, he's a picture of smugness as he strokes me until I whine for him to stop.

"I'm sorry. It kind of happened too quick to warn you."

He shakes his head. "Don't be sorry. I almost did the same to you." He runs a finger through my load and puts it to his lips. "I don't know what I was expecting, but it wasn't this. Do you always taste like this, or is it different every time?"

"Uh, I've never...um, I don't know?"

He nods. Eyebrows drawn like he just made a serious discovery.

"Cool. I'll add it to the list of things to keep trying."

I cough. "You have a list?"

Tapping his head, he grins. "It's up here. Don't worry, big guy. I think you'll like everything on it."

"Do I want to know what's next?"

After surveying the mess on my abs and kissing a few tattoos, he grins. "I've never had anything in my ass before. I've heard it's next level."

My breath puffs out, and my knees would buckle if I was standing. Dragging his head down, I smash my lips to his. As always, Heath is eager and returns the kiss with wild abandon. Hands everywhere and pressing so close to me, it's like he wants to become one of my tattoos.

"You can't just say shit like that," I whisper when I finally release him to breathe. "You're gonna kill me."

"You keep saying that. I need you alive, Marko. No harm from me. I'm as gentle as a fly."

Leading us into the shower for the second time, the smile on my face grows as I crowd him against the tile. We can't stop kissing or touching.

Heath drew me to him for who he is inherently. The way he gives zero fucks about the way people look at him while he tucks a peacock into the back of his car. His genuine want for me to feel comfortable in this town and show me all the places he loves. How he learns about my home country just because he wants to.

His soul is beautiful.

With his long lashes wet under the spray of my shower and his sunshine smile as he slides a soapy hand down my chest, it hits me.

I'm the happiest I've ever been.

It has nothing to do with the sex and *everything* to do with Heath.

***

"You've been smiling constantly for a week now. Spill it." Curtis plops into the chair in my station. "What happened with you and peacock boy?"

"Don't call him that." I scowl and Curtis holds up his hand.

"Sorry. But a guy needs to know. Are you and Heath a thing now or what?"

Curtis's gaze is on me and a bead of sweat runs down my back before I steel myself to say the words out loud.

"We are officially dating."

Curtis whoops and pops up to clap me on the back.

"I'm happy for you! I think it's time you stop working and hiding and enjoy what love might bring you."

"I didn't say anything about love."

"You don't have to." He snickers. "You, my friend, are an open book."

"Don't you have work to do?" I grumble.

Again, he laughs and shakes his head. "Got it. Boss man isn't ready to talk about his feelings. But if you change your mind, I won't give you a hard time."

The front door chimes and I return to the sketch I'm working on for my client tomorrow. They asked for something rodeo and on short notice. It sounds like someone with a tight schedule, and I'm happy to oblige. Although I still don't know much about rodeo and that reminds me of something Heath said. He said he'd take me to a rodeo and one was coming soon nearby.

Opening another browser on my phone, I search for rodeos in the area. If this is the same one, it's in two weeks. I'll have to ask him about it tonight when we ride.

The day slides away quickly as I do a series of consults and before I know it, my phone is chiming with Heath's tune. *Tarzan Boy* by Baltimora because I make him want to beat his chest. His words, not mine, and I went along with it because, well, Heath.

My smile can't be hidden as I read his text.

> **Tarzan:** I'll be there soon. Running behind. Jeff was moody.

> **Not Jane:** I'll start winding down now and meet you at the house.

He sends a selfie with Jeff, who appears unimpressed. But then again, do birds ever look happy? I really need to learn more about peacocks.

After finishing my task and checking in with Curtis, I'm on my bike and racing home. For years, I never wanted to share my life with anyone. No one romantically, at least. I still had my *baka* for family and a few distant cousins, but it was safer to just keep to myself. Taking my bike and feeling the wind race by was all the comfort I needed or wanted.

Reaching my driveway, I kill the engine and coast into the carport. Heath changed everything. As I place my helmet on the seat, a smile forms when I set eyes on the helmet Heath wears now. Black with a smiley-face sticker on the side that he insisted he wanted just in case someone thought he was intimidating on a bike.

The thought makes me snort out loud.

Tossing my wallet and phone on the kitchen island, I strip as I walk to the bathroom. I'm tempted to linger, so Heath catches me half-dressed, but I'm too excited for today's ride. He wants us to visit an artisan market the next town over. Apparently, there's a woman there who makes goat's milk soap, and he needs to research for Dante. To assess the competition, he said, since Dante makes llama products. I love it when he gets fired up for his friends. His loyalty is one of his best qualities.

As the water washes over me, I reflect on how much my priorities have shifted since meeting Heath.

I'm happy and no longer living in the shadows. For once, I'm enjoying my success with the tattoo shop, and coming to a small town from the city has worked out well.

Although I do owe my *baka* a visit still. It seems like it's been forever since I called her from the lookout in another spiral because I was afraid I'd be shoved out of yet another location. And I need to tell Heath about my family. The rest of it.

Until now, I've dodged it. He knows about my mom and *baka*, but I held back about my dad. We're still new and fragile. I'm in so deep with him and already terrified of the thought of him walking away. Most people don't want to be involved with someone tied to crime. It's deceitful to keep it from him, but I'm just so damn scared to make my voice say the words.

A knock on the front door has me rush to finish dressing, but at the last minute I decide to leave my T-shirt off. Maybe I can still tempt Heath into bed and skip the ride.

But it's not Heath at my door.

"You must be Marko. Goin' somewhere?"

The man stands tall with his Stetson on his head, mirrored sunglasses and a charming smile. Glancing in the driveway, I notice the truck with a Broken Horn Ranch symbol on the side and my first thought is panic that something happened to Heath.

"Yes, I am. Is Heath okay?"

"Oh, he's on cloud nine. Right as rain." The man smiles. "Can I come in?"

"Uh, sure."

"Nice ink." The man nods at my naked chest, and I pull on my shirt, still hanging from my hand.

"Thanks. Uh, what, ah...who are you?"

He looks around my place before he lifts his sunglasses and crosses his arms.

"I was supposed to meet you when Heath brought you by for your horseback ride but somethin' came up and I didn't make it. I'm Blaze."

He holds out his hand, and I take it. "Hi. It's nice to meet you."

Blaze doesn't let go of my hand immediately.

"We've already met, but I doubt you remember." He drops my hand and I wrack my brain, wondering how I could have met a man like him and not remember.

He wags a finger at me. "I know what you're thinkin' and I look a little different, but let me jog your memory. It was a sunny day in July about fifteen years ago or so. Gosh, the time just kinda gets away from me. I had a meetin' with your father...at your house."

Black spots dance at the edge of my vision.

"You know my father?"

"Regrettably, I do. And because of my gut, I chose not to take him on as an investor in my company. Good thing too."

I look at Blaze with fresh eyes. In a suit and trimmed hair. Clean shaven. The yelling from my dad mostly, as Blaze and his assistant left. Dad was angry that day. It's also the day he verbally admitted what he was doing and my entire world collapsed.

"Blaze Porter. You turned him down that day for no reason. He was pissed. I remember he said you'd never make it without his help."

Blaze laughs with no humour.

"Yep. He was mighty high on himself and there was just somethin' about him I didn't trust. Has that ever happened to you, Marko? Have you ever just had a feelin' about somethin' or someone and you don't understand, but you listen to it?"

"I have."

Blaze's gaze strips me raw. If he knew Dad, he likely followed the news and knows my involvement too. I already see Heath drifting away. Of all the people in the world, I had to find the one with close ties to someone who almost did business with my father.

He hums and pops a toothpick from a wrapper before placing it into his mouth.

"I know Heath would have come to me if you had already told him this. When do you plan to tell Heath who you are?"

"I'm not lying to him, if that's your insinuation."

"No, it's not. I understand why you don't shout about it from rooftops. Trust me, I get it. But Heath trusts people, Marko. He's kind and good and all the things we hope for in life."

My gaze finds his as I swallow.

"Ah, I see you already know that, son. I'm happy you appreciate that about him." He flicks his toothpick around a few times as the cold dread settles over me. "I know you're not askin', but I'm givin' you some advice. Heath will be fine if you tell him. He values honesty and he won't judge you. If he doesn't find out from you…he's gonna be hurt, Marko. Then I don't know how he'll react."

"I'm not like him." I blurt because that's what this always comes back to. I'm his son by blood only, not his carbon copy.

"I know you're not. Heath will know that, too, because he's just figured out he's not quite straight. Which is a huge thing to trust someone with for the first time. You get what I'm sayin' Marko?"

Sort of. It makes sense. Heath has already shared with me his history of breaking the law and what wasn't a very nice home life. He won't turn his nose up. I know that. But…

"Do you know everything about what happened, Blaze? Did you follow it closely? In the news, I mean?"

"Close enough. I'm not a billionaire because I ignored things. I paid attention, but what are you gettin' at?"

He flips the toothpick in his mouth again, and the scent of spearmint hangs in the air.

"I was involved and made a deal with prosecutors. That day you were at the house, he confirmed what he was doing. I was hoping it wasn't true, but I…I turned him in not long after that."

Wow. That was hard to say out loud after all these years.

"Has he been in contact with you since he got out?"

Shaking my head, I bark a humourless laugh. "Not directly. But my last shop in Rosevale was vandalized. I don't have any proof, but I know it was him. That's why I came here. Fresh start and all that."

Blaze's face softens, but there's no mistaking where his loyalty lies.

"Talk to him, Marko. Don't start off somethin' with a secret."

Without another word, he leaves my house, closing the door behind him.

Chapter 15

HEATH

"Thanks for looking in on Jeff. I'm not sure how long I'll be gone."

Zane eyes Jeff in his enclosure.

"It's not a problem. You deserve to have a life too, Heath." Jeff pecks the mesh and Zane jumps back. "I like animals. He just doesn't like me."

"Yeah. He's pretty fierce when it concerns me. I don't know why he won't be friendly to other people. I really need to find other peacocks for him, but it's been hard."

Zane clears his throat as we step outside the small barn. I've stabled Jeff two hours earlier than he's used to in order to meet up with Marko. It broke my heart to do so, but I'd only worry about him out here without me to round him up. He has a tendency to not listen. And he can sometimes attack. So, yeah, it's a bit of a pain in the ass to anyone else here. But Marko deserves to not be second place to a bird. As much as I love Jeff, he can't kiss me the way Marko does.

Not that I've tried. Birds don't even have lips, so that's just weird all around.

"So... we're hoping you'll invite Marko over tomorrow for the bonfire." Zane stuffs his hands in his pockets. "Will you? We'd all like to spend some time with him and get to know the guy who has you asking to take time off."

Zane chuckles, and I do too. He's not wrong. Since I've started dating Marko, I've found it easier to step away from the ranch more often. I've trusted others to my job and, like tonight, I'm asking for help with Jeff. He's always been my responsibility and I'm fine with that, but actually stepping away here and there has been...eye-opening.

But the fear of them not approving of Marko claws at me more than when I told them I'm bi.

Puffing out a breath, I scuff at the ground with the toe of my boot before meeting Zane's gaze.

"I want to bring him for that, but I'm nervous. I really like Marko and it scares me to think you might not like him. I don't know how anyone can't like him but also...what if you don't?"

"If you vouch for him and like him, I think that's all we really need. We all care about you and want to know the man who makes you happy." He chuckles and runs a hand through his hair. "That, and we want to know if he has what it takes to be part of the ranch."

Wagging a finger at him, I let a laugh slip. "See! That's why I'm nervous, Zane. It's just like you guys to put on the whole dad act and scare him off."

He holds up his hands. "Never. I promise to behave. Besides, I'm more of a big brother and less of a dad." We both laugh at that because it's true, and he softens his voice. "But please invite him. If he comes here, then Jeff doesn't have to be in his pen so early, either."

"I'll talk to him and let you know."

Zane smiles. "It's all we ask. Now get going. I'll check on Jeff later. He'll be fine."

"Thanks Zane. I trust you. Now I need to get going!"

He waves me off and I almost add that I have tattoos to lick and a dick to suck, but that's probably too far.

But it's not a lie and I can't get there fast enough.

***

After parking my car in Marko's driveway and carefully closing the door, I frown at the sizeable chunk of rusted metal that falls at my feet.

"Well, that's not good."

With my toe, I push it under the car and hope Marko doesn't notice, but when I spin around, he's leaning in the doorway of his house watching me. With his arms crossed across his chest and a small smile on his lips, I know I'm busted.

"You're right, *dragi*. That's not good."

My skin warms whenever he calls me anything in Croatian, and I meet him at the doorway.

"Can we not discuss it now?"

Marko closes the door behind us and gathers me into his arms. He's such a large man that he makes me feel small in his embrace. But he also makes me feel safe and cherished; something that's new to me and I very much like it.

"We won't talk about it now. I want us to enjoy the afternoon planned. But Heath," Marko pulls back and his warm brown eyes radiate concern. "You really need to address the car situation. It's serious."

Stretching up on my toes, I kiss his lips.

"Let's talk later. Promise."

Marko nods in agreement, and I puff a breath of relief. My car is a sensitive subject and most people don't get it. Just like they don't understand how I have a peacock. But Marko deserves his say in it... just not right now.

He presses his forehead to mine with a soft sigh.

"I spoke to a client today who said if we want to watch the sunset, then we should drive towards Rosevale and take the route closer to the lake and stop at a rest stop. I have it marked down. Could we do that tonight and go to your market another night?" Marko places a kiss on my forehead before moving to his living room and picks a leather jacket off the couch.

"Yeah, it's fine. Dante probably went by himself, anyway. The market sometimes has the mini donut truck, though, and I wanted that more than to spy on the goat soap lady."

Which is kind of true. I always want donuts.

"Um, it's going to be colder on the bike near the water and later in the day. You should wear my other jacket."

"You want me to wear your jacket?"

He shrugs, likes it no big deal, but I've heard the teenagers talk at the ranch. If someone you're dating gives you a jacket to wear or even a hoodie, it's a big deal. I don't know why, but if the flush on Marko's neck shows how he feels, I think he agrees.

"I don't want you to get cold."

Taking the worn leather coat, I meet his gaze. "Thank you. I bet it's the next best thing to having you hug me to keep me warm."

"Make sure you hold on tight."

"Always."

Slipping into Marko's coat, I inhale the scent of him that lingers in its fibres. Thankfully, he doesn't see me as he's already moved to the door to slip on his boots.

Following him out, he turns when we reach his bike. Rather than handing me my helmet, he places it on me instead. Tenderly, he tucks the hair under the sides and clips the buckle into place.

Then he boops my nose.

"You're so cute." A bit of his accent comes through as he smiles at me. Boyish almost, and my heart flutters in my chest.

"I try."

Marko laughs and his smile drops before he turns from me. I don't get to ask him if anything is wrong because he fires up his bike and motions for me to climb behind him. Which I'll always do. I love our weekly rides and tonight is extra special with a sunset. He backs us out of the driveway and as we travel down his road, I snuggle as close as I can and hold on tight.

***

Marko sits on a picnic table at a roadside stop. His sketch book and pencils out he's been drawing for twenty minutes as I lay on the top of the table, taking in the last bit of sunshine before the sun starts its descent for the night.

Marko's client was right. This will be a gorgeous sunset.

"What's inspired you to sketch today?"

He lifts his head with a start, like maybe he'd forgotten where he was.

"Um...a few things. It's..." He clears his throat and motions for me to sit up. "I'll show you."

After sitting up and switching to sit beside him, I wait patiently. Marko is rarely nervous. He's always confident and so in control. But now he's a little fidgety.

"Heath...I want you to see how I see you."

He slides the book to me and flips back the page. It's me. Laying on the picnic table just now. My eyes are closed, but I'm smiling. It's a black and white sketch, but I know the details are the sun shining around me, making me appear almost angelic, almost perfect, if I had to put words to it.

"This is beautiful, Marko. I love what you create. Paintings, tattoos, drawings. All of it. You're so talented." My gaze finds his, and that cloud I saw earlier passes, and an uneasiness settles. "Marko...is something wrong?"

He brings my hand to his lips and kisses my knuckles. How does he make me so loopy with one small kiss? It's such a small gesture, but it says so much. "You make it easy. You're beautiful, Heath. Inside and out. I'm so fortunate that you let me share my life with you."

"Marko...."

God. My entire body breaks into a shiver and that weird ache blooms in my chest again. Setting his sketch aside carefully, I scramble off my seat and tug at him to stand. Looping my arms around his neck and pushing up, I meet his lips in a deep kiss.

"Is it weird that I feel like you're the only one who gets me? The only one who...who..." I can't think of the word because his lips are on my neck and his hands are under my shirt. Fingertips dance over my skin, setting it ablaze. "You're the only one who has ever made me feel like I can't breathe without them."

This intense need to be next to him, to feel his skin on mine, is so overbearing it's not until he steps back from me that I notice I've been undressing him.

"*Ljubavi*...we can't do this here. I want to, fuck I really want to, but I also don't want to be interrupted." He pulls me to him again and kisses me softly. "Let's watch the sunset and continue this later."

His smile still doesn't quite meet his eyes and rather than poke again for him to tell me what's wrong, I let it slide.

"You know, if you had a car, we could just make out in the back and nobody would see a thing."

"But then I couldn't feel you hold me so tight whenever we ride. I don't want to give that up." He spins me around and wraps his arms around my waist so we can both watch the sun. "Now that I have you, I want to have this for as long as I can."

His words don't sound right to me, and he tightens his arms so I can't turn around. And even though we're still as the sun dips below the horizon, bathing the water in a gorgeous glow of orange, a restlessness radiates from Marko.

"Do you know why I like sunsets?"

He drops a kiss on the top of my head. "Why?"

"It's a reminder that even at the end of a shitty day, there's still something beautiful at the end."

Squirming around, I break from his arms and peer up into his warm eyes.

"Would you come to the ranch tonight? Will you stay with me?"

He cups my cheek and smooths his thumb over my lower lip.

"Is that what you want?"

"Yeah. I want…" I swallow hard, not sure what I really want. Until now, he's not been to the ranch except to ride a horse. I want him in my space and my routine. "I want you to be there in my bed when I wake up because I want you to…I just really like you and I want you there."

Ugh. That was so lame.

Marko gazes at me and takes my face in his hands. His lips take mine and he slowly kisses me, turning my knees to mush and making me pant so hard I fear I might pass out.

"I want to be there for you, *ljubavi.* So much."

"What's that word mean?"

Marko hesitates.

"Love."

My breath stops after hearing that word from his lips. Love. He called me love. Dammit. Is this what it's about? Do I love him? I don't know, but it's something new and scary and so fucking thrilling I want to chase it.

"You always call me the sweetest things. I need something to call you. What word describes a handsome tattooed man who says all the sweetest things and makes me feel like someone important?"

"Yours. Just call me yours and it's all I need."

Fiddling with the hem of his shirt, I let my fingers dip under it and caress the smooth skin above his waist.

"Heath…"

"How long will it take to get home?"

"Don't blink those lashes at me like that."

"Listen, I've been hot for you since we got here and I watched you sketch. That's oddly arousing, by the way. I want to get you naked, and I'm not one bit shy about that."

Marko's throat works as he swallows, and I know he's calculating the best answer.

"It's about forty-five minutes until we can get to the ranch."

"Is that going fast or the speed limit?"

He chuckles and kisses my neck again. "It's driving at a safe speed. And I hope you hang on extra tight."

Pushing away, I walk to the bike and put my helmet on. Marko still watches me with a darkness in his eyes I can't place, and I pat the seat.

"Chop, chop Mr. Tall, Dark, and Handsome. There's dick to be sucked, and I'm getting impatient."

That makes him laugh and move, thank god.

I might have been trying to lighten the mood, but I'm not kidding.

Chapter 16

MARKO

Heath wasn't kidding when he said he was impatient to get home.

We've barely made it into his loft and he's on me like a spider monkey.

"Fuck, I've edged myself all day thinking of you in my mouth." Heath's lips trail down my neck as his hands fumble to unzip my jeans. "And your ink. I want to lick it all. See my cum on you."

He groans when he drops to his knees and yanks my jeans to my thighs.

My dick springs out, and Heath says softly something that sounds like, '*Thank you, baby Jesus.*'

"Did you just say a prayer to my dick?"

He pauses long enough to blink up at me. His cheeks are flushed as he licks his lips. He whispers, "I'm just thanking the powers that be for delivering me this bounty."

Before I can respond, his lips are around me and he's working to get me all the way down his throat.

"Oh my god...Heath...you shouldn't be this good at this." He responds by taking me deeper and I slam my hands to the wall behind me to stay upright. I swear he's smiling as he works me over, but at this rate, I'll be too spent to reciprocate.

His hand works under my balls and I want to spread my legs, but I can't because I still have jeans on. Frustrating.

"Heath..." Sliding my hands into his hair, I tug until he finally releases me. "Come here."

He stands up, and I shuffle us backwards until his back hits the kitchen counter. My lips tease his neck and I work my hands under his shirt before yanking it off and tossing it aside.

"You're a natural, *dragi*. You suck my cock like it was made for you."

"I've been practicing." He drops his head back and grips the counter behind him.

I step back with a raised brow. "Um...what?"

Heath lifts his head, brows scrunched. "To be good at it? I practice."

"I thought that we..." I motion between us.

"Oh, god. No! Not with other people, Marko. With my cock sucker."

He tries to wriggle away, but I shake my head and press my hand against his bulge.

"Tell me later?"

He shakes his head. "No, let me show you."

Heath is so intent on this, I relent and ease away so he can move behind his kitchen counter. He opens a drawer and removes a substantially sized cock-shaped sucker wrapped in plastic wrap.

"Colby said if I wanted to get used to having something deep in my throat, I needed to practice and train my gag reflex. It's cherry."

Heath unwraps the sucker and then shows me just how good he is at it.

"Fucking hell, Heath," I breathe when his throat bulges with the sucker's length—on the inside. "Remind me to send Colby a thank-you card. Put that thing down and get over here."

He licks his lips with his signature grin before placing it on the plastic again.

"I prefer the real thing." He snort laughs which is adorable. "Never thought I'd say that, but I do."

Heath wraps his arms around my neck and pulls me down to him. His kisses are now soft as he uses his body to steer me through his loft until my legs bump into the edge of his bed. Which is perfect timing because my pants have slid down to my knees, and walking was growing difficult.

Perched on the end of his bed, Heath again kneels and removes first my pants and then my socks.

"You have nice feet."

"Um, thanks?"

"People never notice feet. Just thought I'd tell you that is all."

"You're always so thoughtful, you know?" I'm aiming for a joke, but it's true. Kind and thoughtful and perfect.

"Thank you."

Heath grins and lifts my leg. He kisses my calf, then my knee before setting it down and motioning me to move up on his bed. After he strips off the rest of his clothes, he crawls up my body and traces the olive shrub tattoo on my thigh with a fingertip. He kisses it with such tenderness I can barely swallow the lump back in my throat.

"Are you going to tell me what's bothering you tonight?" he whispers and moves up to trace the pattern of waves over my ribs with his tongue.

"Nothing's bothering me."

Heath's deep brown eyes lock on mine, and he presses a kiss on the Croatian flag tattoo, lingering there before raising on his elbows to kiss my nose.

"I won't ask again, because I really, really want to get dirty with you right now, but I know something is on your mind." He kisses me with more force and my hands grab his hips, holding him against me. "Just know I really like you, Marko."

Heath whispers his confession before trailing his mouth down my neck and kissing random patterns along my body. Everywhere he touches me, my skin sings and I arch to keep his mouth on me. Every second he leaves space between us, I want to reach out and grab him to place him back.

This time when he sucks me in, he goes slower, like he's savouring it, just like his giant sucker. Which might not be far from the truth knowing Heath.

"*Jebote*, Heath...I'm gonna come."

He hums and flicks his gaze up to me and he won't release my dick even when I pull on his hair with a rough yank. "Heath!" I come so hard that spots dance in front of my eyes, and he coughs and sputters, letting cum drip down his face as he licks his swollen lips.

"That was even hotter than I thought it would be. Wow." He wipes at his face as my body still shivers from the best blow job I've had in my life. He reaches for his erection and strokes himself, brown eyes drinking in my naked and spent form.

"Wow, is right." My hand reaches for his neck, and he moves it away as I sit up to kiss him. He pulls back. "My face is still...I mean..."

Rather than use words, I grasp his neck and pull him forward, tasting myself everywhere. Heath shudders and gasps against my mouth, eagerly meeting my tongue. His cock pokes into me and I slide my hand around it. A low, animal-like growl vibrates his entire body.

"Lay down, *ljubavi*. I want to make you fall apart just like you did for me."

Heath flops to the side and rolls to his back. His breath comes in shallow pants as his dark eyes watch me. Reaching over to his nightstand, I pull open the drawer and find what I want. After tossing the lube on the bed, I imitate what he did to me. First, kissing his calf, then knee, and up the inside of his thigh. I tease at his shaft with my tongue and he tilts his hips.

"Shit...Marko..."

His voice is still raspy after he abused his throat with my cock. So fucking sexy. Wrapping my lips around him, I slide my finger down his taint and stop at his hole. He inhales a sharp breath and I flick my gaze up to find him watching. Lips parted with a delicious glow on his cheeks, and fuck me, my cum still on his chin.

"Tell me if you don't like it."

He nods and licks his lips. Easing next to him, I take the lube from earlier and squirt some into my hand. Taking his cock back into my mouth, I tease him with a fingertip and he moans so beautifully I know it's my new favourite sound.

I alternate teasing him with my mouth and a finger until he's babbling nonsense, and his cock is so hard it has to hurt. Scrambling to my knees, I reach for more lube and Heath spreads his legs even further.

Sweaty curls stick to his forehead and his chest has a strawberry glow.

"Please don't make me wait any longer, Marko. Please."

Contorting myself so I can do everything I want to at once, I bend down to his lips. His hands pull my neck down as I slide my fingers into his slick hole.

"Oh god." He kisses me and mumbles against my lips. "Don't stop. Please, please."

I can't answer him because his tongue is down my throat, but I awkwardly reach in with my other hand for his cock while he presses onto my fingers.

One stroke.

That's all it takes to have him scream my name so loud as he comes that I hope nobody knocks at the door. His back arches off the bed and I lose my balance, almost crashing down on him.

His hands shake as he slides a palm over my chest and I ease down next to him.

"You just fucked me with your fingers."

"I did. You told me it was on your checklist."

His eyes refocus on me, and he smiles. "It was!" Fingers trail down my arm and his eyelids droop. "Will you help me shower and sleep over? I think I'm too weak to do it myself. I think I used all my remaining energy to come."

Chuckling, I lean down to kiss his forehead. "Of course I will, *ljubavi*."

He stares at me for a few beats. "I really like that word, Marko."

"Me too."

He threads his fingers in my hair. "I think you're turning into my everything."

Heath is so open with his thoughts and feelings it's overwhelming in the best way. He kisses my cheek and rolls out of bed, bending himself and trying to keep his mess contained to his belly.

"Good lord, that's a lot of cum. I didn't know I could do that. Next time warn a guy."

I burst out laughing as I follow him into the shower as he requested. After we're both clean and snuggled under his covers, his breathing evens out quickly and he falls asleep with his head on my chest.

***

My eyes peel open and slam back shut when the sun greets them. A quick swipe with my hand around the bed confirms I'm alone. The disappointment is real for Heath's smiling face and bed-rumpled hair, not being the first thing I see this morning. But the sounds of a tractor chugging and muffled voices below reminds me I'm on a farm.

And things start awfully early.

There's no clock to be found, but there's a folded sheet of paper with my name on it on the nightstand.

Hi!

I didn't want to wake you up at 5 am!

Please don't leave until I come back. I should be back up by 9 am and I know you don't have to be at work until noon today.

I hope you'll still be here and make yourself at home.

Heath

I certainly don't mind sticking around to see him. He's just like my morning caffeine. I need my dose of Heath before my day feels right.

With a snort, I shake my head and start gathering all my clothes strewn around his loft. I wonder if Heath just rolls out of bed and out to work because even his clothes are still all over the place. Wandering around, I pick up his clothes too and place them on the bed.

Searching his tiny kitchen, I find not a single sign of coffee. Not even instant. Does he seriously go into town every day for coffee? Needing something to drink while I wait, I find a hot chocolate package but no kettle, so I resort to a pot on the stove.

Once it's made and cooling I pull up a chair to his kitchen counter and fish my phone from my jeans. It vibrates in my hand with an incoming call from my *baka*.

"Hi, *bako*."

"Don't you '*hi*' me, Jura! Where have you been?"

Shit. I'm about to get a severe tongue lashing.

"Sorry, I know I said I'd visit, but I've been busy."

She unleashes a string of Croatian about how she thought something happened to me when I never made plans and lays the guilt on extra thick.

"I miss you," she finally ends with. I miss her, too. There's so much I need to tell her and just when I'm about to, Heath bursts through the door with a laugh. Jeff follows behind him with a squawk and drags his feathers across the floor while throwing some huge bird shade my way.

"Jura, where are you?"

"Oh, crap. I didn't notice you were on the phone. Sorry."

Reaching for his hand, I squeeze it and mouth *it's okay*, but I don't drop his hand.

"I'm at a friend's house, *bako*."

"It's early. What kind of friend are we talking?"

Heath overhears, and he bites his lip.

"A very special one. I want you to meet him."

Heath remembers to breathe, and I pull him between my legs with the phone still pressed to my ear.

"You should have told me." Her voice softens, and I can tell she's excited. "This weekend. The neighbourhood is having the lamb roast. You'll both be here."

"We will. I need to get ready for work and I'm sorry I didn't call. I'll fill you in soon. Tell the fellows I won't miss it."

After ending the call, Heath leans in to kiss me. "I didn't want to wake you up this morning, but I love coming up here to find you in my kitchen in all your sexy glory. I could get used to that." He kisses me again and, like our kisses always seem to do, they go on forever with roaming hands and soft sighs and an incredible desire for me to never let him out of my sight.

When I pull away, I force him at arm's length, so I don't get distracted. I need to tell him.

"So, um, that was my grandma you heard, and um, I hope you're free this weekend to meet her?"

"If I wasn't free, I'd change my plans. I'd love to meet her. Who else will I meet?"

"Mostly the Croatian immigrants who settled in the same area when my family came over. Most of them worked in the silver mines there or owned small businesses. A lot of business owners."

A few were my father's friends but took mine and *baka's* side. "And I need to tell you something."

"Okay. Tell me anything."

Swallowing hard, I start with the easy stuff.

"My first name isn't Marko. It's really Jura."

"Okay. Not life-altering Marko; lots of people go by their middle names. Especially when they're named after their dads." He just smiles and shrugs, but I tug his hand to get his attention.

"That's true. I was named after my dad and my grandfather. I legally changed my last name to my mother's maiden name because it was too much always being recognized or mixed up with him. Heath...my dad stole a lot of money from people. He's the biggest financial criminal in Canada."

My guts tighten. Fuck. There. I said it. One more to go, but I can't be here to watch the disappointment form on his beautiful face.

"So? Are you just like him?" Heath's smile fades. "Is that what you're trying to tell me? I'm confused Marko."

My hands shake as I pull up an old news article and text it to him.

"I just sent you a news article that explains it." Rushing to pull on the rest of my clothes, I step around Jeff who looks like he's hoping for more cranberries but might want to peck me again instead.

"Marko, please. Don't rush out. I wanted to—"

"Heath, please. Read that article and if you can forgive me, we'll talk, but I can't..." My voice hitches and I need to get out of here. I can't watch his face when he reads it. "If I'm still worth it to you, call me."

Like a coward, I rush out of his place and hurry to get my helmet on. I rev the engine of my bike and hightail it home.

Chapter 17

Heath

"Heath! Hi! Come on in."

"Is Blaze here?"

After reading Marko's article, I still wasn't sure what it all meant. There were loads of words and shit I didn't understand. But I knew someone who could explain everything better than this article did. I somehow got through my work today, but barely. Was this Marko ending things before they even got going? I just don't understand.

"Yeah, he is. Would you like a glass of wine? We were watching *Jeopardy* reruns and arguing like an old married couple." River snort laughs as Mando, their cat, races out of the kitchen to see me. After greeting him properly and acknowledging how he's the cutest cat in the house, he saunters back where he came from, tail held high.

"Heath?" Blaze scans me quickly as he enters the hallway. He motions for me to follow him and turns back to the living room. "I think I know why you're here."

"Um, beer if you have it, River?" I motion to Blaze and gesture with my phone, likely not making any sense.

"We do. Go sit. I'll bring it over."

Blaze reclines in the couch's corner. A half-empty wineglass sits on the side table along with a piece of wood and a jackknife.

"Do you still carve things?" I ask as I settle in the recliner next to him.

"Just spoons. I'll never be good at anythin' else." He pulls the drawer on the table open. "Would you like one?" It's filled with carved wooden spoons, and I can't get over how cute it is to have a drawer full of his creations in the living room.

"Sure! A Blaze original."

Blaze passes me one, and it's small enough to tuck into my pocket. It's kinda cool.

"Thanks. So, I need your help to explain something to me."

"Sure. Is this about your new friend? Sorry I didn't get to meet him on your ride. I was hopin' to be there, but I took longer helpin' River than I thought I would."

"Are you two talking about me? I can leave."

River sets a beer next to me on the side table and then tops up Blaze's wineglass before kissing him.

"You're not goin' anywhere, Riv." He looks to me. "Unless Heath prefers it?"

"No, it's okay. I should get more than one opinion, anyway. And yeah, it's about Marko."

River joins Blaze on the couch and Blaze puts an arm around his shoulders while River turns the volume on the television down. Mando joins us, watching his wildlife shows on his own floor-model television. This cat is #lifegoals.

"So, um, Marko told me today his dad was a financial fraudster or something. Then he sent me an article to read and took off. I've read the article, and I don't understand what exactly he did. Or Marko's involvement. I was hoping you could help me understand."

"He took off? What do you mean? Did he leave town?"

Blaze knits his eyebrows together, and I shake my head.

"No, no! Not like that. He slept over, and, um, he left after telling me this. Took off from my place like Jeff was on his ass."

Blaze nods in understanding and River chuckles.

"He slept over. That's so something you would say, Heath." River raises his glass in a toast to me. "Get it. He's hot."

Blaze raises a brow at River, who sips and shrugs. "I just speak the truth, babe."

Blaze sighs and leans forward. "Marko's father is Ivica Dasovich, and yes, he scammed many people out of millions of dollars. He would convince people to invest with him but never invest that money."

"So, he just stole it?"

Blaze teeters his hand back and forth. "The short answer is yes. He would use it to buy investments or property, but not what the client thought. He forged statements and would pay them money when they asked, but he could never repay the full amount. Just enough to make you think all was well. It's all part of the scheme."

Jeez. That doesn't sound nice, being lied to for money like that.

"Why would he do that?"

Blaze sips his wine and leans back again.

"Only he can answer that, but when people do it, there's usually somethin' small it starts with. Maybe they made a mistake or needed money at home, so they dipped in once and got away with it. Then they do it again. Or they wanted to inflate the book of investments so they can attract bigger fish."

It's still a bunch of gibberish to me, but Marko's dad isn't what I care about. It's what Marko thinks he did.

"Well, I still don't understand what would make someone do that, and I probably never will. But Marko seems to think I'll want nothing to do with him and I don't understand why. This article he sent said he...crap, I need to look it up again."

"It said he turned evidence for immunity. Is that it?"

"Yeah! Wait...how did you already know so much about this?"

River nudges Blaze with his thigh, and they exchange a look. He nods before exhaling.

"You know I'm a billionaire and you know my company. I started one of the first online payment processin' platforms. In the beginnin' I needed investors to help me. It was me who contacted them and made proposals and sat through long meetin's gaining their trust. But there was one man who approached me. Ivica, Marko's dad. Without tellin' you all about that, I will say that Ivica isn't a nice guy."

"I get that. Marko didn't sound very fuzzy talking about him and I knew something was off with him yesterday, but he didn't want to tell me until today. What's Marko all scared about here?"

"Well, I imagine he's afraid you'll judge him and push him away."

"I could never! Why? This is stupid. He's, he's..."

My everything.

But I'm not going to say that out loud just yet. I think.

"He thinks I won't like who his dad is? Hell, I don't even know mine. My dad could be a serial killer for all I know!"

"Heath," River's soft voice draws my attention. "He thinks you won't like him when you find out he helped his dad steal."

"What? No...did he?"

Is the air leaving the room? It feels like my lungs are deflating. There's no way Marko would do that. He's so gentle and kind. And sexy and funny and he brings Jeff cranberries and...

"Heath? Are you okay?"

"No," I croak and shake my head. "What did Marko do?"

"Immunity is asking to be spared punishment for providing evidence against someone else." Blaze moves and stretches out to grab my knee. "Heath, look at me and breathe please."

I do as I'm told and find Blaze and River, both with concerned faces, watching me. Gosh, I think I forgot to breathe. A gulp relieves the burning in my lungs and River sags. "You scared us, Heath."

"Sorry, I just...like...spell it out for me. Please. Is Marko a good guy or not? Because I think I fell in love with him and...and...I need to know what this means."

Blaze leans back, and I remember the beer next to me. A few swallows provide a brief distraction while I wait for the verdict, and it smacks into me. The enormity of it all. I love Marko. I think I have for a while and just never clued into it. Long before we ever kissed, and I realized we were dating.

So much for not saying it out loud.

Should I be happy he told me this or angry because he already stole my heart before he did?

"I follow my gut instincts a lot, Heath. It's how I became a successful businessman. When I met Marko's dad, it was a strong feelin' not to trust him. Has that ever happened to you?"

"Yeah. Remember the guy who said he didn't know his uncle had those horses we rescued last year? It was like I could see through him, see his black heart. I didn't buy a word of his excuse and it's like I could feel the cruelty coming off him in waves." That guy was just gross. "I knew we had to get the horses out of there fast."

"And how did you feel meetin', Marko? Any gut feelin's?"

Smiling, I remember he was nervous with the animals, and he waited forever to talk to me. His hand on the cup for Jeff, and the way I had that swoopy feeling when he smiled at me. No warning bells. If I have to be honest, I was drawn to him like a magnet. Not just his tattoos, but maybe a vibe? It felt like he was a man I wanted to know. Immediately.

"All of them good. Not a single bad feeling."

"If it helps, I sort of know how he feels. It's sometimes hard to tell people where you come from or your past because you think they'll judge you. You're an exception to that. You put yourself out there all the time and it doesn't matter to you. *'I'm Heath, take it or leave it.'*" Blaze pauses. "Those are good qualities, by the way."

Blaze and River both laugh softly, and a genuine smile fills my face.

"That's true. I don't *always* put it out there, but when I do, it's just the way it is."

"I think Marko has spent too much time runnin' from the pain of what his father put him through rather than focusin' on the good things."

"But what does *your* gut say, Blaze? Does Marko give *you* a feeling?"

Blaze swirls the wine in his glass and is silent for a while.

"My gut says he's a good man. Just maybe confused about the black and white of life." He sets his glass down before assessing me again. "You know you're like a son to me and Dan. Hell, even Alec.

We want to see you happy, and Marko does that. He balances you. Life can't always be about the ranch animals and Jeff. Yes, you love and care for them. It's your job. But at some point, Heath, you need a life of your own. Another outlet and interests. Since you've been datin' him, we've all noticed a change in you, and it's not bad at all."

"Thank you." A giant lump sits in my throat and I stand. "I need to think about things, I guess."

Standing, Blaze meets me and pulls me into a hug.

"We're here for you. And I'm glad he finally told you. I knew you'd struggle with this and it's not the way to start off a relationship. Come by again if you need to."

Blaze walks me to the door, and while I put on my shoes, all I can think about is how great it would be to take a drive on Marko's bike, but my car will have to do. Which means I won't go far.

"Can we talk about my savings next time? I hate to admit that it's time, but I think I need a new car." Blaze handles all the ranch employees' savings and benefits, and I don't think I've ever cared about what he did. Maybe it's time for that to change.

"Oh, thank god. You don't know how long I've been waitin' for you to say that. And yes, we can do that. It would make us all happy to see you drive somethin' safer." He squeezes my shoulder. "You can still keep it. Just don't drive it. We'll find a safe place for it."

Again, I'm swamped with emotion and can only nod.

"Thanks again, Blaze. I'll call you."

In the evening sky, I look up at the stars before getting in my car. It's a clear night and I know exactly where I want to go.

***

There's no way my car would make it quietly into Marko's driveway.

Instead, I pulled over on the shoulder and then walked along the darkened road up to his house. As I drew closer, the light from his house spilled outside. I stood at the end of his driveway for a while, wondering if this was what I wanted to do. Every time I thought of no Marko, I didn't like how that made me feel.

After sending him a text, I continued around to his backyard.

I spread the blanket from my car on a spot to the side of his pond. Hopefully, the bugs aren't bad out here tonight. The slide of the patio door draws my attention and the light from his sunroom illuminates Marko as he steps out.

He really is a beautiful man. Even now, when he shuffles over in a pair of low-slung lounge pants and bare feet.

"Hi. I have another blanket."

Patting the spot next to me, I smile.

"Good. I hope the bugs aren't bad here."

Marko folds his giant frame down next to me. I miss a lot of signs. I'm not always quick to pick up on things, but I notice the space Marko leaves between us and I don't like it.

"I don't spend a lot of time out here, so I'm not sure about bugs."

Leaning back on my elbows, I stare up at the stars. They're so bright tonight. It's been far too long since I took the time to enjoy them.

"Do you know why I don't want to get a new car?"

If Marko thinks my conversation topic is odd, he doesn't acknowledge it.

"You said it was complicated."

"It is." Lying all the way onto my back, I fold my arms behind my head. When Marko remains sitting all tucked up into himself, I poke him with my foot. "Lie back with me and look up."

He manages, and I keep my laugh inside. He's really trying not to touch me. I don't like it, but I think I understand why he's keeping some distance between us. I'll let it go for now until I've said what I need to.

"My car is the last and only thing my mom ever owned. When I was really little, there were a lot of nights we'd fold the seats back and pretend we were camping. But before that, she'd spread a blanket on the hood of the car, and we'd lay there looking for shapes in the stars."

"Like constellations, you mean?"

"No. Shapes. Mom was…different. She liked to be free and make things up. We'd try to connect the dots in the sky to make different things like animals or letters or whatever." It's funny how easily children can be distracted from the truth by funny games and stories. "Anyway, I didn't know any better, and I always thought those weeks of camping were fun, but the truth was, that car was our home now and then. Mom rented furnished apartments or rooms because we had nothing. When she didn't pay rent and we had to leave, she'd pack our stuff in boxes and garbage bags and say, *'Hey, Heath baby, it's time for another adventure.'*"

Thankfully, because of the regulations around renters not being evicted during the winter, we never had to adventure in the snow.

But those adventures were never something I hated. Not even when I was old enough to realize we were homeless.

"The point to all this is, I don't want to let it go." Reaching over, I find one of his hands and tangle our fingers together. "It's a hunk of junk, a falling apart heap, but when I left juvenile detention, it was all I had. No pictures or teddy bears. No memories of fancy trips or knick-knacks. Just a car that my mom tried to turn into some wild adventure to shield me from the truth that we were homeless more often than we had a home. She didn't always make the best choices, but she loved me. And that car is all I have."

His fingers squeeze mine and tears slide down my cheeks. It's been a long time since I shared that with someone. Even the good memories can hurt sometimes.

"*Ljubavi*...don't cry. Please."

Marko's gentle thumb swipes at my cheek, and I turn to face him. His brown eyes mirror my sadness, and there's no way I could let him walk away.

"I know it's not the same as whatever it is you think you did, but I don't blame you for your choices. Your father should never have put you in that position." Marko stiffens, and looks away, but I yank on his hand. "Hey, I'm here for you. Why did you think I'd run away when I've been nothing but open with you?"

His sigh is heavy. "I guess because it's all I've known since then. My friends turned away from me. People who I thought liked me for me when they learned the truth were all suddenly gone."

"They weren't your friends then." My voice is a hiss and a fiery anger like I've never, ever felt spreads in my chest. "You shouldn't be judged on things in the past that you've paid for. That's...that's...garbage!"

Marko's lips tilt into a small smile.

"That's a pretty powerful word. Garbage."

"I'm not always good under pressure."

He brings my hand to his lips and kisses each knuckle. "It's not just that. I feel like I didn't pay for my part in his crime because I made a deal. Sometimes that bothers me and you're so full of...sunshine and light. You always do good. I was afraid I'd change your outlook or tarnish you somehow. I turned my dad in, Heath, while I remained free."

There's so much guilt in his voice it physically pains me to know this is how he feels.

"More garbage talk. What bothers me the most here, Marko, is that you had the opportunity to tell me this, and you didn't trust me. I can understand why, but when you love someone, you have to trust them with all the crazy shit in your head and in your life. That's what it's all about. It had to be so hard for you to watch a man you looked up to lead you astray like that. My heart breaks for you. And you paid, Marko. You lost your father. Don't you think that's enough?"

"I try to think that, but I'm sure the families who lost their life savings don't think so." He rolls over to his side. "But can we go back a minute? Did you just tell me you love me?"

"Not exactly." I guess I really am no good at keeping the big stuff inside. "But I'm telling you now. I shared about the car because I trust you. And maybe it's crazy, but, yeah, I love you. Pretty sure anyway. You're like no one I've ever met. Ever. And you kiss great. So fucking great."

When he smiles in the moonlight, he's so damn beautiful. The scruff and the tattoos, the way he makes me feel just being with him. If I'm not in love, I'm in something, and whatever it is, I don't want to let it go.

CHAPTER 18

MARKO

He loves me. Holy shit.

"I think I've loved you since the day you brought me to the lavender gardens."

Heath's lips part in surprise and I can't help swiping a thumb across them.

"Really? But that was like our second non-date date."

Shaking my head with a small laugh, I bring his hand to my lips and dust my lips across his wrist. "I still can't believe you didn't think that was a date. It was the sweetest, most romantic thing anyone has ever done for me. I wanted to kiss you that day—so bad."

My confession makes me overheat and want to turn away. But not Heath. His palm presses against my cheek, holding my gaze to his.

"Why didn't you?"

"Well, I wasn't sure you were into men, for one thing."

Heath snorts. "At the time I wasn't."

"I think I suspected that. You were...naïve, yet giving me all these mixed signs. I didn't want to screw anything up, so I waited. And hoped."

"Hoped for what?"

"For you to like me that way because you make me laugh. You're so fresh and beautiful. So damn unique that just thinking of you makes me forget my own black clouds." His eyelashes, still wet from his earlier tears, make my heart ache and bloom at the same time. How could I have doubted his reaction to my news? "I was afraid it would all end if you knew about my past."

"No one has ever seen me like you do," he whispers. Heath's fingers scratch into my scruffy beard. "You fill this space for me. This empty feeling that's been bothering me goes away with you. I don't want that to end."

"I love you, Heath. You are...*moja sreća*."

It fits him perfectly and the words feel so right across my lips.

"What does that mean?"

"My happiness. And you are, Heath. Without you, I just go through the motions of life. You make everything about it better. You're my happiness."

"That's the sweetest fucking thing anyone has ever said to me."

A single tear rolls down his cheek and I wipe it off.

"I'm sorry for not trusting you. I should have just told you the day you shared about your mom with me. But I was so infatuated with you, I didn't want to risk losing you. I had it bad for you, *ljubavi*. Still do."

Heath closes his eyes with a breath and the hand on my cheek trembles.

"Thank you. So much. Don't doubt me again. I'm not going anywhere, Marko."

Heath leans forward and kisses me. Soft and gentle, the hand on my cheek drifts down to my chest to rest over my heart. "I will never hurt you here."

"Heath…"

What do I say to that? He forgives me for causing him pain and promises never to hurt me all in the same breath. After I ran like a coward.

He silences me with another kiss and slides us closer. The blanket bunches a little under him as he moves, and he huffs the cutest little growl.

"Stupid blanket. I just want to be next to you."

Wrapping an arm around him, I roll onto my back, taking him with me.

"Is that better?"

"For now. I just want to kiss you under the stars."

"I wouldn't mind."

And we do. It makes me feel like a kid again, breaking curfew and making out in dark alleys or, a few times, even the woods. Heath's weight on me reminds me he's real and we have something so special growing between us that making out on a blanket in my yard isn't the same as those trysts.

He makes me want to do better.

With everything.

"Did you just feel a drop of rain?" Heath pauses his kisses and lifts his head. When he does, a single raindrop splats on my forehead.

"We've been out here so long we didn't notice clouds roll in, I guess."

The rain is light now and Heath laughs with his full body.

"How cliché." He laughs even more. "Can we stay out here like this? I want to live the fantasy of peeling you out of wet clothes and towelling you dry before I slip you under the covers and hold you close."

"I will purposely stand in the rain every day if that's my reward."

The rain now falls harder, and he shivers as his T-shirt clings to him.

"Okay. You know, it's kind of cold out here in the rain. Maybe we should do this on a hot evening in July instead."

Heath sits up and together we scramble, gathering the blankets and dashing into my sunroom, laughing. And we don't stop laughing as we work our wet clothes off, stealing all the touches and kisses in between.

But his towelling-off fantasy needs to wait.

Backing him up against the patio door, rainwater still dripping from his hair, he gasps when the cool glass meets his bare skin.

"*Woo!*" Heath steps away from the door. "That's cold. What are you doing?"

"Not waiting to dry off. I want you right now."

Wrapping my hand around his cock, he leans into me with a moan. "I'd be agreeable to your plan."

Smiling, I kiss his neck and back him into the glass again. "I thought you might be."

"You think I'm easy, don't you?"

"Not at all. You're eager." A kiss to his cheek. "And sexy." A stroke on his dick. "And so damn ready for anything. It's my fault that you test my patience."

"I was never good at tests." Heath's voice is serious and I pause. Is he wanting to talk about this now? "Tests give me anxiety. What if I didn't study enough? What if—"

"Heath...stop talking and let me make you feel good."

He wraps his arms around my neck, and it always makes me melt when he does that. I don't know why, but I love it.

"That's a solid plan," he murmurs against my lips and tilts his hips, sliding his cock through my grip.

With a firm hand on his chest, I pin him against the patio door before dropping to my knees in front of him. Nipping his thigh, I don't wait a second to taste him, taking him in my mouth right away.

A loud thud sounds as he drops his head back against the door with a groan. His fingers tangle in my hair.

"Oh, hell...Marko..."

There's nothing skilled right now. I'm slobbering all over him like a dog with a bone and desperate to the point of pain to make him come. To make him mine. Mine. It flashes in my head like a sign on the Vegas strip.

I almost fucked up and the blender of emotions is spinning with the lid off. Everything is out.

Love. Want. Mine. I'm sorry.

"Close...Marko..."

Heath's moan isn't sexy. It's like a wheeze of an asthmatic donkey. When I release his dick and stick out my tongue, he gasps and wheezes again before he unloads on my chin and face. He slides down the door, ass squeaking, before he hits the floor with a sated smile.

"Let me finish you. Don't let my practice go to waste."

He offers his mouth and I rise off my knees. Gripping my thighs, he urges me forward. It won't take me long, not with Heath wet and naked on the floor and his cum all over me. I curl my fingers into his hair and let him swallow my dick.

"*Tako*...fuck, Heath..."

Fuck, his throat is heaven on earth.

He does the same as I did, popping off my cock and offering his tongue when I'm on the verge. My knees quake as I come with a roar, and Heath leans back with a tiny smirk, watching me jerk myself through the mother of orgasms and paint him with it.

Ragged pants are the only sound as we both catch our breath.

"I had no idea I was this filthy, you know. But new discovery unlocked." He takes my hand and I pull him up off the floor.

"And what would that be?"

"Having you come all over me. It's so...primal. Like you want me to smell like you or something and I'm bonkers for it. You don't even have to ask to do it. I like it that much."

"Yeah?" I bring my lips to his, and he loops his arms around my neck again, pressing our sticky, sweaty bodies together.

"Yeah. Seems you're at the heart of most of my discoveries these days and I'd like to keep it that way."

"You might change your mind after meeting my *baka* and the old Croatians this weekend. They might send you running for the hills. What if it's too much for you?"

"Won't happen. You know why?"

"Why?"

"Because nothing will ever be too much for me to be with you. Those things don't matter. What matters is us and how you treat me. How you make me feel. People can say all the things they want about you, Marko, but I know who you are. I *love* who you are. Crazy family members won't ever change that."

His soft gaze searches my face, and I lean down to press my forehead against his.

"I believe you. Just be prepared for an inquisition."

Leading him to the shower, I add, "Oh, and be prepared to talk about when the wedding is."

He stops dead in the hallway, and I bite down a laugh.

"Uh, what?"

"You'll see, *ljubavi*. You'll see."

***

"Shit. Sorry."

I groan as Heath fumbles with the alarm on his phone.

"What timezit?"

"It's 4:30. I need to get to the ranch for chores and make arrangements for the weekend." His lips brush my forehead. "I was trying to sneak out."

"Don't ever sneak out. I don't care what time it is. I want to wish you a good day and kiss you goodbye." My hand finds his in the dark, and I pull him back to me, placing a lingering kiss on his lips. "Have a good day, srećo. Text me when you get there."

"Sweet talker." Heath kisses me back and untangles our hands. "I will." The rustling of clothes in the dark brings a smile to my face. It's just a little thing, but it's a comfort listening to him let himself out of my place.

But Jesus Christ it's early.

And I'm probably not going to get back to sleep until I know he's made it to the ranch okay.

With a sigh, I flick on the bedside lamp, and after my eyes adjust, I fish out a pair of lounge pants from the mess of clothes on the floor. In our haste last night, we knocked over my basket of clean laundry and never picked it up.

Heath was...insatiable. I wasn't ready for another round, but I was more than happy to satisfy him. When we knocked the basket over, it was because I couldn't see where I was going since he insisted on climbing me like a tree and carrying him. Another turn on, apparently.

Shaking my head, I pile the clothes back into the basket and set them on the bed to put away later. Much later. Maybe three coffees later. Because I'm not used to late nights and sex that leaves me wrung out. It's all good though. If I'm going to drag my ass, being tired all day, there's no other reason I'd prefer.

Curtis will totally call me on it, too. I should consider my reply to his taunts now.

When I finally make my way to the kitchen, the light over the stove is on and scrawled on a paper towel is a note from Heath.

We need to clean your patio door. I left ass prints.

With a snort, I head to the sunroom and there it is. When the light hits it just right, two cheeks and two handprints. Farther up I think is a bit of shoulder rub and my skin flushes as I recall everything we said and did.

I don't think I'll clean that door just yet.

After making a coffee, I settle at my easel. A rush of inspiration hits, and I reach for my sketch pad and a pencil. I could paint this, but that would take me too long, and I really want to finish what just came to me before I go to work.

My phone sings Tarzan Boy and I smile like an absolutely deranged person as I reach for it.

> **Tarzan:** I'm here safe and I still smell like sex. Can't say I hate it.

> **Not Jane:** Thank you. I can make you smell like that whenever you want.

> **Tarzan:** Every. Damn. Day.

Ah, fuck. This man is something else.

> **Not Jane:** Will I see you and Jeff for coffee this morning?

> **Tarzan:** I'll let you know for sure, but I'm planning on it. Talk soon.

He adds a heart, and I acknowledge it before setting the phone aside and returning to my sketch. Whatever I don't finish now, I can do later.

When later finally comes and I need to get ready for the shop, it's almost done. I just hope Heath likes it.

CHAPTER 19

HEATH

"Come on, Jeff! Let's go!"

Any other day, the dang bird will follow me so close I practically step on him, but today he's just a shithead, either running to hide or trying to bite me. Maybe it's best I just leave him here.

"That bird is sketchy today, Heath." Dante stands beside me as Jeff paces near the chicken coop, feathers fanned out as he ignores me.

"More than usual, you mean?"

"Definitely." Dante leans closer, even though we're the only two around. "You smell like a night at a cheap motel and no soap."

I shrug. "Not a cheap motel, and there was plenty of soap. I chose not to use it...the second time."

Dante chortles and bumps my shoulder. "You dog! Gotta say I didn't think you had that in you."

"Neither did I." Turning to him, I grab his arm. "Is that weird?"

"You should know by now I don't judge. I like to roll in cherry-flavoured powder for Colby and be an all night *lik-a-stix*. You do you, my friend."

I forgot about the weird thing those two have with *FunDips*. I'd like to forget again, but it's quite an image.

"Um, right. So why do you think Jeff is so odd? He usually loves to go for coffee and a car ride. He's acting like a dick."

Dante bobs his head in agreement. "Mhm. He sure is, but I'm not sure what the issue is. Maybe he smells Marko on you and is jealous." He slaps his thigh with a snort, but I'm not amused.

"Be serious. Should I call the vet or something?"

The bird has always been strange, but never like this with me.

"I don't think so. He's still eating and drinking and all the other stuff birds do. Maybe leave him here, though, today. You wouldn't want him doing something stupid."

"Yeah. You're probably right." It shouldn't be the end of the world, but I'm sad he won't be joining me today. It's our thing. "Do you want me to bring you anything back from the Screaming Bean?"

"Ooooh! If they have any of those shortbread cookies, I could go for a few."

"Will do. I'm going to head in then. Keep an eye on Jeff for me."

Dante nods and heads off to Dan's place for his morning coffee visit with Dan. Jeff still struts around the chicken coop and screeches here and there. But Dante is right. It's best to leave him here as much as I don't want to.

After locking the door of my car from the inside and making sure it's secure, I head for my morning coffee.

Without Jeff.

***

After dropping a bag of a dozen cookies for Dante in my car, I walk over to Dark Horse Tattoo. I only left Marko a few hours ago, but the same fizzy feeling washes over me, knowing I'll get to see him again once I step through the doors.

It's still weird for me to feel like this. But I love it. Since I met Marko, so much has changed, and I feel like the luckiest guy on earth.

The door chimes as I enter. A man waits in the seating area, flipping through a design book, and he nods. Smiling back, I walk down the hall where Marko's station is.

I find him there, hunched over a sketch pad, his coffee next to him.

"Knock, knock. Is this where I find the handsome owner of this tattoo shop? I need to lodge a complaint."

Marko turns with a smile that could guide ships in the night and takes the few steps to greet me.

"Hello, *ljubavi*. What kind of complaint can I help you with?"

"It's been too long since you've kissed me."

He laughs softly and grips my chin with his thumb and finger.

"Let me fix that. I don't want an unhappy customer."

His lips brush across mine with a tenderness that makes my heart leap. Marko deepens the kiss, and my tongue chases his while I forget where we are until a throat clears.

Marko presses his forehead to mine and slides his hand to the back of my neck, like he needs me to stay connected to him. And right now... I think I need that.

"What is it, Curtis?"

"Sorry lovebirds, but I just wanted to ask if you'd like me to take the Friday afternoon client so you can leave for your grandma's earlier. They're new and you always get first dibs, but I can call them now."

Marko lifts his head and nods.

"Thank you. Go ahead, and if they're okay seeing you, then take it."

Curtis raps his knuckles on the door frame.

"You got it. I'll let you know." He pauses. "Nice to see you, Heath. You make the big guy smile more. I like it."

He leaves us just as fast as he came, and Marko's fingers massage my neck.

"What's wrong? You seem like you're not your normal self. Where did your sunshine go?"

I huff a small breath and allow my finger to trace the horse pattern on his shop-branded T-shirt.

"What gave it away?"

"You have a light that follows you everywhere, *ljubavi*, and it's not here right now. I can just tell." He takes my coffee cup and sets it aside before pulling me into his arms.

"I think something is wrong with Jeff."

Marko's arms settle around me, and I rest my head on his chest. While I'm still upset with my bird's behaviour, Marko just makes it better.

"How can I help? What might make you happier?"

"This helps. I like this. But you can't hold me all day while I have a mini meltdown."

Pushing away from him, I reach for my coffee. After taking a drink, I tell him all that happened today with Jeff. The attacking and weird stuff and how he seemed to not want anything to do with me.

"It wouldn't hurt to find someone who specializes in birds to talk to about it."

"I think that's what I'll do when I get back. We rescued him because he was probably going to be killed, and Blaze couldn't let it happen. None of us know anything about peacocks, but he just seemed to like me, and he's been fine all these years."

"I wish I knew what to say to make you feel better." He reaches for my hand, twining our fingers together. "If you want to stay with him this weekend, don't feel you have to come with me. There will be another time, and I don't want you to worry about him while you're away."

Why does he have to say sweet stuff like that? Nobody I've dated before ever gave me that kind of advice. If there was a problem with Jeff, it was brushed off. *He's just a bird. Let it go.* But he's not. Before meeting Marko, Jeff came first and taught me I was important to people. Well, important to a bird, I guess. But Jeff gave me the confidence to explore new things. Like trying my hand at being a travel consultant. I wasn't good at it, but I tried.

"Thank you for saying that. I'll let you know. But I really want to go with you."

Marko smiles again and tugs me closer. Leaning on the counter, he pulls me between his legs and runs his nose up my neck.

"I want you to as well, but there's no pressure, okay?" He kisses my neck. "And by the way…you smell amazing." An appreciative rumble in his chest vibrates against me. "Did you do that on purpose?"

"I did it for me. I like the reminder that I'm yours. Dante said I smelled like a cheap hotel with no soap, though. So I might need to do something else."

Marko chuckles before kissing me again.

"There are many, many ways I can claim or mark you, *ljubavi*. And I'd be willing to show you every single one."

Fuck. Me.

"Yes, that," I breathe. "Let's do that next time. Soon. We'll do that soon."

I don't know what all these ways are, but the blood is already rushing south just thinking about it.

"Marko, your client is here." Curtis pops his head in the door and whistles. "You two are adorable. But work before play, boss man."

Marko gives him the finger and kisses my neck once more before easing off me with a sigh.

"Will you be okay today?"

He brushes his thumb across my cheek, and my chest tightens.

"Yeah. The guys are around and will help me. I have support." Stretching up on my toes, I kiss his cheek. "I'll keep you posted."

Grabbing my coffee, I slip out of his room before I run into his arms again and beg him to tell me about his other ideas of claiming me. It's one way to distract me from the Jeff issue.

When I reach my car and I don't have a bird's feathers to tuck into the back, the distraction vanishes.

Then my phone buzzes with a text, and it's Dante.

Dante: You need to get back here. Jeff just had a short circuit.

My thumbs are a blur as I text my reply and I drive my car faster than I should to get there. Just as I pass under the ranch's archway, there's an ominous clunk and bang under the hood, and my car loses all power. Steering the car to the side of the lane, I let it coast to a stop before getting out.

Deep inside, I know there's no babying this thing back to life. My car just died and I don't even know what the issue is with Jeff. What's that saying? It's gone from bad to worse?

"Heath!"

Dante waves from across the yard and jogs over to me.

"Sorry to bother you, but Jeff went berserk and attacked one of the barn cats. Dan got her and already took her to the vet, but Jeff is...I don't know, man. Something is up and he won't let anyone near him. We need to get him penned before he does something else."

"Where is he now?"

Dante doesn't get a chance to answer. The loudest screech I've ever heard sounds from behind Alec's house and I take off towards it. Lord, let this be something I can deal with.

Out of breath, my gaze finds Jeff on the fence post with what looks like a squirrel clutched and bleeding in his talons. He's killed the odd mouse over the years, but never anything bigger than that. First, the barn cat, and now a squirrel. He's never hurt multiple creatures in a day, either.

"Jeff. Hey buddy. What's going on?"

He tilts his head back and forth at the sound of my voice and drops the squirrel. Its lifeless body thuds on the packed grass and I wince. Poor little guy.

"What's going on with you? Do you want to talk over some ice water? I missed you today."

I know he doesn't actually understand what I'm saying. I *know* that. But I swear when he hops off the fence post and walks toward me, he's agreeing to my suggestion. It's almost like his little bird brain is saying, '*You know what Heath? I'd love some water and to talk this out. I'm not quite myself today.*'

Dante stands a safe distance back, and I wave him back towards the barn.

"I hope you're not mad at me for staying out last night. Is that it?"

Jeff keeps walking and stops once he reaches me with a tilt of his head. My breath catches in my throat as he fans his tail while staring at me. It's... unnerving. Almost like he knows damn well what I was up to, and it makes me feel guilty that I left him for a sexfest.

"I like your feathers. Prettiest bird I know." I figure it's best to keep walking in case he turns on me. Probably easier to fight him off. But he lets his feathers droop as we walk towards the barn. It's like he knows he did something wrong and my heart breaks.

I want to pat his head and assure him it's gonna be okay, but the vision of that squirrel hanging from his claws is a fresh memory. Instead, I just talk to him in a calm voice and walk alongside him until we reach the barn where his pen is.

This low grumble, like a growl, comes from him and he spins his head like I've betrayed him for leading him here. With my heart in my throat, I reach for the shovel near the door just in case he comes at me. I hope like fuck I don't have to hurt my best feathered friend with a shovel.

"Jeff...you're not well. I'm gonna get you looked at. Trust me, okay?"

He doesn't move for the longest time, and we stare each other down; all the while he growls at me continuously. Every second that ticks by is a tiny tear to my heart at the thought that he hates me.

"Please, buddy. It's not safe for you to be out."

I'm just talking to convince myself now, and he finally turns into his pen. Closing the door and sliding the lock behind him, the air rushes out of my lungs and fresh tears burn behind my eyes.

My poor bird.

Shit. Dante is still outside, probably wondering if everything is okay. Rushing out of the barn, I find the ranch yard full. Everyone is there.

"Are you hurt?" Blaze comes up to me and grabs my arms. His gaze sweeps over me, assessing for damage and his concern only makes me feel worse.

"Not on the outside." Fresh tears well in my eyes and Blaze wraps his arms around me. Not as good as Marko's arms, though. "I think he needs help, Blaze. What do I do?"

Blaze releases me, and I wipe at my tear-dampened cheeks.

"I made some calls the other day when you came by. Good timin', I guess. But there's a guy comin' by today to talk and see Jeff. He has a breedin' farm and is into producin' show birds. Mostly chickens, but exotic birds are gainin' popularity. Did you know there are huge chicken shows just like dog shows?"

"Um, no, but I don't understand. What's this guy want to do with Jeff?"

Blaze motions for me to follow him up to Dan's, and he fills me in as we walk.

"I think he wants him to stud."

"So he's not sick?"

Blaze laughs softly and pats me on the shoulder.

"Not with something that needs medicine. It sounds like he needs to get laid. But let's let the bird guy explain it."

A small cargo van rolls into the yard and Blaze turns, waving at the driver. The van parks in front of Dan's and a smiling man with light brown hair and a moustache climbs out. He bounces up the steps and smiles as he introduces himself.

"Hey! I'm Terry. I hear you have a peacock that needs some loving."

Blaze takes his hand. "I'm Blaze and this is the bird's keeper, Heath. Come on in and explain to him everythin' you told me."

Terry follows us into the kitchen and after we've had the required small talk and my skin feels far too tight, I can't maintain the polite control any longer.

"Can you help Jeff or not?"

Terry focuses on me, and when he reaches for my hand and squeezes, my shoulders relax.

"I can. Let me explain."

CHAPTER 20

MARKO

"**O**kay. You're all finished, Jamieson."

The cowboy takes the mirror I hand him and positions it to see the completed tattoo on his chest. It was easy enough for me to design and, from our conversations, this is something that carries a lot of weight for the cowboy. People don't ink initials on their body permanently unless it's something serious has been my experience.

He's quiet for a while and when he clears his throat and hands me the mirror back, there's a tremor in his hand.

"I really love how you made the bull's hoofprint part of the initial like that. It, ah, it's exactly how I feel."

"I'm happy you like it. But I'm more happy that I got it right."

After applying a thin layer of ointment and a bandage, he pulls on his shirt and buttons it up as he talks.

"Griff is the best thing in my life. He and bull riding make my world complete. I need nothing else."

"That's a wonderful gesture. How long have you been together?"

"Together?" He laughs as he stands to tuck in his shirt. "We're not together. He's my best friend. Without him, I don't think I'd be as good of a bull rider as I am."

"My apologies. He sounds like an amazing friend."

"The best."

I'd say the smile and the way he described what he wanted in a tattoo the first time means Griff is more than a friend, but I'm in no position to point that out.

"I'm really glad you fit me in. A week is still okay before I'm riding again? The big money happens at the Kissing Ridge Rodeo in a week, and I don't want to miss it."

We walk to the front, and when I present the terminal for him to pay, I ask him more about the rodeo.

"I've never been to a rodeo. My boyfriend works on a ranch and told me I need to. We had planned to go to one this weekend nearby, Colton Creek, I think it was. But we can't make that one. Should we wait for Kissing Ridge? How far is that?"

You know when people get all lit up when they're excited about something? That's how Jamieson is as he grabs a pen and asks for a *Post-it note* while he scribbles out the name of the rodeo and dates. Even adding names of his friends we need to watch when we go and what events they're in.

"Anyway, the season is almost over, but Kissing Ridge is the best. But if you've never been to a rodeo before, maybe don't show up without a cowboy hat. Blend in a bit."

"Thanks for the tip, Jamieson. Good luck and if there're any issues with the ink, just call and arrange something."

Jamieson places his cowboy hat on and tips the brim.

"Will do Marko. I hope you get to a rodeo. If you do, look me up."

Tucking his note in my pocket, I return to clean up my station. No sooner do I step into the room, my phone rings and it's Heath.

"Hello, *ljubavi*."

"Marko…" Heath's sniffles immediately make me snap to attention and abandon my clean up. "Can you…I hate asking you this, but are you able to come to the ranch?"

"Of course I can. Are you okay?"

I'm already pulling my jacket down and searching for my keys. There's no way I'll make him wait longer than he has to.

"I'm okay. I'll explain when you get here."

"As soon as I can. Hang tight."

"Thank you."

His voice cracks and this giant squeeze in my heart threatens to leave me breathless. Heath ends the call, and I stop at Curtis's workstation. He's working on a full sleeve for a buttoned-up businessman type and they talk quietly, but he senses me at the door and lifts his head.

"Sorry to interrupt, but I have to run out to the ranch. If I'm not back in two hours, can you call my appointment and reschedule for me?"

"Sure. Is everything okay?"

"I don't know."

He nods and we share a glance.

"I'll take care of it. Keep me posted."

Without another word, I leave my shop and drive to the ranch as fast as I can.

***

Heath is running over to me before I've even removed my helmet, and when I step off the bike, he throws himself into my arms.

No words are said, but he holds me tight, and I dip my head to inhale everything that is Heath.

"I'm so glad you're here."

"I'll always come when you call. Always." Cupping his face, my thumbs brush under his reddened eyes. "You've been crying."

He huffs a small laugh and turns his face to kiss my palm.

"Yeah, but it's so stupid. I should be happy, really."

"It's not stupid." Shaking my head, I press a kiss to his forehead. "Jeff is important to you, and you care about him. If you weren't upset, I'd be concerned."

Heath releases a large puff of air and takes my hand as he leads me up to the main farmhouse.

"Dante texted me as soon as I left you after coffee this morning. Jeff attacked a barn cat and when I got here, he'd already killed a squirrel."

Heath's shoulders slump with sadness as he tells me everything that went on this morning with Jeff as we walk up to the ranch house. The devastation in his voice that it's not something he can fix crushes me.

"I think I know what's going to happen, but I excused myself from the discussion until you got here." He stops outside the front door and turns to me. "I don't know how I'll react, and I need you to like...just be my rock, I guess? These guys are amazing, and I love them. They're my family. But you...you make me feel different when you're around and not just in an '*Oh my god, my dick is hard again*' kind of way. I feel tied to you, maybe?" He shakes his head as he reaches for the door. "I'm probably not explaining it right. I just know I need you."

That was quite the revelation. I know what he's trying to say because I feel the same way about him.

"Oh. This is Dan's place." Heath says over his shoulder as he leads me in. "I don't think you've met him yet. He's like a dad." He perks up as we step inside. "Actually, all three of them are here! You can meet all the guys at once." He snorts. "My three dads!"

If he wasn't the man I was head over heels in love with and who had already agreed to meet my Croatian family this weekend, I'd be making excuses to get out of here. But I suppose this is as good a time as any to prove my worth to the three men Heath thinks the world of.

We enter the kitchen to find four men talking around the kitchen table, and they all pause their conversation as we enter.

"Hey guys. This is Marko. You know Blaze and you met Alec, but this guy here is Dan, and that's Terry. He's going to help with Jeff."

Dan stands and offers his hand. He's smiling and not at all imposing, but his grip on my hand is punishing. He hasn't said a word, but I get the message already.

"Nice to finally meet you, Marko. I hear good things. Thank you for being here for Heath."

"I wouldn't miss it, sir."

Dan's grin grows as he turns to Blaze. "Hear that? He called me sir!" His smile is genuine as he motions for us to join the table. "I like you already, Marko."

"He calls everyone, sir. Don't spit shine your belt buckle over it, Dan." Blaze drawls as he shakes his head. Dan shoves his shoulder, and I enjoy their teasing until Terry clears his throat.

"So, is everyone we need here now? Can I explain to you what your options are for Jeff?"

Terry looks around the table and I notice the three older men are waiting for Heath's response. Heath clutches my hand and nods.

"Please. I'm ready."

Terry opens a folder in front of him and passes a small stack of photos to Heath while he speaks.

"From what I've learned before seeing Jeff, he's a single adult male peacock living on the ranch. He's been here alone for several years. The thing with male peacocks is they reach sexual maturity around three years of age. When that happens, they can become aggressive. I've been told he's attached himself to you and you've been a...suitable mate for a few years. Is that right?"

Heath's cheeks pinken as he nods. "Um, yeah. A few times he'd really get, um, in the mood? But I could usually tell when it was coming, and I'd wear chaps for a few days in case he really got into it. Then he'd be fine. Like, he'd always follow me and show me his feathers and stuff. But it was only a few times that he...wanted affection."

Terry's eyebrows almost fly off his head. "So...you...let him breed you?"

Alec pulls his hat down low as he bites back a laugh. The other two keep it together and listen as Heath recounts his story of letting Jeff do exactly that. But clearly not having sex with a bird, just acting as an outlet for him, much like a dog humping a leg. Which is so like Heath to put himself at risk for Jeff's happiness.

"I knew what he was doing, but I couldn't just let him hurt people, and he seemed to like me and be okay with it. I just...I don't know, put up with it and let him do his thing. The breeding, I guess, if that's what it's called."

Terry nods in disbelief. "Um, well, that's...commendable."

Blaze snorts and immediately schools his expression. "Sorry. Heath has always been good at people pleasin'. I can't say I'm surprised it extends to birds." Blaze's gaze finds mine over Heath's head and he winks.

"What I think happened when Jeff came here is that he imprinted on you, Heath. But instead of thinking you're his parent, he saw you as a mate."

Heath nods as he listens.

"He'd get really territorial sometimes and fan his feathers and peck at people when they got too close to me." He squeezes my hand and smiles. "Like when you came over the first time and he pecked your thigh? Remember? I had to get you to drop your pants so I could put ointment on it."

Heath's innocent remarks make me shift in my seat. Of course, I remember, but I don't want his dads to know this stuff. Blaze smiles like he's enjoying my reaction, and Dan... well, I'm not sure how to read him, but if anything else happens, Alec will have to leave the room. He might bite through his lip soon if he can't laugh out loud.

"We tried getting a peahen once, but he just wasn't interested. I figured he didn't like them or they weren't his type. Then I guess I just never bothered looking into it again."

Terry, bless him, soldiers on. "What today sounds like is that Jeff is sexually frustrated. Peacocks have multiple mates. Most people think they mate for life, but they're actually polyamorous. The males have a usual group of peahens they rotate through, but they sometimes take favourites. In your case, Heath, he was content with the arrangement. You acted as a favourite."

"But that's not good enough now, is it?"

"It's not, I'm afraid. His need to mate and reproduce is finally catching up. I'm impressed he didn't get aggressive before this, to be fair. It's highly unusual."

Heath twists his hands in front of him, and I rub his back. His voice is so gloomy. His shine is all gone.

"So, um, the attacks today were because he needs sex?"

"Yes. In the most blunt way possible. Yes."

Heath puffs a breath and reaches for my hand. He nods like a sage old man processing the words. It's cute, but he's working hard not to fall apart. We all know what has to happen and we're just waiting until Heath catches up.

"Blaze said you breed birds and want to have peacocks? What would your plan be for Jeff?"

Terry's face lights up as he takes back the photos of his operation that Heath barely looked at and replaces them with pictures of... peacocks, I think. Or peahens. I'm not a bird guy.

"Well, I have many interested people in establishing their own peafowl places, mostly for bird shows. It's a very popular hobby. Bird shows, that is. I need another peacock to service the hens and keep up with demand. When Blaze contacted me, it was perfect timing."

Heath remains silent for several moments as he slides through the photos.

"Would I be…" He trails off and swallows. "Could I visit him there?"

"I've never had anyone ask, but I don't see why not."

"What about, like, could I take him out sometime? You know, like a family visit or something? Because he loves car rides and ice water at the coffee shop. It's our thing."

A single fat tear slides down his cheek, and I wipe it away with my thumb. He's breaking my heart.

Terry switches off business mode and reaches across to hold Heath's hand.

"We could definitely work out visitation. Whatever would make you comfortable, Heath."

Heath nods and turns his attention to the men across the table.

"It's the right thing to do, right? He needs this or he'll be unhappy. I don't want him unhappy."

"He's still an animal, Heath. I know how much you love him, but none of us can give him what he needs," Alec says with a kind smile.

"You know I'm sad about your situation, but we've talked about this." Blaze softens his voice. "We always do what's best for the animals here, Heath. Be it a horse, cow, chicken, or peacock. Their care is always first."

Dan remains silent, but I know Heath wants his assurance too. Not like there's any other option, but Heath is so sensitive and sweet. I've watched him with this bird for months and seen firsthand his care of it. The way he talks about Jeff, he's attached just like anyone would be to a pet. Hell, even I'm going to miss seeing the dang thing during our coffee breaks.

"Jeff needs to be happy, Heath. You did everything you could until now. Terry will let you visit. He might even send you photos often."

Heath sighs and pushes the photos back to Terry.

"He really likes cranberries and those meal worm things. He likes to drink ice water from a Styrofoam cup and if you have a car with an open door, he might jump inside." His watery smile as he offers his hand to Terry nearly breaks me.

"You seem like a good guy, Terry. I trust you to take the best care of Jeff. And I'd like to ask, no, I *demand* weekly updates and photos."

Terry shakes his hand and smiles. "I will absolutely do all that, Heath. Trust me. He'll be happy and I know you aren't right now, but you will be when you see how different he'll be. He'll be a better peacock."

Heath whispers, "I know. It's just hard." He wipes at his wet cheeks. "Come on. I'll take you to him."

I stand to follow Heath, but a hand pats my arm.

"Can you stay for a minute?"

My eyes meet Dan's and Blaze calls out that we'll join Terry and Heath in a few minutes. Heath smiles at me, assuring me it's okay, and I retake my seat as Alec leans forward.

"Marko, I'm the nicest of the three of us, FYI. Heath is a grown man, but he's important to all of us. I've never seen him this happy to be with someone. Please come by for supper one night. That's all I need to say." With a tip of his hat, he leaves.

Blaze grins and flips the toothpick around his mouth before standing.

"You already know how I feel. And you passed the test. I like you. But I'm not afraid to make your life hell if you do wrong by that man. He's the gentlest human you will ever meet. He says things like it is and sometimes he takes a while to catch on...but he will. Be patient. And love the fuck out of him because he has so much love to give. You're a lucky son of a bitch."

Blaze exits and I'm left with the final one of the threesome. The man Heath has only ever said kind things about and holds the highest esteem for. He's like the godfather of the ranch.

"I'm glad those two left because I might cry and they'd never let me forget it. That's how much I trust you, Marko. Heath loves easy. He always has and I never say it out loud, but I love him like a son." He clears his throat and chuckles. "Dammit. I'm already getting emotional. I'm not giving you a speech about burying your body in the yard if you hurt him. Instead, I'm going to tell you all the things I love about him as quickly as I can so you can get out there and ease the broken heart he's about to have when Jeff leaves."

Turns out Dan couldn't really keep it short, but I got the picture.

And Heath is one lucky guy.

Chapter 21

Heath

"Did you see how happy Jeff was when he saw that peahen in Terry's van? I was almost jealous. He never looked at me like that unless it was snack time."

Making the choice to have Jeff live on a bird breeding farm wasn't as hard as watching Terry drive off with him. *That* hurt. A lot.

"I did. Like a kid at Christmas. I've never seen him move that fast. Guess Terry brought the hottest fowl from his farm."

Marko's arm tightens around me, and I snuggle into his chest. After Jeff left, Marko didn't even ask what I needed. He made some calls and told me he was staying. I overheard him talking to Curtis and I know he rescheduled a client to be here for me. While I appreciate his willingness to be here, I feel guilty about him giving up work.

"You're sure your business is okay with you taking all this time off? I feel bad. You're losing money because of me."

His hand cups my jaw, and he tilts my head back so I can look at him. His brown eyes flash with something unfamiliar.

"Money will never be more important than you, srećo." Marko's gaze is fierce. It makes my skin flush, and, in a surprise twist, my dick hard. "I know what valuing money over your family can do to a person. I've lived it and it's not something I ever want to do again."

Marko bends to kiss me, and his hand tightens on my jaw. Even with the punishing grip he has on me, his kiss is tender and exactly what I needed. One kiss eases my worries over Jeff and brings me back to my other new reality. A man who I've fallen hard and fast for. He accepts my quirks. Loves them even. Nobody has ever made me feel the way he does.

When he releases me, he smooths his palm over my cheek and kisses my forehead.

"It's been a long day. We should get some rest before tomorrow. You still want to keep our plans for the weekend?"

"I do. I can't stay here and wallow. Besides, Dan told me to take the time off. Apparently, I don't take vacations, so he said for me to not rush back and relax for once. Honestly, I know I need the time away too. It's all too much to think about right now. I never thought there'd be a time I'd never have Jeff with me."

Realistically, I know he wouldn't have been with me forever. Life ends sometime. But I really loved that bird and now that he's gone, I feel like I'll never be able to look at a Styrofoam cup of ice water again.

Marko stands from my sofa and turns off the TV. I don't even know what we were watching. I was just happy to be snuggled into his arms and trying to focus on how happy Jeff will be in his new home.

"Come on, *ljubavi*. Let's get to bed."

Marko offers me his hand and when I take it, he leads me to the bathroom and turns the shower on.

Without another word, he undresses me, and I get it. For the first time in my adult life, I think I understand what he's doing. Even though my dick gets hard with his hands on me like this, that's not what it's about.

"You're kind of incredible, you know?"

Marko smiles, and the lines around his eyes deepen at the sides.

"Thank you. So are you." His hand guides me towards the shower. "Take some time and decompress, Heath. Let the water turn cold if you want. I'll be right outside if you need me."

"Oh. You're not joining me?"

"Don't bat those lashes at me. I would, but I think you should take some time alone. Be with your thoughts." He kisses me softly. "I'm here for you, okay? I think you need this. I might be wrong, but just in case..."

With a nod, I step into the shower, and Marko closes the bathroom door as he leaves. I have to admit, he's right. The hot water feels good and the tightness in my shoulders fades. Jeff is gone, my car is dead, and I'm in love with a man who's taking me to meet his grandmother tomorrow. I'm in this weird place of impossibly excited and a little bit broken.

Everything is happening at once and while I feel like I should be overwhelmed, I'm not. I'll miss Jeff. I know I'll struggle to find a new routine without him, but... it's life, right? When Alec had his favourite rescue horse pass away, he kept going. We've all had hurdles to overcome, and that's what this is for me.

My car can wait. Blaze said he'd find the perfect place for it. I trust him.

But the man in my loft can't wait.

After turning off the shower, I pat myself dry and wrap a towel around my waist before brushing my teeth. Steam billows out of the bathroom when I open the door and turn towards the corner where my bed sits. Marko waits there with the lamp on and his phone in his hand.

"Feel better?"

"I do. You were right. I just needed time to think things over. Shocking even myself, I'm okay."

Dropping the towel on the floor, Marko's gaze rakes down my body and he lifts the blankets for me. After sliding under them and snuggling next to him, he turns on his side to face me.

"You're capable, Heath. I hope you know that."

"I do. I didn't before, but I do now. When Jeff came here, he taught me I could handle anything; I just didn't realize it until now." Sliding my fingers through Marko's dark hair, our gazes lock. "You taught me there's more to sex than just getting off."

His palm trails down my side and rests on my hip. "Did I?"

"I never connected with any of my partners like I do with you. Not just in bed, either. Maybe I'm naïve again here, but...I think that's what makes us so great together. We've got this vibe or this—"

"I like to think of it as a pull. Like a tide. It always comes back to you."

"Yeah. It always comes back to you, Marko. I may be capable of handling things on my own, but I always look for you." Pressing my lips to his, a small sigh escapes his mouth.

"I've never seen the ocean," I whisper.

"I'll take you to the sea. You'll love it."

His hand squeezes my hip before sliding to my ass and pulling me closer. Our legs tangle together, and our kisses are gentle. It's like the first time all over again, exploring the touch and taste of someone new. Not pushing ahead to sex, but keeping us in this moment of tender vulnerability.

When we finally settle for the night, it's with a new sense of purpose in my heart.

***

Marko kills the engine on his bike after parking on the curb outside of a very skinny-looking house. All the houses here press together and seem to be taller rather than wider.

After we've dismounted and removed our helmets, he motions towards the house.

"This is *baka's* house. Leave your helmet here and we'll come get our stuff after saying hello."

Marko takes my hand and leads me down a path to the back door. I pause before stepping up onto the porch and admire the postage stamp of a yard.

"Marko, this is gorgeous. Your *baka* likes to garden?"

He grins. "She does. If you tell her you love the garden, be prepared for a tour with plant history."

Marko holds the door for me, and I step through into a tiny alcove. Even the doors are skinny here. I'm only 5'10" and Marko is easily 6'2". He knocks before opening the door and ducks his head to step inside.

"*Pazi na glavu.*" He grins when he turns around to motion me inside and places a hand on the top of my head. "That means watch your head. We say that a lot here, since all the doorways are so low."

I don't think I need to duck, but I do it anyway.

"*Bako*! We're here!" Marko leans down and whispers. "She speaks English perfectly fine, but often speaks Croatian when I'm around to '*keep me sharp*,' she says. I promise she's not saying bad things."

"Jura!"

A tiny woman in a navy-blue dress shuffles from a back room into the entrance where we stand, which is actually the kitchen. And it smells amazing.

Watching Marko bend down to hug his tiny grandmother and do the double kiss on the cheek thing is nothing short of adorable. They speak a few rapid sentences in Croatian before Marko takes my hand and pulls me a step forward.

"Heath, this is my *baka*. You can call her Lucy."

Lucy steps forward, and I greet her with the same double kiss. "It's nice to meet you. Marko speaks of you often."

"He needs to speak less and visit more." She holds my hands in hers and her eyes, still bright even with the obvious signs of cataracts, bore into mine. "Heat." She can't say the '*th*' part of my name after a few attempts and huffs. "That's a hard name to say. Hal is better."

"You can call me whatever you'd like." I say with a smile.

She drops my hands abruptly and turns back to Marko. "*Lijepe oči.*"

I don't know what that means, but Marko blushes. He actually turns pink as he agrees with his grandmother and we sit at the tiny kitchen table. I catch his eye, and he leans over.

"She said you have pretty eyes," he whispers as he grips my thigh under the table.

"So, Hal. My grandson brought you here to meet me and the rest of the old country people. Did he warn you about the work?"

"Work?" I cock an eyebrow at Marko. "He didn't. But I'm happy to help. What do you need?"

She and Marko speak in Croatian again, and one word I recognize, the name of the almond cookies I made for Marko.

"Do you want me to bake? I'd love to."

She nods, showing that she has decided, and Marko frowns.

"Are you sure? I didn't bring you here to put you to work. You're supposed to be relaxing. Well, as relaxing as meeting your boyfriend's family can be."

"Baking is fun. I don't mind."

A loud knock comes at the door, and a giant man with white hair enters. Lucy turns and the two of them talk while Marko leans in to steal a kiss. "Let's get our things upstairs and I'll explain what's about to happen."

A few more Croatian men enter and it's loud and crowded in the small kitchen. Marko chimes in and pulls me along after him reminding me to *pazi na glavu* and we leave the kitchen gathering behind.

Once outside, he huffs a breath and turns to me.

"Are you okay?"

"Of course, I am. Why wouldn't I be?"

"Well, you weren't supposed to get roped into cooking. *Baka* said she wouldn't. That's what we were arguing about."

"You were arguing? Huh. I didn't pick up on that. I just heard the cookie name, and you said to just chime in, so I did."

He bends down for a quick kiss. "I did say that. Thank you. I'm just sorry I didn't explain how this all works before coming here."

We've reached his bike, and he removes our small duffle bags out of the saddlebags. Really, it's more like an extra-large shave kit in size. Duffle is far too generous for what we have.

"I'm here with you, Marko. That's all that matters."

"Yeah...about that. When you offered to bake, you'll be in the kitchen with a bunch of older Croatian women for most of the day."

"Well, that's not bad. Where will you be?"

"With the men at the spit helping to cook the lamb. Which is really just sitting around and drinking while we watch meat cook." When I laugh, he shakes his head. "I'm not even kidding."

"Oh. It's fine. I'll learn about your country at the very least."

My phone chimes with a message in my pocket, and I fish it out as I follow Marko back to the house. When I see who it's from, I call out for Marko to stop.

"Terry sent pics of Jeff and says he's settling in splendidly. He already has a small group of hens he favours and no aggressive behaviour so far. He's eating and drinking well." Clicking on the attached photos, my heart swells. Jeff stands proud in a group of six females. It might just be me, but he looks relaxed. Can a bird get sexed out?

The next picture is...bird porn. Jeff is actively mating and I feel like I violated his privacy by opening the picture.

"Looks like he's doing more than eating and drinking well." Marko chuckles over my shoulder and with his free hand, pulls me against his chest and kisses me below the ear.

"He's living the dream, isn't he?"

"He's in bird heaven. Look at his face."

I'd rather not, at least not while he's impregnating his lady friend, but Marko is right. There's something about him in all the photos Terry sent that tells the story of a content bird. As much as I hated seeing him go, I love that he's living his best life. This text sets the final bit of guilt free, and I shove the phone back in my pocket. Missing him will take longer to go away, but I know he's where he should be now.

"I'd rather look at your face." Turning in Marko's arms, I loop my arms around his neck and push up on my toes to kiss him. "While I suck your dick. The best sight ever is how you look at me when I'm on my knees for you."

Marko groans softly and squeezes my ass with his free hand.

"Heath...don't give me a hard-on before we have to visit with my grandmother for a few hours. I'm begging you."

"It's usually me begging. This is different."

Sliding my nose along his, a wave of longing for this to be my everyday life slams into me. It's like the time I accidentally got a hole in one playing mini golf. I was aiming for a bank shot and missed. But the ball bounced over the small moat on the course, off the cement elephant, and into the hole. It took me by surprise.

Just like Marko. I wasn't aiming for him, but I'm sure happy about where I landed.

"This *is* different." His voice is raspy as he chases my lips. "But let's get through the next several hours before either of us begs."

Laughing, I step back and take his hand.

"I'll hold you to that."

Chapter 22

Marko

Thank god Heath is a morning person.

He was downstairs before me, bright-eyed and ready to go. When I left him with my grandmother and a handful of other Croatian women, I could tell he'd already charmed her. She patted his arm as he sat at the table, shaping the cookies like a pro.

Seeing him with her and the other women I've known since I was a boy lodged a massive ache in my chest. He fit in so well, even with Vera, who only spoke broken English. He smiled and tried to paraphrase and make gestures, never getting frustrated.

I felt bad leaving him with the women like this. I wanted him with me all the time. To hold his hand and show him the things I did as a boy. I didn't want him to feel like they had slotted him in a woman's role in all this, either. The old country people had a way of gender stereotyping, but it wasn't because of narrow thoughts. It was simply the way it was. I'd certainly helped her in the kitchen enough as a child.

I'm sure *baka* will give me the play-by-play tonight.

But right now, we have a lamb to roast.

"Marko!" One of my grandfather's closest friends, Petar, slaps me on the back. "What have you been up to? I was so happy when Lucy said you were coming. Come sit with an old man."

Petar already has a beer and motions for me to get him another one. When I sit across from at the picnic table without one of my own, he raises a bushy eyebrow.

"No *pivo* for you?" His Croatian is thick as he teases me for not drinking beer at 10 A.M.

"I usually work this time of day. Beer for breakfast was never really my thing."

Petar, always blunt, just gets to the point. "Lucy says you found someone to make you happy. A man?"

Petar is the most understanding of the group. I wouldn't say they're homophobic. I remember shouting to them all at a lamb roast over Easter when I was thirteen that I liked boys and if they didn't like it, they could pour their own damn beer. While I got in trouble for cursing at my elders, Petar rewarded me for being brave. The rest of them were polite, and it took years for me to feel accepted with them again, but they did.

"Yes, Petar. His name is Heath. *Baka* already calls him Hal."

"That's good. He's in the kitchen with her. Did you want him here?"

"Yeah. I wanted him to see how we make the lamb and just be here like this, but he's happy with her too. He fits everywhere."

He pats my hand. "I'm happy you're smiling." He drinks from his beer as we watch the others at work. The lamb has been on the spit for hours already and basted with more butter than I'm comfortable to admit. Some of the younger men stand nearby, running pieces of bread along the cooking animal to soak the juices before eating. I still don't understand the appeal of eating that.

"It's good to be smiling. It's been a long time since I've felt this...free."

People have set up tables around the park, and soon all the other food will begin arriving. Every Croatian family in the area will bring their favourites. Fresh baked bread, homemade noodles for chicken soup that was made from scratch, cabbage rolls with minced ham, boiled potatoes, stuffed peppers, and enough sweets to last a year.

"Have you heard from your father?"

Shaking my head, I press my lips together.

"No, and I'd like to keep it that way."

"I heard he may be in town, Marko. I don't know if he'll stop by to see Lucy, but...he will be managed if he does."

Petar's disdain for my father is just as big as mine. He held my *baka* together while her son was convicted of a crime and his name splashed all over the papers. I changed my name to avoid some of the attention, but *baka* wasn't that lucky. The entire community helped her, really. But I know Petar has always been sweet on my grandmother. He was the biggest pillar of support for us. There's no doubt in my mind if my father shows his face here, he'd not be welcome.

My phone chirps with Heath's sound, and I quickly swipe to read his message.

Tarzan: I think your grandma has said we're about to bring food out. She said something about a wagon?

Not Jane: She wants to use the wagon from the garden. It should be out in the small shed.

> **Tarzan:** And we put all the food on it?

Chuckling, I hit *Call*. It's easier to talk this out.

"Hi." Heath's sweet voice brings a smile to my face. "Sorry. I'm not sure I understand."

"We're at a park two blocks down the street with the spit. They bring all the food here and we eat in the park. If the weather was crappy, we'd all just go to our individual homes."

"Oh! So it's like a community picnic! This is fun!"

Heath's smile comes through the phone and I huff a small laugh.

"Yes, I guess it is. I know how you love picnics."

"So, is this all supposed to fit on the wagon? There's a lot of food here."

"We eat big lunches. It's our thing. I hope you're hungry."

"If I wasn't, I'd eat anyway. I've already sampled everything."

Heath laughs, but my heart melts. *Baka* would never allow tasting. She'd always make us wait. Letting him eat already doesn't seem like much to him, but it is to me.

"Let me know if you need help. I can run back if needed." My grandmother's voice in the background raises and Heath chuckles.

"I think she told me to get off the phone and come help."

"She did. See you soon, *ljubavi*."

Ending the call, I return the phone to my pocket to find Petar grinning at me like the *Cheshire Cat*.

"Make sure you introduce us properly when he gets here." Petar excuses himself to the washroom and I walk back to the spit to help with removing the lamb and carving it. Someone hands me an apron and four of us get to work.

These men are closer to my age, born here and returning to visit elderly parents and extended family. I don't remember their names, but they're still familiar. We settle into easy chatter, English mixed with Croatian as we pile plates high with the roasted meat and connect over food and our shared heritage.

I've missed this. For too many years, I've stayed away. Ashamed for what my dad did, knowing some of these families were affected by his thievery. It never felt comfortable for me to join these celebrations because I wrongly assumed I'd be an outcast.

Once we've finished carving, one man grabs a large olive oil bottle with no label and several plastic shot glasses.

"We've not had enough brandy today! My dad made this one."

He pours us all a shot and we toast to health and happiness.

"*Živjeli!*"

"Oh, that sounds fun! What are you toasting?"

Heath's hand on my arm startles me. I didn't even know he had arrived.

"A toast to happiness and health." I press a soft kiss to his cheek. "A good wishes kind of thing. Did you want to try the brandy?"

"Of course I do!"

Someone passes a shot his way, and he raises it with a smile and tries his best to say the toast. Then he swallows back the whole shot of brandy.

"Oh, good lord! What did you just have me drink!? You said it was brandy. That tastes like gasoline that's on fire." He coughs and sputters as the other men laugh and I find something non-alcoholic for him, which is difficult because we love our alcohol at these parties. After finding some juice boxes nearby, I poke the straw in it and hand it to him.

"It's not that kind of shot. You're supposed to sip it."

Heath narrows his eyes. "Next time warn a guy. That shit is nasty." He rubs at his chest. "Fuck, I think it corroded my guts. How do you drink that?"

"I guess I'm used to it. Are you okay?"

"Yeah, just...don't give me anything gross. I might puke." He waves a hand at the tables with all the food dishes. "Tell me what all the food is."

The park is full of at least fifty people and the food tables are exploding with all the favourites. Heath goes up and down the tables and takes a little of almost everything. He turned his nose up at the brown beans and spaghetti. Not that I blame him.

Finally, with full plates of food, we join Petar and *baka* at a table.

"Hal! Do you like red wine?" *Baka* sets a glass in front of him before he answers.

"I'm not a big wine drinker, but I'll try it."

"Heath, this is a family friend, Petar."

Heath moves to get up to greet him but Petar waves him down.

"Eat first. Talk later. But it's nice to meet you. Any friend of Marko and Lucy's is a friend of mine."

The four of us enjoy the food while someone turns up a radio with music. The men who've been here since 6 A.M. cooking the lamb are well into being hammered and dance along to it, laughing and drinking more.

Heath has seconds and raves over how good certain foods are. *Baka* glows with his praise even if it was something she didn't make.

And he loves the wine.

As Petar pulls another bottle from a box next to him and tops up Heath's glass, I'm trying to add up how much he's had.

"You guys sure know how to throw a party. And cook! Wow! How often do you do this kind of get together? I love food."

"We try for twice a year." Petar tops up Heath's wine glass again, and it's almost overflowing. Heath stretches forward and slurps from the cup before lifting it in his hand. "But usually it's only once. We're getting older, so it's harder. The younger ones move away and they don't continue it."

"Oh. That's sad." Heath swivels to me, wine sloshing in his now half-empty cup. How fast is he drinking this stuff? "Zane will make you lamb. Remember I asked, but it was too short of notice." He leans forward to kiss me. "Maybe that's what I'll call you. My little lamb."

My *baka* chuckles as she watches us and I gently take Heath's hand, which is fiddling with the buttons on my shirt absently.

"I need to thank you, Lucy. Your grandson is ah-mazing. Did he tell you my peacock bit him?"

"Peacock?" Petar furrows his brows. "Like a bird?"

"Yes!" Heath shouts entirely too loud and a few people turn to listen. "Turns out I couldn't satisfy his sex drive and he needed to go to a stud farm." He frowns as he gestures for Petar to add more wine in his glass. "Do you think I could ever make the stuffed peppers like Marica?"

I'll have to make a note for future Croatian gatherings that Heath needs to monitor his alcohol consumption better. I don't think he realizes most of this stuff is homemade and is more potent than anything he's used to.

Petar is amused and winks at me, a huge smile on his face as Heath rambles on. *Baka* sips her wine, hiding a smile, and I keep removing his wandering hands, which is a shame. But it's awkward being groped in front of your grandmother.

"Mama. Can we talk?"

The bile rises in my throat and my spine stiffens at the sound of my father's voice.

"You're not welcome here, Ivica," Petar grates as he stands.

"I can talk to my mother. It doesn't concern you."

"You're the guy who put his son through hell? Marko, this is your dad?" Heath bounces from the table with an ease I didn't expect, considering his level of intoxication.

"Who the hell are you to talk about me like that?"

Standing to join Heath, I face my father for the first time since he went to prison. He's been free for two years, but I've avoided him until now. His hair has thinned, and he carries a pot belly that he never used to. He was always so vain and it's odd seeing him not perfectly put together and dressed in jeans and a T-shirt. I idolized this man once. Now I wish he didn't exist.

"Jura, you look well."

"It's Marko. Why are you here?"

My grandmother speaks sharply in Croatian, telling my father if he wants to talk to come by the house later. Her disapproval of him being here is clear in her tone. She's always struggled with the balance of loving her son and protecting me. As a mostly private person, I know she'd prefer this conversation in away from curious eyes.

"I thought you'd be taller," Heath blurts as he gestures to my father. "Marko is so tall and strong. And kind. He's not like you."

"You don't even know me."

Heath steps up and pokes him in the chest. "I know enough to not like you."

My father grabs Heath's wrist.

"Don't fucking touch him," I growl and step between them. I'm not a man to condone violence, but if he even thinks of throwing a punch at me or Heath, I will lay him out without a second thought.

By now, the rest of the people gathered have noticed what's going on and a small group has formed behind us.

"You should go, Ivica. Nobody wants you here. You heard your mother." It's a man from a family my dad fleeced. John, I think.

My dad glances at my *baka* with a nod. "I'll see you this evening then, mama."

"Not if we can help it!" Heath calls out and a few laughs sound. "*Bako?*"

We exchange a glance as she sips her wine, completely unfazed.

"I'm fine. He can have his chance to talk away from the village later."

"I need more apple strudel." Heath declares. "Lucy makes a killer strudel. I'll be back."

Heath leaves us watching after him. He gets sidetracked and speaks with a woman for a few minutes before finally finding the strudel and eating it as he stands next to the table.

"He's going to have a killer hangover," Petar says with a hearty laugh. "But he's loyal. He loves you."

We watch as Heath dances with a few of the younger men and women, still laughing like he has zero fucks to give to anything.

His gaze catches mine and he raises his piece of apple strudel in my direction before taking a bite, all while dancing.

"I like Hal."

I snort a laugh as my grandmother's gaze collides with mine. Her approval means everything to me and knowing she likes Heath is the best gift I could ask for.

"Why don't you take him back early so he can sleep off a bit of the alcohol? We'll catch up tonight."

Having some alone time with Heath sounds like a great idea.

Especially in an empty house.

Chapter 23

Heath

A gentle hand on my arm squeezes.

"Heath? You should wake up, *ljubavi*."

Blinking open my eyes to the sound of Marko's voice, I groan.

"Fuck me, my head is about to pop off. How much did I drink?"

Marko chuckles and it's like a bomb going off.

"Not much, but homebrew packs a punch. I should've warned you how it sneaks up. Croatians take their homemade wine and brandy seriously."

Marko sets a glass of water and two ibuprofen on the bedside table as I sit up.

"What did I do? I think I remember everything." I swallow the pills and raise a finger. "Until here. I don't remember us getting here."

Marko's lips tilt in a sexy grin. "No? You don't remember calling me your 'Croatian Sensation' as we walked home...loud enough for everyone to hear?"

"Well, no. But it's not wrong. You are sensational."

He laughs as he sits beside me.

"Then you promised you'd 'ride my dick like a real cowboy' and passed out while I was in the bathroom. You've been asleep ever since."

"That sounds like something I might say. Sorry."

Marko takes my hand in his and threads our fingers together.

"Don't be. There's lots of time for that, and I will most definitely take you up on the offer." He kisses my hand while locking his gaze with mine. "My father will be here to visit *baka* shortly." Marko's voice is soft and hesitant. "Do you think you could join me?"

"Of course. It's just a little hangover." He rubs his thumb along mine.

"Thank you for standing up to him like you did. That wasn't the alcohol. I know you would have done it sober."

"You're welcome and you're right. I'll always do that, you know. I know how he made you feel, and you don't deserve that. You're such a good man, Marko. You know that, right?"

His throat bobs with a swallow as he nods.

"I do, but sometimes I don't feel like it. I broke the law for his approval, Heath. While I've made amends as best as I could, sometimes it's hard to move on from."

The paper-thin walls in the house announce doors opening and closing, along with a male voice. His father, no doubt, by the way he squeezes my hand.

"I know how you feel, but I'm here. Give me a signal if you want me to punch him or something."

"No violence needed. Just be there."

"I can do that."

But I still want to punch the guy.

***

When we enter the tiny kitchen, Marko's father and grandmother are in a heated discussion. It's all in Croatian, and Marko frowns as he walks to the stove to remove the boiling kettle.

His father stops speaking and snaps his head in our direction.

"I wasn't sure if you'd join us. You've always preferred to hide."

Marko stiffens as he makes a mug of tea and passes it to me. I hadn't even noticed he made it the way I like it before he pours one of his own.

"Don't speak to him like that, Ivica. You're in my house."

His *baka* may be tiny, but she's fierce and his father presses his lips together.

"Why are you here?" Marko's voice is so quiet I'm not sure his dad even hears him until he answers.

"To see my mother. I didn't know you would be here."

"Where have you been since you got out?" Marko doesn't take a seat at the table with them, so I don't either. Call it a sense, but my gut says we won't be here long, and his making tea is just something to do while he collects himself.

His dad shrugs. "Here and there."

"Are you working at anything?"

"Nobody wants to hire someone with a criminal record. You'd know that if you hadn't sold me out."

The guy is itching to lash out and fight with anybody, but Marko doesn't take the bait.

Marko hums and sips his tea. "Some do. I guess you haven't found the right place yet."

His father mutters in Croatian and Marko laughs without humour.

"Listen, Dad. I'm not about to sit here and let you make me feel guilty anymore. I've spent the last fifteen years running and hiding because of what you did. I worshipped you!" His hand trembles as he sets his mug down. "Hell, I wanted to be like you, and you betrayed my trust in a way no parent ever should." Marko runs a hand through his hair and his fingers curl, pulling at the strands. "You didn't just fuck up your life; it was mine, too. That's not fair."

His dad remains silent as his *baka* watches. This is the first time he's actually spoken to his father in fifteen years, and I have to admit I'm impressed with his calmness.

"So you're right. I hid. Not because I was a coward who used his family like you did, but because losing everyone I once held close was too painful to allow again. People viewed me as another version of you and I'm not. I didn't want that."

Ivica's expression remains stony. There's no love for his son there, and I think Marko knows it.

"I wanted to give you the world, Jura. You always wanted something. Ever since your mother died, you pulled into your shell. This kid who only wanted to paint and draw. I needed to prepare you for the reality of life!"

"By having me do illegal things for you?!" Marko's voice rises and he curls his hands into fists at his side. "You could have played with me. Or maybe sat with me to read a story. Dinner together. Anything, Dad. Literally *anything* would have been better than what you did. I never wanted money and all the fancy things. I just wanted my father to be proud of me and notice me."

His voice only wavers a little, but my heart cracks open for young Marko. Oh, how he must have been so alone. My mom wasn't always present, but at least when she was, I knew her heart was in a good place.

"I need help," his father says, like he didn't listen to a word Marko just said. Just says it bluntly and Marko freezes.

"What?"

"I know about the money Mom has. I need some to start over. Just a small loan to get started."

Baka shakes her head. "No. I can not do that, Ivica." Her lips press into a thin line.

His father's face turns an angry shade of red.

"You're my mother. Part of that money is mine. I need it now."

Baka shakes her head again and unleashes a spew of Croatian. I don't know what she's saying, but it must be good. Marko's shoulders droop and he reaches for my hand. *Baka* falls silent, and a tear runs down her face.

"If you need food, I will feed you. If you need love, I will give you what I can, Ivica. But I cannot and will not allow you to take advantage of me. You're my son and I love you, but I will not do that for you. You're not entitled to anything I have. When you put your son at risk, when you betrayed all those people, you gave that up."

Marko squeezes my hand before walking to his grandmother and placing a hand on her shoulder.

"Would you like to stay for a meal, Dad? Heath and I leave in the morning. You're welcome to stay."

Oh, my heart. After being so broken by the man, he still has the courage to offer a branch of love, and I hold my breath.

His father pushes his chair back, and it grates along the kitchen floor. He stands for several moments. His gaze flicks between *baka* and Marko and for a brief moment I think he might apologize. "No, thank you." He nods towards them. "I'm sorry I came."

Ivica just... leaves. *Baka* stares after him and Marko remains silent as he drops into the chair next to her.

"I'm sorry, *bako*. He hasn't changed, and I was willing to let him back in my life, but only on my terms. I thought dinner would be a place to start."

"Jura, you're a good boy. I don't know where I went wrong with him. But like you, I hoped he was here to visit his mother and not to get money from me." She sighs a heavy sigh. "Sometimes it's hard to let go."

She and Marko sit holding hands until she peers around Marko to find me still standing near the stove.

"Hal, come here. Sit."

Doing as she asks, I pull out a chair across from her and she offers me her hand. I take it with a smile and sneak a glance at Marko. This has been a very intense evening, but he seems almost serene.

"How's the hangover?"

I bark a laugh, even though my headache is still there, and she laughs with me.

"It's not too terrible. I'm sure a good bowl of your chicken soup and a lot of water will make it better."

"Then that's what we'll do."

The three of us work together in the tiny kitchen to warm up soup, and Marko finds the plate of leftover lamb for sandwiches.

While I slept off my booze, the community packed up leftovers, cleaned the park, and went home. It was definitely an experience I'd love to have again.

But what I love the most is sitting here with Marko and Lucy like an actual family and eating dinner. Watching how much he dotes on her makes my heart double. He's such a loving man. It's a shame his father couldn't see who Marko is.

"What are you thinking about?"

Marko pokes my foot under the table, and I look up from my empty soup bowl.

"About eating more soup." I wink as I reach for the ladle and fill my bowl.

"That's not it, *ljubavi*. Are you okay? Still want to be a part of this circus?"

Lucy pauses her eating and watches us.

"If you must know, I was thinking about how much I love sitting here like this and being part of your family. It's a shame your dad can't see what a genuine gift he's missing here. In both of you."

"Heath..."

Marko drops his head and swallows hard. His grandmother pats his shoulder.

"Hal is right. You should listen to him more often."

"Yeah, you should." I smile and Marko raises an eyebrow.

"Uh-huh. Something tells me listening to everything you say might not be a good idea."

"Lucy, tell him he needs ducks for his pond."

"If Hal says you need ducks, then maybe you should listen."

"*Bako!*"

She laughs, and Marko shakes his head. "You two will never be allowed to spend time alone together. You'll gang up on me."

They trade a few sentences and Marko slips into Croatian with her, but I don't mind one bit. My man has had an impossible weight lifted today and I love watching him like this.

***

Marko hugs his grandmother one more time before we leave.

"I promise to come visit more."

"I'd love to see you more, but you have a life to live, too. Especially once you get ducks."

Marko rolls his eyes, and I laugh as I bend down for a hug.

"I'll wear him down. Don't worry."

His grandmother stands on the sidewalk while we put our helmets on and mount his bike. With a last wave, we pull away and leave this tiny town behind. Marko planned to take me on a scenic tour, he said. With pretty fields and lakes and lookouts and maybe even farm animals.

The countryside rolls by and I squeeze my arms around him. Marko brings a hand back and rubs my leg before resting it there for a few moments. He may love it when I hold on tight, but I love it when he reaches back to touch me. It's something he's done more of, and I don't know what it is about the gesture that does it for me. Maybe it's seeing his tattooed hand grip me like he owns me, or maybe it's just him touching me. Either way, I'm here for it.

When we stop at a station for fuel, he checks the weather.

"We might get wet on the way back. There's a storm moving in and it looks like we might hit it about an hour from home. What do you want to do?"

That's a fucking loaded question.

"Let's get wet."

I grin through my helmet and wiggle my eyebrows. It's hard to flirt with this thing on. So instead, I grab his junk and his eyes widen.

"The good kind of wet."

"Fuck, Heath. Warn a guy."

"I thought I did?"

He shakes his head as he pulls us away and back onto the highway. But he puts his hand back on my leg and waiting to get home just might kill me.

Chapter 24

Marko

The rain starts about forty minutes from home, and I need to slow down a fair bit to travel it safely. I'm regretting not packing rain gear for us, but I'm also not disappointed about the prospect of a wet and naked Heath.

There's so much I want to say to him since this weekend at my grandmother's. So much has changed for us both and maybe I'm moving too fast, but Heath needs to be with me.

I want that smile every morning and his hugs every night. He brings joy to my life like I've never known and if I could just keep his sunshine around forever, I'd die happy.

As we turn onto my road, the skies open up, and the rain arrives in sheets. If we were still on the highway, I'd have had to search for cover, so the timing couldn't be more perfect.

I pull into the driveway, throwing up a thank you to the gods that we made it home safe. Soaked, but safe.

When I tap Heath to signal he can get off, the rain hits the carport roof with a roar. When he removes his helmet, his curls poke all over and he shivers.

"I might regret the choice to drive in the rain. I'm freezing."

After placing my helmet on the bike, I peel off my light jacket that's soaked through to my T-shirt and now clings to me like a second skin.

"Or maybe not," Heath purrs and I find his dark gaze roaming my body. "Tick the box for something else I didn't know I'd like." He steps closer to me, still in wet clothes, and the rain continues to fall. "A literal wet dream, Marko." His fingers brush the hardened nubs of my nipples under the shirt. "Lord, love a duck. You're sinfully hot like this."

"Is that your way of talking about ducks at an inappropriate time to convince me to get some?"

"Huh? No. Maybe." He bites his lower lip, always playful. "But if it works, then yes."

He dusts his fingers over my nipples again and smooths my wet shirt against my body. "Even your tattoos show though when it's wet. Fuck..." Heath's hands drift to my zipper, but I take his hands in mine.

"Can we take this inside? I really am cold."

"Oh. Yeah. Solid plan."

Heath turns and tries to open the door, but it's locked. He holds out a hand for the key and I place the entire key set in his hand.

"Which one?"

"The one with the little house on it."

He flicks through my keys and sighs. "Aww...you marked all your keys with little symbols. That's so fucking adorable."

He finally opens the door and as soon as we're inside, he hangs them on their hook while I lock the door behind us. We stand dripping in the area off my kitchen and the earlier playfulness from Heath is gone. Vanished, and I reach out to him.

"Are you okay, *moja srećo*? What happened?"

Heath shivers and I help him out of his jacket. My mind is whirling, trying to figure out what changed in the last thirty seconds to have his silly chatter grind to a halt.

"I love you, Marko. I mean, like, with everything I have. If my heart could give you more, it would." His warm gaze finds mine as he shivers. "I've known for a while that this was different. Not just because of the same sex thing, but because...because my heart beats for you in a way I've never felt."

"Heath..." Lifting a palm to his cheek, I dip to brush a kiss across his lips. "I love you, too. More than anything. I can't even compare it to something because it's different from anything I've ever known."

"Oh, thank god. I was hoping you'd say something like that. I know I say a lot of random shit, but that was as good as I could come up with." He loops his arms around my neck. "It also sounded a lot better than *'my dick is always hard for you, and I want to make good on my promise to ride you like a real cowboy would.'*"

My entire body shakes with laughter as I kiss this random man. This man who just blurts out how he feels, but also does the sweetest things for me. He's such a wild card some days and I think that's what makes me love him more.

"I won't say no to that."

It's all hands and tugging off wet clothes. Laughter and stolen kisses as we leave our soaking clothes on the floor and get our bare asses to the bathroom to towel off.

"I'm not cold anymore at least," Heath says as a fingertip traces the Croatian flag tattoo over my heart.

Tossing the towel on the floor, I grip his hips, pulling him into me.

"No? I hear skin to skin is the best thing to warm up with, though."

My hands massage the globes of his ass, and he presses a kiss to my neck. "I forgot, but I'm not opposed to the idea." He groans when I drag a finger down his crease. "Yes. Do that. Please, Marko."

Heath's hands grasp my neck and tug me down to his lips. His kisses are frantic, like he's afraid I won't be here when he opens his eyes. "Up." I press my hands under his ass and he gets it, jumping to wrap his legs around my waist and I carry him to my bedroom.

"You have no idea how hot that makes me. I love it when you carry me."

Laying him on the bed, I pull away to find the large pool of pre-cum between us.

"I have an idea. Look at you leaking for me."

Running a finger through it, I bring it to my lips and Heath slams his eyes closed.

"Stop being so hot. You're killing me."

With a chuckle, I lean down to kiss his jaw. "I think that's usually my line, isn't it? You're the one who usually pushes all my buttons and unravels me. Usually with a single kiss."

He cracks an eye open and his lips tilt ever so slightly.

"It only takes a kiss for me to do that?"

Dragging my tongue down his neck, his breath hitches, and he stretches to allow me better access. "Yep. Sometimes not even. A well-timed grope or even the scent of your aftershave. It makes me gone for you." I whisper in his ear before nipping at his lobe.

"It's *Old Spice*."

"What?"

"My aftershave. Sometimes people think it's just for older men, but I like it." Both eyes open now and a small smirk plays on his lips. "Seems it helped me snag an older man, so maybe they weren't wrong."

"I'm not old!"

"You're older than me."

"Yeah, but it's like five years. I'm not old."

He rocks his hips. "Prove it."

Heath grabs my neck and smashes his lips into mine. He writhes under me, creating a heady slide of our bodies, and I'm gasping within minutes. How do I stand a chance to have any staying power with this man when that's all he needs to do to turn me all the way on?

"I meant it before, Marko." His hands grip my cheeks and he holds my face in front of his. "I want you to..." Somehow, he blushes, his cheeks growing more pink right up to his ears, and he appears so naïve and innocent my heart stops. "I want to ride you. I've...researched things."

"Have you now?"

Heath nods slowly. "I have. According to various chat boards, I'm either a cumslut or a size queen."

Okay. So not exactly naïve then.

"What kind of chat boards are you *on*?"

"Something Dante told me to check out. Reddit maybe?"

His hands slide down my sides and he lifts his head to kiss me. "The point is, I liked it before when I rode your fingers. I want more, Marko. I know it might hurt at first, but I know I want it, so don't be afraid to give it to me because I'm new to this. Nothing we've done has ever made me feel...not good."

Heath wraps his legs around my waist and lifts his hips up. He rocks slowly but with a need, I feel deep in my chest.

"I can't ever deny you, *srećo*. But you can always change your mind. Just tell me."

Heath nods and lets his legs drop away from my waist. My body trembles. When a gorgeous man like Heath asks you to be his first experience with anal sex, it's a lot of pressure.

But it's not a hardship to worship his body.

All of it.

Every inch of him I cover in tender kisses and, remembering how he said he likes to be marked, I suck hard to bruise his skin. Heath splays himself across the bed and reaches over his head to grip the slots of my headboard. He's giving me his entire self freely and knowing he trusts me so completely has me floating higher than any cloud in the sky.

My tongue slides down his cock, across his sack, and I linger, flicking across the sensitive skin above his hole.

"Oh god. Marko...this is already better than I imagined."

His breath is ragged, and he shamelessly spreads his legs wider.

"Well, you're probably going to like this then."

Rimming Heath is both a source of pleasure and entertainment. I've never had such a vocal partner before and I can't say I hate it. He's like a cheerleader and play-by-play announcer in one. And it's great for my ego.

"Oh fuck, you just stuck your tongue in my...gnhh...oh shit. Do that again. Holy noodles, Marko...you're really good at this."

Of course, I don't respond. My mouth is busy anyway, but when he plants his feet and grinds down on my face, babbling nonsense, I need to check in with him.

"*Ljubavi*, I didn't understand that last part. You okay?"

Glazed brown eyes meet mine and his lips tilt in a lazy smile.

"I'll be better when you fill me with dick."

"Jesus, Heath. What's got into you?"

"Hopefully you. Can I?"

Climbing up the bed beside him, I settle and he turns his lust-blown eyes to me.

"You can do whatever you want to me."

Heath kisses me with a loud groan. Pushing me onto my back, he straddles my waist and runs a finger across the crease between my eyebrows. "Don't worry. I'll be fine."

His body glistens like a slicked-up gladiator. The curls of his hair stick to his forehead and after he's found the lube in the nightstand, he's a vision from heaven as he coats his fingers and reaches back to finger himself.

I'm kind of in awe that he just goes for it and loses himself to his own touch so completely. He's beautiful in his inhibition and in the way he lives his life. It shouldn't surprise me at all that he just goes for what he wants with no shame.

"You've been practicing, haven't you?" My voice is so thick I need to clear my throat. "Did a message board tell you to do that, too?"

"Oh, yeah." He drops forward and plants his hands near my head before planting the sweetest kiss on my lips. "Help me with the rest."

My hand slaps around the bed to find the lube, and I coat my dick before teasing him with my fingers a little more. He sighs across my lips.

"God, it feels so much better when you do it."

Notching my cock at his entrance, he sits up with a clenched jaw. "You're bigger than I thought."

He doesn't let me say anything. Instead, he eases himself over the tip and rocks back and forth, teasing both of us as he adjusts. Each time he lowers a fraction more and I can't tear my eyes away from his face. Every emotion, every sensation, plays out across his features. Heath is hedonism personified.

"Marko..." My name is a breathy plea from his lips as he sinks a little deeper. "Oh wow. Oh..." His chest heaves again and his gaze meets mine. "I want you to kiss me."

Raising up on my elbows far as I can go, he dips his head to meet me and takes my lips in a lust filled kiss. "Do you want to kiss me while you ride me, *ljubavi*?"

"Yeah, I...how?"

"Let me sit on the edge and you climb back on."

Heath reluctantly slides off my cock with a wince, but as soon as I'm in place, he wastes no time getting back to it. The first part is easier this time. He moans so sweetly every time he takes more of me, and it breaks me open in the best possible way. He buries his fingers in my hair and crushes his mouth to mine.

I'm hanging by a thread by the time he finally lowers himself all the way and his ass hits my thighs. Heath gasps against my lips. His chest heaves with shallow breaths as I smooth my hands up his muscled back.

"Marko..." He gently rolls his hips with a moan. "Oh, fuck..."

"You're doing so good. You feel amazing."

Heath pulses his hips in short pumps, increasing the speed and depth to something he's comfortable with and maintains his rhythm.

His lips find mine. Over and over, he kisses me and grips my hair in a tight fist.

"Are you close?" His words are a pant as he drops his forehead to mine. "I'm gonna come."

"Fuck yes. Come while I'm in you, *srećo*."

"Marko!"

Heath's ass strangles my dick as he floods my stomach between us and wraps his arms around my neck. It's enough to push me over the edge and I unload inside him, my arms wrapped tight around his waist so he can't move—even if he wanted to.

"You just came in my ass."

"I did. Another one of those marking things I told you about. I never asked if—"

"Shush. I knew what I was doing. I wanted it."

We release our holds, and Heath stands up in front of me. Several purplish red marks decorate his chest and sweat shines on his body.

"My legs are on fire and my ass is kinda sore, though. I think now would be a good time to try your fancy bathtub."

"I couldn't agree more. I'll meet you in there."

Heath turns away and my breath catches as I watch my cum run down his leg. Hickeys all over his chest and filled with my cum. I smile to myself.

He said he wanted to be marked by me.

Guess I'm an overachiever.

Chapter 25

Heath

"Here are the keys. It's all yours."

The salesperson hands over the keys to my brand-new *Jeep Cherokee*.

"Thank you so much for your help."

The salesperson wishes me the best again, and I step out into the afternoon sunshine.

"How do you feel?"

Blaze waits outside, insisting I do this part on my own, and I'm grateful. He still hasn't told me where my old car is but promises something is in the works and I'll love it.

It's been a weird two weeks, though. My car died, Jeff left, and I met Marko's family. Blaze reviewed my savings with me, and it turns out he's a great advisor and I have more money than I ever thought I would. More than Mom had probably ever seen in her life. Buying the new-to-me Jeep wasn't an issue with Blaze's help, but it's been almost too much to process. Too much change in a short time.

"I'm a little out of sorts, to be honest." The keys weigh heavy in my hands. "Do you have time to talk?"

"I'll always have time if you need me, Heath. Where would you like to talk?"

"Could we go to the brewery? Maybe walk the gardens?"

"Sure. Want me to ride with you now or meet you there?"

"I'll meet you there in about thirty minutes?"

Blaze nods and returns to his truck while I climb behind the wheel of my new ride. A new vehicle should make me excited, but it reminds me of things I no longer have. No more car with memories of Mom and Jeff. No more peacock filling the back seat. Memories of our pretend camping trips no longer close.

After adjusting the mirrors, I send Marko a quick text and selfie from inside. He has several clients today, all back-to-back. Since we took a week off together to visit his grandmother and explore our relationship, Marko booked himself heavily in the coming weeks to catch up. I don't expect him to reply, but when he responds with a heart, I rub at my chest before connecting my phone to the *Bluetooth* and pulling away from the dealership.

Me and Marko have connected with each other in the evenings because going for coffee without Jeff is still too raw for me. I didn't think the little things without Jeff would hit me so hard, but when three people in one day asked where my bird was, I cracked. I'll need more time before resuming that routine, and I'll get back to it when my heart is a little less bruised.

I've spent every night at Marko's, though, since. When I leave at the ass crack of dawn, as he likes to say, we kiss each other good morning and see each other by suppertime.

Marko has definitely helped ease the sting of not having a peacock rule my life. But Jeff still left a Grand Canyon-sized hole in my life. While Jeff can't be replaced, not having to be responsible for him anymore has resulted in a shift in my priorities. For once I've thought about my future seriously.

And that's what I need to talk to Blaze about.

He's already at the brewery waiting for me, leaning against the side of his truck. After parking next to him, we fall into step, towards the garden paths. He says nothing. Just walks with me, and that's what I like about him. He has more patience than the other guys and lets me sort my shit without interrupting.

At the top of our first small hill, next to Jacob's favourite lavender garden, I stop and lean on the railing at the top. Blaze does the same, and I smile.

"I know I've thanked you for taking over my savings and helping with all the car shopping, but thank you again, Blaze. It's changed my life."

He dips his head with a smile. "You're welcome. Again." He pokes me with his elbow and chuckles.

"You probably know I'm in love with Marko. Like, head over heels for that man. It's so strange how it creeps up on you sometimes."

Nodding, he flips the toothpick in his mouth over and it hangs from the side of his mouth.

"I figured. He's good for you. I know I've said it before, Heath, but we're all happy you've found your person."

"I know, and I owe you guys so much." My eyes burn, but I don't want to cry. This isn't a sad time. Not really. "Um, I've been thinking a lot about...my life, I guess. I'd like to..." Fuck, I can't even say it.

Blaze turns to face me with a soft smile. "You let the tears fall if you need to, Heath. It's a big change to leave. It's okay to be emotional about it."

Shaking my head, I wipe at my unshed tears. "Not the ranch. I can't leave the ranch. The animals are my babies, you know? And Hank. He's mine. I can't walk away from him. Working at the ranch, I think is what I'm meant to do. But...I don't think I want to live there anymore."

Blaze hums under his breath. "We expected this day to come, Heath. We're not mad. Not even disappointed. We're fuckin' thrilled for you."

"It's just hard to say out loud. It's the only home I've known for ten years. I've stayed because I love everything about it. Jeff needed me and I knew I couldn't just leave him, but..."

I sigh and look out over the gardens below. Jeff had to leave anyway. It was one of life's inevitable happenings. But I was there for him when it mattered. I found myself through that bird. Which sounds so completely stupid, but Jeff taught me a lot about myself. That I was valuable and had a purpose. And that my heart is likely bigger than my brain. Watching him leave was damn hard, but seeing him thrive with Terry makes me so happy. This must be what parents feel like when their kids grow up and move away. I'm just happy he's happy even though I miss him like crazy. With Jeff thriving somewhere else, it feels like I have permission to do something for me.

And that was a revelation I felt a little uncomfortable with.

"But the one thing you love the most isn't at the ranch." Blaze mirrors my stance and finishes my sentence. "It's hard to be apart from your person. I get it, Heath. Me and Riv did the same thing. Swappin' nights at each other's houses before I begged him to move in with me. He had his business and his dad to keep him busy and he was only at the ranch for peak times." Blaze runs a hand over his face. "Jeff was a lot of work, and you were there when we needed him wrangled. He gave you what you needed, and you did the same for him. It's okay to want something just for yourself now."

Which has been my greatest struggle since spending time with Marko. I want to spend all my days and nights with him. My loft is a place I never want to sleep alone in again. I loved it, but I was there for Jeff. Blaze is right; I need something for myself now.

"So you don't think Dan or Alec will be upset when I tell them I'm moving out?"

"They'll be sad they won't see you in their kitchen at all hours, but they won't be mad about you havin' a life."

"I never told you this before, but the three of you are like the dads I never had. You've all been so patient and cared about me. Your advice, your job help, everything. I don't know how to thank you for any of it properly. Without Dan taking me in, I'd probably be homeless and an addict like Mom was. You rescued me just like everything else on the ranch."

Blaze looks away and clears his throat. He says nothing for a while, but when he does, it's with wet lashes and a gruff voice.

"You don't have to thank us. Just love us, like you said. That's all we need."

"I will, Blaze."

I hate seeing the big guy all teary, so I hold out my arms and he wraps me in a hug. "I'm so proud of you, Heath."

I needed this bit of time with just Blaze more than I realized. My chest is a little lighter now.

"Why don't we round up the guys tonight and you and Marko can come over? It's the perfect time to show you what we've done with the car for you."

"Really? Yeah, okay. I'll check with Marko, but I think he's free tonight."

Blaze and I walk back down the path and with every step, the future seems more clear. When my phone buzzes with Marko's message telling me he's free, I reply that I'll meet him at his place so we can come back together.

"Marko is in."

Blaze smirks. "I had no doubt, Heath. He'd move mountains for you." He pauses at his truck and hesitates. "You know, when I heard who you were datin' ...well, not datin' at the time, because you couldn't see it."

He chuckles when I punch his arm. "Don't remind me! I'm surprised he kept coming back. He must've thought I was the thickest guy in the world."

"Maybe. You should ask." He laughs before schooling his face. "When I found out who Marko was, I knew you'd have no problem gettin' past his history. I hope you're not angry that I interfered a little and pushed him to tell you. From what the boys at the ranch were tellin' me, you seemed pretty smitten. I didn't want you to get hurt with secrets."

"I'm not angry at all. Kind of happy you did, actually. It gave me the push to examine what I wanted, too. Besides, there's not much you could do that would make me angry."

"That's true, I suppose. You're the most laid-back guy I know." Blaze opens his truck and slides in. "See you both tonight."

As he drives off, I lean on my Jeep, smiling and taking a few minutes to myself.

One hard conversation down, and I'm feeling confident.

Now… I wonder how hard it will be to convince Marko we really need ducks.

***

Marko's fingers tap his thigh as I drive. Since we decided I should move into his place, the plan was to pack a few things from my loft and bring them over after dinner at the ranch tonight.

But Marko doesn't like enclosed vehicles.

"Would you prefer to drive? I don't mind."

"What? No. You drive just fine. Maybe a little like my *baka*, but your driving is fine."

I snort because yeah, okay. I was so used to babying my old car and driving slowly. It's just natural for me to drive like I'm eighty and on my way to the coffee club on a Sunday morning. That car needed to last.

"But you're all fidgety. What is it?"

Marko reaches over and rests his palm on my thigh.

"It's just a little claustrophobic for me. When I was a kid, I developed an irrational dislike of cars since my mom died in a car accident. That's why I like bikes instead." He shakes his head. "I know it doesn't make sense. Sometimes I'm okay and sometimes I guess I fidget. Before you ask if I've talked to anyone about it, yes, I have. It comes and goes, and it's just a weird little hang-up I have."

"You never told me that before."

He shrugs like it's no big deal and I flick the signal light on to pull onto the shoulder.

"What are you doing?"

"You're driving. Get out." I don't even give him a chance to reply. I've already walked around to the passenger seat and Marko still has his seatbelt on. He finally exits when I knock on the passenger window.

"Heath, it's your new Jeep. You should drive. I'm fine."

"I'm sure you are, but don't forget I've been your passenger for a few months now and I know how much you love driving a bike. So let's make this be like a bike."

"I don't—"

"Get. Out."

Finally, the man walks around to the driver's seat and slides in. After he adjusts the seat and mirrors, his fingers flex on the steering wheel and his lips twitch.

"Put the windows down, please. Even the back ones."

Marko lifts an eyebrow, but does as I say.

"Now drive."

After pulling off the shoulder and back on to the road, I stick my hand out and tap on the roof. The cool air rushes into the cab, ruffling our hair and making me laugh. Marko sticks his arm out, too, and I turn up the radio.

"It's good, right?" I shout over the rushing air and music.

Marko glances my way before reaching over and holding his hand palm up for me. After lacing our fingers together, he brings my hand up to his lips and kisses my knuckles.

"The best, Heath."

***

"Thank you so much for this, Zane. Delicious as always."

Blaze and the others at the ranch had arranged a BBQ at Alec and Zane's. When Blaze said to come over tonight, I didn't think it would be for something like this. Zane had made all my favourites, and we sat in their gazebo laughing and eating.

Alec and Dan played horseshoes off and on outside and showed Marko, too. Watching Marko fit in and laugh along with these men made me all squishy inside.

"Hey, help me carry these dishes in and quit mooning over the guy. Do that later."

Laughing, I scoop a load of dishes off the patio table and follow Zane inside with it. After placing them on the counter, Zane asks me to sit on the couch for a minute while he disappears.

When Zane returns, he finds me getting a closer look at one of Alec's violets. They're so pretty up close.

"You can take one. Consider it a housewarming gift. Plants make a house a little more welcoming, I think. I started that one from a sprout a few years ago."

"Really? Yeah, thank you. I'd love one of these. It will make me feel like I'm still here."

"Um, so...Dan has something to show you shortly, but before he does that, I wanted to give you something." He holds a small box in his hand, and I place the violet on the table to take the box from him.

"I know how much you'll miss Jeff. I sort of do too. Mainly because I'll never forget how that bird chased you all over when he first got here, and you insisted you knew what you were doing." He laughs softly. "One time you lost a shoe. Do you remember that?"

"I do! That was the first time he...ah...tried to mount me and his toe ripped off my shoe, but I was so freaked out I just kept running without it." I laugh hard at the memory. "And that's when I knew the bird was mine. I just didn't understand what was happening then."

Zane motions to the box. "Open it. And promise you won't cry."

"Okay. Promise."

Zane waits with a smile as I peel off the paper and lift the lid on the box. Inside is a man's necklace with a dog tag-shaped pendant like someone in the military would wear. Etched on the pendant is a photo of Jeff in the front of the chicken coop.

"Zane..." My voice hitches as I run my finger over it. "This is gorgeous. Thank you."

"You said you wouldn't cry." He swipes at his eyes.

"I'm not crying. You are."

He pulls me into a hug and both of us laugh as he releases me and reaches for the tissue box.

"I'm super happy you found the next part of your life, Heath. I hope you're as happy as me and Alec because I love that man more than life itself. If Marko makes you even a fraction as happy as that...then I'd be thrilled."

"He's great, Zane. Really. It was odd at first when I finally clued in that I was attracted to him that way. But he's just so thoughtful and kind and—"

"He's hot, dude. You can say it. And I agree."

"Five alarm fire, Zane. Like so hot I just want to drop to my knees when he —"

"Stop!" He laughs as he pushes the wrapping paper into the recycle bin. "I don't need details." He looks at his phone and abruptly pushes me back to the patio. "Dan's ready. Come on."

When we head back onto the patio, everyone is seated and there's a folder on the table. Dan and Marko stand shoulder to shoulder, whispering, and when the door closes, they turn to me.

The chatter stops amongst the others, and Dan clears his throat.

"Heath, I don't need to tell you again how much we care about you. When everything went down with Jeff and your car, we insisted you take time to deal with that for a few reasons." He picks up the folder on the table. "One reason is in there." Dan squeezes Marko's shoulder. "The other reason is right here."

"I told you I'd take care of your car," Blaze chimes from the corner. "So, all of us sat together one night and threw around ideas until we found one that we agreed on."

"Nobody is more dedicated to our animals than you, Heath." Alec, who usually keeps quiet, comes to stand near Zane. "You're a friend to everyone; animal, bird, and man. We've all watched you grow from an unsure teenager into the confident and caring young man you are now. We all love you. I think you know, it's not just as a friend, but as family."

Marko beams at me and holds out a hand, so I take it, and he kisses my forehead.

"I get the fun part, *ljubavi*." Taking the folder from Dan, he opens it and there are a series of sketches inside. "Your family said the car should stay on the ranch because you love it here, and I agree. When you told me what this car meant to you, I came up with this idea."

Three sketches, all slightly different in design, illustrate my car as part of the landscape around a pond.

"Duck boxes?" My gaze finds Dan, and he nods eagerly.

"We have that spot of land that's too marshy to plant in. At the back of the pasture where Hank plays. So I thought it would be cool to put the car on a platform to slow the decay of the body and plant some vegetation the migrating birds like to eat. We'd build a few bird boxes, take the doors off and leave the body open for anything that wanted to nest inside."

Dan's excitement is palpable and I'm still trying to wrap my mind around what exactly he's proposing.

"So you want it to be a place for ducks?"

"A place for any bird or wild animal seeking refuge. Maybe it's squirrels—"

"Or a raccoon!" Zane adds with excitement and Alec rolls his eyes.

Dan continues. "Birds, ducks, animals, whatever needs some stuffing for a nest or a burrow for their young. The sky is the limit out in the wild. Your car would give them something they need; a home."

"I added these duck boxes because I read some ducks like them. And songbirds. Did you know the ranch is right under a popular flyway for migrating birds?"

Marko shrugs when I stare at him. "You researched birds for this?"

"I wanted it to be perfect for you. That's why there are three designs. You choose the one you want and we'll build it."

"We?"

"Well...I want to help."

"You don't need to decide now, Heath," Dan says. "Until the spring, the car is in the machine shed and we'll remove all the fluids over the winter, so it's ready and safe to be there. But what do you think?"

Closing the folder, I look around the patio where every person I hold dear to me sits. My found family in every way possible. Brothers, fathers, and the man next to me who has slotted into my heart in a way I didn't expect. Boyfriend doesn't feel right. He's far more than that.

"I think I'm the luckiest guy in the world. But one question."

Turning to Marko, I grip his hand. "You researched ducks and birds. Does that mean we can get ducks now?"

The guys all laugh at Marko's expense, but I'm serious.

"I'll think about it."

"That's not a no."

Marko shakes his head and kisses me.

"It's not a yes, either. One step at a time, *ljubavi*."

"I'll take it. Now let's pack some stuff and go home."

Marko smiles softly. "I like the sound of that."

CHAPTER 26

MARKO

The following spring

"Y ou're sure Terry knows we're coming?"

Heath gives me 'The Look' and I hold up a hand.

"I was just asking. I know when you get excited, you sometimes forget stuff."

Which is an understatement. The last time he started talking to the guys at the ranch about the duck car, as I refer to it, he forgot he had started a bubble bath. We had bubbles oozing into the hallway and half an inch of water on the bathroom floor. The time before that it was watching the wild partridge that wandered into our yard, and he went outside naked as a jaybird to throw down birdseed and damn near froze his balls off.

Which would have been a shame.

"Okay. That's fair. But yes, I spoke to him this morning, and he said it's perfect timing because Jeff was...extra busy the last few days. A *'prolific breeder'* were his words."

Heath puffs his chest like a proud dad, and I slide a hand onto his thigh.

"Sounds a lot like his dad."

Heath's cheeks flame bright red, and I smirk. Sex with Heath has been nothing short of amazing. He's a dirty one. Don't let the boy next door smile fool you. More often than not, he begs for his own breeding, and I'll never deny him.

"Marko..." He warns as my fingers slide dangerously close to his zipper. Hands at ten and two like a good little driver, he's also helped me be more comfortable as a passenger in a closed vehicle. I'll still always choose a bike, but this road trip is longer than either of us wanted on a bike. Especially since Jacob filled Heath in on the pleasures of road head. Another friend of his I need to send a thank-you card to.

"What?"

"Don't do it. I...don't laugh...but I don't want Jeff to know I just came down your throat before we visit."

Am I disappointed to be cock-blocked by a bird again? Absolutely.

Do I press him like I might other times when it's a game for us to make each other horny out of our minds just to see how far we can take it? No.

Because it's been several months since we've been to visit Jeff and it's important to Heath. Instead, I relax back and leave my hand on his knee. He picks it up to kiss the back of my hand before placing it back on his thigh. His signal that he enjoys me touching him and I still have a shot later.

"I won't laugh. I understand."

"So...are you excited to go to your first rodeo?"

The other reason for the road trip. My first rodeo. The one we didn't get to last year.

"I am! I'm not entirely sure what to expect, but I'm looking forward to it. Jamieson told me there are tickets at the gate for us."

When I met the bull rider last year and finished his tattoo, I didn't think I'd ever hear from him again. But he sent me a few clients over the winter and one of them told me I needed to come and see him and friends in a real rodeo.

"Was he the one who's a steer wrestler?"

"No, Jamieson is the bull rider, and Jackson is the steer wrestler."

"Well, that's confusing."

"They look totally different if that helps."

Heath slows the Jeep, and signals to turn into the lane for the bird farm where Jeff now lives. It's a gorgeous place that I'm envious of. Surrounded by amazing scenery to fuck the rest of your days away. I thought I'd like to be a spoiled house cat in my next life, but a stud bird could be the way to go.

Heath parks in a visitor space and meets me on the passenger side after grabbing a small bag of cranberries from the back seat.

"Heath! Hi! Right on time." Terry exits the small building we parked in front of and shakes our hands. "Good to see you both again."

I like Terry. He's way more into the bird talk than I am, but Heath soaks up everything he says. He comforts Heath in a way I can't, and for that I'm extremely grateful.

"Jeff has been a star, Heath. An absolute star."

"Oh? What did he do?"

Terry leads us along a path towards the enclosure where Jeff spends most of his time with his feathered harem.

"I've had six peahens lay eggs this week alone. As long as they all hatch, the birds have homes already. Male offspring bring more money and Jeff is already making a name for himself as a good stud. His kids will be sought after to start other bird farms."

"Oh, wow. I'm happy to hear he's helping you so much."

"A good stud like his dad," I whisper in his ear and Heath swats at me to be quiet. But he's trying hard to hide that smile.

Terry opens the gates and lets us inside the large enclosure. Heath's face lights up when he sees Jeff. "Hey, buddy!" He waves, whistling, and Jeff stops mid-step, snapping his head in Heath's direction.

"I'll wait inside. Take as long as you need."

Terry leaves us and I fade to the side as Heath focuses on Jeff, who now struts towards him with purpose. Once he's a few steps away, he pauses and lifts his feathers. Jeff shakes them and cocks his head as he slowly comes closer to Heath.

"He remembers me," Heath whispers, and I think he's right. We hadn't been here over the winter and Heath was so worried Jeff would forget who he was. "Hey, buddy. I've missed you. Looks like you've got a nice setup here. Cute girlfriends."

Jeff makes a sound I've never heard before. A low purr. Maybe a coo? It's not a screech and Heath reaches out to pet his head. Which still blows me away that he can do that. The bird keeps his fan up and Heath pulls the cranberries from his pocket.

"I brought you a treat. Your favourite." Jeff makes the same cooing noise as Heath shakes them on the ground. He pecks at them and a few peahens have drawn close, but Jeff turns and squawks, sending them running before cooing again as he eats and struts around Heath some more.

Heath keeps telling the bird all the things we've done since he left like he's catching up with an old friend. Which I suppose he is, and I enjoy watching Heath with the bird that first caught my attention. After my shock of seeing a peacock in town, Jeff led me to the beautiful man whom he followed around every day.

"You know, Jeff is a matchmaker. Did you ever think of that?"

Heath pauses and looks over at me. "No. What do you mean?"

"I first saw him. A peacock on Main Street. He caught my eye and led me to you. Maybe I wouldn't have met you if I hadn't noticed Jeff first."

Heath nods as he thinks it over. "What do you think, Jeff? Did you unintentionally find me a partner while you were strutting around?"

If a bird could throw daggers with a single look, Jeff nails it as he reacts like he understands what Heath says. He continues eating the cranberries, and once he's done, he stands for a moment, staring at Heath before swivelling back to the peahens still milling around behind him.

"It's okay, buddy. I get it. You can go. I'll see you in a few months, okay?"

Jeff drops the tail fan and saunters away while Heath silently watches him leave.

"You okay, *srećo*?"

Heath unlatches the gate, and we step out of the enclosure before he finally wraps his arms around me.

"I'm okay. Better than okay. He remembers me. I wasn't expecting that."

"I'd say he remembered. I'm happy for you."

Hugging him close, I kiss the top of his head before he releases me. I thought he'd cry, but he's beaming the smile I fell in love with and throwing his arms around my neck.

"You're right. Jeff led me to you. I never thought of it that way before. Maybe that's what his purpose was in my life? Without him, I may never have met you."

"Fate in the form of a peacock?"

Heath pushes up on his toes to kiss me. His lips brush over mine and I melt into him. Just like every single time.

"I don't know if it was fate. But it was something."

"No, it was everything, *ljubavi*."

"Yeah, it really was."

***

"Ok, which one is the steer wrestler again?"

Heath and I take seats in the stands of my very first rodeo. As suggested, I wore a cowboy hat, and I still feel like I stick out like a sore thumb. Although it could be the tattoos. Anywhere I go, new people stare like I have broccoli in my teeth.

"Jackson is the steer wrestler. His tattoo was some kind of champion symbol. He brought it in. Jamieson is the bull rider. His tattoo had initials."

Settling onto the bleachers, Heath turns over his arm where his very first tattoo, inked by me, sits.

"Initials sound so serious. I like ours."

Last year for Christmas, Blaze insisted on tattoos for their core group at the ranch that matched. Even Colby sat with his husband and white knuckled through it. Not that he didn't want to, he was just nervous. Now they all have the Broken Horn Ranch symbol on them somewhere with the year they became a part of it.

Blaze joked it was an advertising expense, but I'm pretty sure he was serious about it.

The announcer's voice comes over the speaker and music blasts across the arena as the show starts. It's a Saturday afternoon rodeo, and the crowd is bigger than I thought it would be.

Heath explains to me bull riding is the premier event and will be the last one on the schedule, but steer wrestling will be towards the end of the first half. Not that it really matters. There's enough here to hold my attention outside the action in the ring.

The man beside me.

Heath swapped his ball cap for a cowboy hat, and I don't know what I like better. His faded jeans and worn cowboy boots, along with his faded black T-shirt, make it all work for me. A lot.

The first event is called saddle bronc, and it looks painful. I can only imagine what the guys on the back of a bull go through if this is what a horse does.

Heath hoots and hollers for all the cowboys, and I've probably watched him more than the events.

"Oh, it's steer wrestling next!" He turns to me and smiles. A softness in his gaze when it settles on me. "What's the look for?"

"Nothing. Just admiring the most beautiful thing here."

Heath's deep brown eyes never waver from mine. "Ditto."

He leans in and our hats bump. Both of us laugh and I take mine off before claiming the kiss he was going for. The music fades away along with the announcer's voice until Heath pulls away.

"Family event." He murmurs as he sits ahead to watch the action again. His hand finds mine though, and he squeezes it before stealing another glance. "I think your friend was just announced."

Heath points to the crowd of cowboys on horseback at the one end of the ring.

"I wasn't paying attention because a hot guy was kissing me. Explain this to me."

Heath tries to look embarrassed, but I know he loves my attention. Sometimes I wish I had feathers like Jeff to signal my intentions, but I'll settle for holding his hand instead.

"The steer will come out of the shoot and the two guys on horses will try to keep it between them. The hazer is the guy who doesn't wrestle the steer, and he's just trying to keep the steer running straight for the wrestler. Then your friend will slide off his horse with a fancy move to grab the steer's horns and wrestle it on its side. When all four feet point out off the ground, the timer stops."

"He just falls off a running horse onto something with horns!? Holy fuck."

Heath nods. "Yep, and then wrestles a four-hundred-pound animal to the ground."

"Wow."

Rodeo cowboys are unhinged.

There's been a bit of an issue with something at the chutes, so the rodeo clown is out there doing what clowns do best and making a fool of himself until the announcer tells him to get lost. The crowd laughs and then it's on.

The first two steer wrestlers have me on the edge of my seat and Heath nudges me with his elbow. "It's cool, right? Alec used to do tie down roping with a guy named Hunter. He always told me to go to the Kissing Ridge Rodeo one day. If you like this, maybe we should plan a trip."

"Jamieson told me about that place, too. Said it's where he's from." I've been watching Jackson on his horse and he's in the stall, or whatever it's called, since he's next.

The steer bolts out, and the two cowboys are on it fast. I've barely blinked and Jackson slides off his horse and just lays this animal down so fast I'm in awe.

"That is...wow. I think I love rodeo now."

Heath laughs before turning to face me.

"That settles it then. Our first official couple vacation will be to the Kissing Ridge Rodeo. And I'll get some new chaps."

He winks at me, and I shake my head.

"You did that on purpose."

"I sure did." He licks his lips. "How bad do you want to stay for the whole thing?"

Standing, I pull his hand and apologize to everyone that we bump on our way down the bleachers. Once on solid ground, I remove his hat and crash my mouth to his.

"I can catch a rodeo any time. But every day with you is precious. You are *moja sreća*, my happiness, and I'll choose that all day, every day."

"I love you," Heath breathes as his arms loop around my neck. "You are my everything."

A throat clears and we step aside for the man who needs to get by and we both hurry away, trying not to laugh.

It takes far too long for us to leave the rodeo grounds and get to Heath's Jeep, but when we do, I can't help but to box him in against the door and make out with him a little longer.

"I thought we were taking this back to the hotel?" He smiles up at me and blinks those long eyelashes. I'm such a sucker for his eyes and the way he says so much with a single glance.

"We are. I just needed a bit more for the road."

"And do you have enough?"

"With you? I'll let you know, but I don't think I'll ever have enough."

He smiles and turns to open the door of the Jeep.

"Well, that's good to hear. I'd like you to remember that when the order of ducks I bought shows up next week."

"The what now?"

He slips behind the wheel and closes the door, forcing me to jog around to the passenger side faster than I'd like.

"Heath...what did you do?"

He snorts as he steers the Jeep out of the parking lot.

"I told you. Ducks."

"Do we need to upgrade to a hobby farm?"

He turns his head to meet my gaze. His sunshine smile blinding my rational thoughts.

"That sounds like a great idea! Can we?"

"I...um..."

He laughs before squeezing my leg. "No, we don't need a hobby farm. You love your studio. And it's just two ducks. For now. You'll love them. I promise."

And you know what? He's right.

He could say he ordered two cows, and I'd be happy just because it makes him happy.

But I won't put that thought in his head.

"I should be angry you didn't ask me first."

"Why do you think I mentioned chaps before telling you?"

I bark a laugh and reach for his hand.

There's one thing I know with certainty: life with Heath will never be boring.

Chapter 27

Epilogue

Two Years Later

Heath

"I can't believe how beautiful it is here, Marko. It must have been hard to leave this behind. Will you be okay when we have to leave it again?"

When Marko asked if I'd ever want to visit Croatia, of course, I said yes. I want to know everything about his life before coming to Canada. It's such a big part of him. Knowing this is the place he was closest to his mother made it an even easier yes.

Our visits to *baka* and the old crew for lamb roasts endeared me to most of their culture. Except for that plum brandy. They shouldn't be proud of that stuff. I learned my lesson, though, and stay far away.

For two weeks, we've toured his home country and for the last few days, we've been staying at his favourite place on the island of Hvar.

"It really is beautiful. I've missed it. There's nothing like the scenery here. I could stare at the blue water all day and never tire of it."

We had our lunch on the balcony off our room. The view deserved to be soaked up while we relaxed in the sun and enjoyed more of the local food. Including a bag of the sugared almonds he likes.

"This is my first ocean, and it's incredible. Remember when you told me we had a pull like the tide and you'd always come back to me?"

"Technically, it's the Adriatic Sea, *ljubavi*. Don't say ocean here. It starts fights." Marko squints into the distance while he thinks, and it's the sexiest look on him. I love all his smile lines and that single dimple that pokes over his scruff. Since we've been together, he smiles a lot more and I see that dimple more often. I know I'm not always the easiest guy to live with, but the fact he doesn't have grey hair yet has not escaped my attention.

Although Marko as a silver fox will be... yeah, okay. That will be a look he'll rock.

"I remember. Why?"

"I noticed the tide here isn't that big. But sometimes it takes a long time to come back. Would you take that long to come back if you ever left?"

He cocks his head as he digests the question. He's used to my randomness, so this isn't anything new to him. And I love how he still takes me so seriously. I fucking adore it, if I'm honest.

"Well, I'm not tied to the moon, so no, I'd come back faster."

Swiping an olive from the bowl on the table, I offer it to him, and he sucks it into his mouth. "Nobody makes olives taste as good as these."

"The olive grove here is your tattoo, right? The one we walked in yesterday?"

He nods and wraps his arm around my shoulders.

"It is. I picked olives here with my *baka* when I was little."

"Right." I kiss his cheek. "And all the lavender here is so gorgeous. The plants inspire you, right?"

"One of the first times I ever did a watercolour painting was here. I loved the blue water and sky, and the purples of the flowers. I've never felt it could be captured on paper well enough. Even that sketch I made for you. When you moved in, remember I had it on the easel waiting? We had that time in the rain and you left me a note." Marko's thumb rubs a spot on my neck. "I sketched that scene, then painted it. Your naked body in the garden. I added lavender because you took me to see the brewery gardens, and I thought it was the most romantic thing you could ever have done."

"So there are a lot of wonderful memories here, then?"

Marko's gaze is soft as he turns to me.

"Yes, there are. Now there are even more."

My heart beats all wacky when Marko looks at me like he is right now. So, here goes, I guess.

"I did a thing."

He smiles and kisses my forehead.

"Okay, *srećo*. What did you do?"

"I wanted to make this place even more happy for you. I hope. If you agree, I'd like you to meet me in the olive grove tonight for a wedding."

Marko squints again, and I run a finger over his brow. He licks his lips and those brown eyes I love to get lost in, blink. Then they widen and blink again.

"Heath...what did you do?"

"God, my hands are shaking so bad." I laugh softly as I stand from my chair to sit in his lap. Taking his face in my hands, I swallow and hope I don't fuck this up. "I kept a secret for months. First, let's acknowledge that."

Marko sucks in a breath and nods. "Okay. That's great. I know that's hard for you."

Understatement. As soon as I spoke to *baka* and had her blessing, I wanted to tell anyone with an ear. But I needed to stay quiet, and that was *so* hard.

"It was very hard keeping to myself how I contacted the resort and arranged for a marriage licence..." Marko's lips part and I keep speaking before the nerves become too much. "And a minister for a sunset ceremony in the olive grove tonight. It was also near impossible not telling you I arranged for a jeweller to be here in a few hours so we could pick rings." Smoothing my thumb across his cheek, I wipe a tear away. "I also asked your *baka* if it was okay with her and she wants us to call her immediately after. That's assuming you don't say no."

Marko releases a shaky breath and wraps a hand around the back of my neck.

"You planned a wedding here? Our wedding? In my Hvar?"

"I did. Are you mad?"

He shakes his head and wipes at his eyes.

"God, no. Heath...you will never stop surprising me, I swear. This is...holy fuck...you're going to be my husband?" His voice cracks and that's what it takes for me to lose my composure and finally shed my happy tears.

"Yeah. Forever, Marko. I had some help pulling strings, and when we return home, we just do it over at the courthouse with our friends. I arranged that too once I had help."

"Let me guess; Blaze."

"He's a closet romantic, that guy." My Marko kisses me softly. His hands shake just like mine as he holds my face in his hands. "So, is that a yes?"

He rests his forehead against mine and whispers, "You didn't ask me the question."

"Marko, will you marry me tonight and be my happiness for the rest of my life? Will you promise to buy me more ducks and forgive me when I put too much bubble bath in the tub? Will you be my husband and promise to come back faster than the tide, should we have a disagreement?"

Marko laughs softly.

"You stuck the part about ducks in there because you thought I wouldn't notice."

"I did."

"Yes, Heath. Even to the duck part. Yes, to all of it."

"Oh, thank god." I pause before kissing him. "Wait. You mean I can get more ducks for real?"

"Shut up and let me kiss my fiancé."

"Fine."

And he kisses me, laughing as we make out on the balcony of our suite and it couldn't be more perfect.

I'm getting a husband and more ducks.

I can't wait to tell Jeff.

***

Thank you so much for reading Heath and Marko's story!

If you're curious about Marko's rodeo friends, you can meet them
in the new series!
Kissing Ridge Cowboys begins with Jackson's story!

Jackson Sutherland may be a champion at wrestling 400 pound
steers to the ground, but wrestling Riley Benton's heart into falling
for a cowboy is proving to be harder than he thought.
Cowboys Can't Kiss – coming early 2025!

ACKNOWLEDGEMENTS

We did it!

Heath finally got his HEA and I couldn't be more proud of his journey. He was a hard character to get a feel for. I tried matching him with a hockey player, a rock star, and an artist before he met Marko. I even tried moving him to Maple Mountain to meet the artist there, and he wasn't having it. Neither was Jeff.

After several false starts, I latched on to the one constant in all Heath's possible matches – tattoos. Marko materialized from there and I just love the two of them together. Originally, Jeff was to stay with Heath. They're inseparable after all and it seemed like the right direction, but again, that damn bird took over and led me somewhere else.

The amount of tears I shed writing the scene where Jeff leaves left me so drained. I didn't want to do it, but it was for the best. I hope you understand why it had to happen that way. Jeff is living his best life, and that's what matters.

A big thank you to Nicki Adkins who suggested the name for Marko's tattoo shop! It ended up being the perfect fit for him.

Menotah, thank you for your support. Your early feedback was the encouragement I needed.

I also need to thank A.M Rose for their help with my Croatian. While Mr.Neill is Croatian, he was born and raised here and only learned a few words growing up. Thank you so much A.M, for giving me your time to review it. Languages are hard. Especially when I don't realize there's a Croatian alphabet and not just accents, LOL.

Most of Heath's trip to meet Marko's grandmother is based on the first time I met Mr.Neill's Croatian family! Mr.Neill's grandmother couldn't say my name and just called me something else instead. I thought she didn't like me for months because she never got my name right, LOL.

Thank you, dear reader, for being on this journey with me.

Heath is a labour of love and I'm so pleased you stuck around for his story. I hope you loved him as much as I did.

Much love,

RM

Also By

Want to read more by me? Scan the code
to find my back list.

Visit my website for signed paperbacks and merch!
rmneillauthor.com

9 781999 851603 2